The Distillery

The Distillery

The First Generation

JOHN ARCHER

To order additional copies of this book, contact:
Xlibris Corporation
1-888-795-4274
www.Xlibris.com
Orders@Xlibris.com
20658

Contents

Dedication

This book is dedicated to "the girls." May God
bless them and keep them, every one, amen.

ACKNOWLEDGEMENTS

Cover and author photos by Allison of Pekin.
Cover art by Cynthia M. Van Dam.
Photo prop, 1932 Ford Model B, by Bob Waight
Technical consultant: Jeremy Styninger
Editing and final proof: Marc Dukes

CHAPTER ONE

It was a power struggle.

The mayor sat at his desk in his second-floor office, peering down at the street in front of City Hall. He wanted to see the Canadians arrive, but he did not want them to know he was interested. It was an anxious moment for all concerned.

They were late! Mayor Adams took a cigar from a box and rolled it in his mouth to moisten it. It was 1934 and the mayor was in his third term. No greenhorn was he.

The bastards were probably late on purpose, he thought. He remembered with cynicism how they had insisted on no press or notoriety.

The mayor reached for the telephone and called downstairs. Trying to make him squirm wouldn't work.

"Mildred," he growled into the mouthpiece. "Send that bunch of citizens from 'shantytown' up to my office. Send every damned one of them at once."

"But Mr. Adams," Mildred protested. "You've got a very special meeting with those distillery people any minute now."

"Just send those 'locals' up, and the Canadians can wait in the rotunda until I call you again," he said as he took one last look at the street and hung up. "I'll show them who's goin' to wait on who," he grumbled.

The mayor prolonged the session with his complaining citizens. Their point was simple – they felt oppressed because their shacks built on Cinder Point along the river were infested with rats. He listened with interest and blew cigar smoke at the soiled ceiling above his head. He supposed the Canadians were downstairs fuming with disgust.

City Hall was a refuge, even to the poor of Cinder Point, and A.J. Adams was their mentor. To resolve the rat problem, he established a dog and cat pound surrounded by fence, and located it between the river and Cinder Point. The impounded animals could feed on the rats, diminishing their numbers and saving the city the expense of buying pet food. Two city problems resolved in one stroke!

Adams put his arms across the shoulders of two of the constituents as he walked the group to the exit. They felt vindicated, and he insisted they register to vote before leaving City Hall.

When they were gone, the mayor fumed. The Canadians still had not arrived!

As the mayor's indignation was growing, six suited men wearing wide-brimmed hats were stepping from the Lafayette Hotel into two waiting sedans.

The oldest man, an ugly bewhiskered hulk, was the obvious leader. He sat in the back of the first auto. The other men scurried into the remaining seats and the cars pulled into the street, heading for City Hall.

The air was blue with stale smoke and the mayor was smoking his fourth cigar when they arrived. He had removed his coat and stiff collar. He sat in his shirtsleeves, his black suspenders outlined on his white shirt.

The negotiations had begun. They were planning a "booze" factory.

Like the town of Logan, the depot was small and cold. It was near midnight and Melba sat across from her mother in the waiting room. Except for the ticking of the clock and the nervous pacing of her father, the entire world seemed still.

Her mother, Lacey, sat erect and looked straight ahead, her hands folded over a worn purse in her lap.

It will be a long time before I see you again, Melba thought as she studied her mother's rigid form. There was much she wanted to say . . . if only Papa was not there! She had never been able to say what was in her heart. Since childhood, conversations with her mother were always impersonal, as if there were an invisible screen between them.

Melba leaned back against the seat and looked at the ceiling of the waiting room. It was dirty and needed paint. Old strips of fly paper hung down, dried with age from last summer, or some summer of the past.

The problem went back to Boyd's arrival. Before he was born, there was just Melba and her parents. These were lighter times. Yet, even then, there was something restrictive about the relationship. Melba had always wanted to be accepted and never quite made the grade.

Melba Starks just turned eighteen and had graduated from Logan High School, hoping that somehow she could continue her education. She even speculated that she might attend a small local church college while living at home with her parents.

Her brother, Boyd, took care of that. He and two of his pals were wanted for looting a boxcar on the railroad siding. Melba's parents scraped up all the cash they could to get Boyd out of town ahead of the police.

Now, Melba had to leave home and go to Riverport to find work. The family needed the money.

In her stocking feet Melba stood five feet two inches tall and was of medium build, although inclined to appear stocky. She sometimes used powder to cover brown freckles across the bridge of her nose. Once, she had tried painting her nails, but this was discovered by Lacey and never happened again. Her skin appeared to be whiter than it was, and she turned red quickly if exposed to the sun.

When Lacey was gone, Melba became the proxy mother. Lacey's jobs included cleaning other people's houses or doing extra work at the pottery. Lacey was never hired steadily there, because Harold worked at the pottery and a company rule prohibited husband and wife from working at the same plant.

Melba's parents were solemn folk, having experienced serious hardship most of their lives. Harold would have preferred being a farmer, but could not afford to buy a place, and refused to work as a "hand" for anyone else.

Papa walked nervously back and forth within the small room. He stopped before the bulletin board. A notice there stated the Illinois Electric Railway would serve Logan only on a whistle-stop basis after December 1, 1932.

The closed ticket window seemed to rebuke them.

"I told the agent she'd be takin' the 'Owl' out of here tonight," Harold said, gesturing toward the agent's window. "He said he'd put the flag out to stop her. Damn him, he's home sleepin' and I'm standin' around this stinkin' station waitin' on a train that's probably runnin' late anyway."

"Where'd you put your watch?" Lacey asked, without looking up.

"I know! I know!" Harold shouted, waving his arms at his wife.

"Don't blame me if this stuff around the I.E.R. ruins it," she admonished.

"The men who work here have watches, don't they?" he demanded.

"Trehee said some of this electric stuff would ruin a good watch. He ought to know, he works for the C. and A.," Lacey said.

Please stop fighting, Melba thought. *Is this the way I'm to remember both of you?* She shifted uneasily on the straight-backed bench. It was hard enough leaving home without having to hear them go at it.

"Have you got your ticket?" Lacey asked. It was the fourth time she had asked the question since they left home.

"Yes, Ma," Melba responded, rubbing her thumb back and forth on the face of the ticket. "I wouldn't be leavin' at all if Boyd had stayed out of trouble," she said.

"None of that," her mother scolded.

"What's done is done," Papa said without turning away from the bulletin board.

"I'd hoped to stay home and work in Logan," Melba said without looking up. "I could pay for my keep right here at home."

"What? Scrubbin' floors for twenty cents an hour?" Lacey demanded.

"I could work two jobs. I've done it before."

"We've covered all of that," Harold scolded as he turned to face the women. "Now let's not belabor the point."

The room fell silent. Melba wanted to cry. Lacey bit her lip, and Harold started pacing again.

Tall and thin, Harold Starks looked like the weathered workman he was. Born in Kentucky, and raised in the remote regions of the hill country, he was not a stranger to adversity. He had enlisted in the U.S. Army in the latter part of World War One, and had been shipped to Europe with the A.E.F. Injured by gas, he had been confined to a military hospital in Illinois. It was here that he met Lacey, whose first husband, the father of Melba, had died in the war. After a brief courtship they were married and set up housekeeping in a farm home owned by Lacey's relatives. Being a hired hand was not to Harold's liking, and he soon moved to Logan where he found steady employment in a pottery.

The Starks had been married almost a year and Melba was four years old when Boyd was born. Times had started to pick up, and when things improved, Boyd came down with infantile paralysis. There was little knowledge about the illness, commonly referred to as polio. The family had no money for medical attention. The disease reached epidemic proportions and was known to be highly contagious. To protect Melba and Harold, Lacey took Boyd and moved to the a place on the south side of town near Sugar Creek. It was little more than a shack, but it served its purpose.

Harold and Melba maintained the home and cared for one another. He did the garden during the summer and fired the furnace and hauled the ashes during the winter. Melba was glad that he neither smoked nor drank. His only vice was a deep fondness for gambling. He often made ridiculous wagers on long odds and produced nothing but losses.

Food and supplies were left in the thicket for Lacey and her patient. She stayed in isolation tending to Boyd for nearly a year, not returning home until the county health department determined that there was no further possibility of infecting others.

Shortly after they were reunited, Harold got in on the ground floor of a chain letter, and received twelve hundred quarters in the mail. He used this windfall as a deposit on a Hudson auto, which he failed to insure. Thieves stole the car from the parking lot at the pottery. His fellow workers felt sympathetic and collected twenty-five dollars. They used this money to buy a flatbed truck being retired by the company. Harold was in the sixth year of patching and driving this relic when he drove Melba and her mother to the depot.

I knew the train would be late," Harold said, looking out of the window into the night.

"Tain't late yet," Lacey said.

"Tis so," he bristled.

Melba stiffened. *Why do you have to fight about it?*

From the night, they heard the horn of the train. Melba looked helplessly at her mother. Now it was too late for talk.

Her mother stood and faced the door. "Come, girl, that's the train. Remember to write when you get settled. Tell your aunt and uncle hello. Don't forget to go to church. Live the kind of life we'd be proud of."

Melba nodded hesitantly as she picked up her battered suitcase in one hand, tucked a cloth bag under the other arm, and followed her parents onto the station platform.

The air was cool and damp. She was glad to be wearing the full-length sweater handed down to her from her mother. Under this she wore a multicolored cotton dress reaching down almost to her ankles. On her feet, she wore white anklets and oxford shoes. Her mother brushed Melba's hair back from her face and attached a cheap silver barrette to the side of her head. Melba resolved to remove it the instant she was out of sight of her mother.

"Train's comin'," Harold said as though they had not already heard. "It'll be daybreak when you get in. Don't take up with no strangers," he admonished.

Melba bit her lip, partially to control her grief about leaving, and partially to suppress her desire to say what she felt to her father. It was just as well that she kept silent at this tense moment, for her mother could only be the loser from such a scene.

At least I'm shed of you, she thought as her eyes scanned her father's face. She turned to her mother. The two women kissed cheek to cheek as the headlamp on the train lit up their faces. Melba was not surprised to see tears in her mother's eyes. She was puzzled about the reflected moisture in the eyes of her father.

The train hissed to a stop and the conductor stepped down from the end of the coach. He placed a stool on the platform and turned toward the Starks.

"Where to?" he asked.

"End of the line," Harold said.

"Riverport? All aboard for Riverport," he called.

The trainman threw Melba's suitcase onto the coach and gripped her elbow as she stepped upon the stool.

"Take any seat you want in the car to your left," he said. "There's a drunk in the other car, and you'd best stay away from him."

The horn bleated twice and the train started to move. Looking down from the coach, Melba thought her parents looked small and pitiful. She waved goodbye from the vestibule until she could see them no more, then she removed the barrette from her hair and turned to enter the coach. All of the other passengers were asleep in various positions of discomfort. She discovered an empty seat and sat down. The train rocked and swayed as it left Logan behind. Melba pulled her knees up under her chin and stared out of the blackened window into the night. Her fear of the future surged with each wail of the horn as the train lurched toward Riverport.

The white Cord Coupe slowed as it approached the main entrance to the distillery. An uniformed guard opened the gate, stepped back, and waved as the sleek machine entered the premises and headed for the officials' parking lot, in front of the administration building.

Dr. Leonard Barstow stepped from the car and hastened toward the building. He was a gaunt, lean man in his fifties. He impressed strangers as the kindly grandfather of a respected family. The chief chemist, he was more than the mixer of compounds. He was, in fact, the supreme authority in this whiskey factory, and those in the "know" knew him as the Canadian Connection. He took the steps two at a time. An ordinary man would have had to trot to keep up with him. He took his hands from the pockets of his cardigan for more freedom of motion. Before entering the building, he knocked the fire from his pipe and disappeared into the hallway.

Once inside, he called for his assistant, Bud McKenna.

"Bud," he shouted above the sounds of the workmen removing construction material from the building. "Bud," he repeated. "Here now!" he warned a laborer who brushed him with a plank in passing. "Bud, where the hell are you?"

A plasterer's trowel crashed down the stairwell and spun around like a top at the doctor's feet.

"Careful there, dammit, be careful!" he grumbled to no one in particular.

"Bud, I've got confirmation on the production schedule. The boys in Canada give us the green light to be in bottling production in two weeks. We can expect them to be here before cold weather."

A stocky, red-faced blond man in his thirties peered down from the landing above.

"Great," Bud grinned, as he descended to his superior.

"By God, we've worked hard for this moment," the doctor puffed.

"When did you get the word?" Bud asked.

"They phoned me at home," the older man responded as he entered his office and laboratory. "I haven't had a chance to tell anyone but you. The others must know this news as soon as possible. Call a meeting in the cafeteria in thirty minutes. Don't leak the news until we are behind closed doors . . . and, oh yes, call the mayor and tell him I'd like to have lunch with him at the club at noon."

"It's done," Bud responded as he left the lab and disappeared into the corridor.

The staff of the Jacob Wasserman Distillery filed into the cafeteria with the drone of anticipation. Each of them suspected the nature of the hurriedly called meeting. The whole scheme of things for more than a year was to prepare for the day when the huge plant would come alive and start producing.

Riverport had been chosen as the site for the new distillery for good reason. First, it was in the United States, which was just making it legal to manufacture and sell distilled spirits again. Also, it offered plenty of good water, transportation, coal, corn and a waiting labor force. Several old distilleries had been located here before Prohibition. They left behind buildings and equipment, not to mention remnants of a staff of experienced workers.

Having had no break in production, the Canadians' experience was more recent, so the nucleus of the new distillery was largely Canadian. Add to this the experienced technicians from the community, and the large number of workers to operate the bottling line, and the Jacob

Wasserman Distilling Company was ready to quench the thirst of Americans from Maine to California.

The bottling house was centrally located, near the buildings which stored the product, and next to the shipping facilities where empty trucks and boxcars waited to be loaded.

All of the buildings were made of red brick; the tallest being the building wherein the actual distilling was done. The bottling house was next tallest, having a tower-like center to contain large tanks of spirits above the bottling lines. Because of their square, squat appearance, the rack houses used to age the product in oaken barrels seemed like rows of red elephants standing on either side of the company street.

All of this was perched on the banks of the river, securely surrounded by woven wire and guardhouses like a penal farm that allowed the tenants to leave at the end of each shift.

Clean, neat and quiet, the distillery squeezed spirits from grain by the application of heat, and in the process altered the lives of those who became in any way associated.

"Good afternoon," Dr. Barstow greeted the group of about sixty people assembled in the cafeteria. "We have exciting news to tell you. This is the day we have all worked for."

The late arrivals found seats. A hush fell on the room.

"Word has come to me from our superiors that all is in order, and as soon as final inspection is completed by the government people, we can start this place humming."

Bud McKenna was first to his feet, clapping his hands and looking about for support. The others followed suit and joined in the applause.

Dr. Barstow motioned with his outstretched hands, palms down, for the group to be seated. The staff hushed again.

"Thank you fellow coworkers," he said. "As you know, we have one rack house filled and ready to supply four lines in production. Very soon, the sound of bottling machines will be music to our ears."

"As most of you know," he continued, "The distilling process in the past has been at best, slipshod. Most of the producers of alcohol before Prohibition adhered to little consistency in quality or process. The finished product often varied in quality because of this lack of control. Our company already produces one of the recognized leaders in whiskey sales, and is among the leaders of other beverages containing spirits."

He paused a moment before proceeding. "We have a distinct advantage in the market, because we are now able, with the end of Prohibition, to produce the leader here in the central part of the United States for easy availability to this new market. We have the equipment in this new facility to produce products for the consumer's palate of such high quality that we are without peer. Let us all continue to work together to present to the drinking public a product they will prefer over all others."

More applause, this time without prompting by Bud McKenna.

"Each supervisor has specific instructions regarding his particular unit. The personnel department has been instructed to start hiring. New faces should start appearing among us in the next few weeks. It is up to you, as the cadre of this organization, to project leadership, pride, and safety in our company operations. This distillery offers you the cleanest, most modern facility of its kind in the world. Run it with efficiency and honor it with accomplishment. We have only two cardinal rules at this plant, the violation of which will remove you from our payroll and our property. One: You must not drink our products while on these premises, and Two: Except here in the cafeteria, you must not smoke anywhere in the plant. Bud McKenna will assign schedules and production objectives at the conclusion of this meeting. I take this opportunity to thank each of you for the fine work you have done thus far. May you, and this company, enjoy a lasting partnership in progress."

He waved and disappeared through a side door.

The room filled with the buzz of speculation as the staff contemplated the future. Bud McKenna dutifully started passing out the production charts.

The 1932 Ford was distinctive for its simplicity, but not for its spacious interior. A black two-door with yellow wire wheels sat parked in the darkness of night next to the football field in Tonica. The windows were heavy with steam, and the car pitched and rolled like a small boat in heavy seas. Through the distortion of the translucent windows, the illumination of a match gave an orange glow, as the activity inside ceased, and the occupants lighted cigarettes.

Sweat appeared to ooze from Roddie's red hair, running across his forehead and dripping from his eyebrows. His brawny shoulders gleamed with perspiration as he sat up breathing heavily while smoking the cigarette.

Francine's right leg was red from being pressed against the back of the seat. Her other leg was missing somewhere under Roddie's knee.

Even so contorted, she was beautiful. Her disheveled hair, large dark eyes, and full red lips appealed to the eye. Just eighteen, her body was strong and yearning. Long slender legs, rounded hips and firm breasts begged for attention, baiting any boy lucky enough to see her.

"Jeez," she cursed. "Get your weight off me so I can breathe."

"Raise your butt off my hand," Roddie insisted. "Can't we please open the windows of this hot friggin' car?" he asked.

"Oh, sure, and let all the goddamn mosquitoes in the county have a bite of my bare ass!" she snapped.

"But, Baby," Roddie pleaded. "Can't you see how much more fun this would be if you could straighten out and cool off, like outside on the ground?"

With the heat, and the discomfort of the position, Francine Ryan was beginning to be less than satisfied with making out in this car with Roddie Dixon. In fact, she was on the verge of quitting the whole scene when the darkness lit up with the beam of a flashlight pressed against the window on the driver's side.

Roddie straightened up abruptly and bumped his head on the headliner as Francine drew her legs up and rolled off the seat to the floor.

"Open up, it's the police," came a deep voice from behind the flashlight.

Roddie looked questioningly at Francine as another light illuminated the opposite side of the car. Someone beat against the glass and echoed the first voice.

"Go away," Roddie said.

"Open it up," came the response, "or we will do it the hard way."

"What shall we do?" Roddie pleaded to Francine.

She was probing around on the floor of the auto, trying to find her clothes under the seat. "Don't open the door now," she threatened.

Rap rap rap against the glass.

Roddie wiped a small circle of condensation off the window nearest him, and peered out. His heart sank. It *was* the cops! Why hadn't he heard their car approach? What the hell was he going to do now?

The car rocked as the policemen demanded the door be opened at once. Roddie had no choice. He wound the window down on the driver's side, and holding his boxer shorts across his groin, blinked helplessly at the beam of light protruding into his auto.

Francine was still crouched on the floor of the back seat. The policeman directed the beam towards her. Her head was hidden under some of her clothing, but her bare bottom was clearly visible to the inquiring officer.

"Okay, come on . . . out of the car," the first policeman commanded.

The car doors burst open and the flashlight beams crossed the interior of the auto.

Francine straightened up, and peered out from under the garments still covering her head. "Do WHAT?" she shrieked.

"Out of the car," the policeman repeated.

"Like this?" Roddie cried.

"Get a move on."

Roddie stumbled out of the car, still holding his shorts in front of his crotch. Francine was not so quick to comply. She sat upright in the car and very precisely straightened her clothing, making sure she was amply covered before she stepped from the auto. The policeman directed the light from her feet to her face and back again.

"Gettin' a good look?" she smirked.

"You ain't nothin' but a kid!" the cop drawled.

"She's old enough to engage in sex," the other officer said, his attention diverted from Roddie to the more attractive view of Francine.

"What's your name, young lady?" he asked.

"Lady Godiva."

"Let's not get smart, now. How would your parents feel about what you two are doin' out here in this auto?"

"You wouldn't!" Roddie exclaimed.

"Shut up!" Francine warned Roddie.

"Spunky lil' mouse, ain't she?" the officer noted to his partner. "Here she is, standing out here on a cold night, hot from screwin' her boyfriend, and she's got the guff to crack wise."

Francine remained calm. She hoped Roddie would do the same.

"Now, once more . . . what is your name?"

"Janet Williams," she lied.

"Where do you live?"

"With my folks on River Drive."

"What is your Dad's name?"

"Judge Franklin Pierce Williams."

"Judge Williams?" the cop asked.

"You got it."

The two policemen briefly went into a huddle and whispered to each other.

"What would your father say about this?" the first officer asked Francine.

"What would he say about a lecherous cop holding a flashlight on the shivering body of his favorite little girl?" she threatened.

"Let us give you some advice," the policeman started in a more friendly tone. "This is no place for you two kids to be out here sparkin'. Now do us a favor and go farther out into the country where there's less chance some whacko will walk up on you."

"Yeah, yeah, man," Roddie agreed.

"Now do as I say, git in the car and skedaddle. We'll be nice guys and forget what's happened here. You do the same. Okay?"

"Sure, sure will," Roddie said as he jumped into the car and started the engine. Francine thought he might leave without her and hurriedly got back into the car. Roddie drove from the field onto the highway, and headed away from town.

"Cripes, what if they hadn't believed that lie you told them?" He inquired without looking directly at Francine, who was buttoning her dress.

"What lie?" she asked.

"The name you gave them. Janet Williams."

"Poop, those two were out for free looks. They never intended to take us in. They just wanted to see what I looked like. When they thought I was the judge's daughter, they got defensive because of their unprofessional behavior. *You've* got the problem."

"I've got what problem?"

"When they find out the real Janet Williams is a spinster schoolteacher living in Chicago, they will be looking for this flashy little Ford to even the score. I'm leavin' tomorrow morning for Riverport to make my fortune in the world."

"Leavin'? You didn't tell me you was goin' away!"

"I intended to after you got your rocks off. I just didn't get the chance when those peepin' Toms came along."

"Riverport? Why Riverport?" he asked as he drove farther from town.

"Because that's where the action is," she declared.

"Action? What kind of action do you want?"

"More than this hick town can come up with," she said, resting her head against the window and staring at the stars as the car lurched along the bumpy road.

"*Riverport?*" Roddie asked again.

It was rumored that the Great Depression was bottoming out. This seemed to be partially confirmed when the Jacob Wasserman Distillery ran an ad for help in the *Riverport Times,* and the townspeople felt partially redeemed. Long lines formed before the temporary hiring hall, located discreetly away from the plant itself.

This is how Riverport newcomers Francine Ryan and Melba Starks came to meet for the first time. They stood in line next to each other, nervously hoping to be hired . . . and this is how their clock numbers and badge numbers happened to be consecutive, a source of conversation between them for three generations.

CHAPTER TWO

THE PAST, THE PRINCIPLED, AND THE PIOUS

Historically, Riverport was one of the oldest cities in the state. The Indians had found the valley to be a good place to hunt and fish. They had named it "a place of abundance," and often occupied the area which later became Riverport. In addition to the bountiful food supply, the Indians enjoyed the river, which allowed them to come and leave from the north or the south. They were not surprised to see the first white explorers, and they met them with friendship and hospitality. It was significant that these early explorers were Frenchmen from Canada, and they recorded the location for future trading posts.

Settlers also availed themselves of the waterway, and arrived in ever-increasing numbers. Some of them, seeing a future in the fertile valley, made homes here. In the early days, a fort was built as protection, not from the Indians, but from warring white men.

When riverboats powered by steam appeared commerce surged. Materials arrived by packet for the town and the surrounding area. Farms began to appear in all directions from the original settlement and much of the shipping had to do with agriculture.

The town was two hundred years old in the roaring 1920s when it became known as a port for vice, bootlegging and gangsters. Its location midway between larger cities made it an inviting stopover for travelers looking for pursuits not allowed in other places. On the heels of the illicit change followed an assemblage of people desiring to further these vices. It was not surprising that vaudeville had made Riverport the brunt of many jokes, and in so doing helped to create the opinion all across the country that Riverport was a wild, lawless town.

Prohibition had been a windfall. Bootleggers appeared on every side street, and several self-proclaimed illegal distillers produced spirits of varying conditions and quality. The consumer bought these products at his own risk, and there was little control over these activities. On at least one occasion, alcohol was delivered to a speakeasy in a hearse escorted by the police.

When the Roosevelt administration kept its promise to end Prohibition, this put the bootlegger out of business and returned the business to the corporate distillers. Now, the way was clear and the Jacob Wasserman Distilling Company made its appearance on the riverbanks at Riverport.

The town was a strange mixture of society. It boasted good parks, schools, churches, theaters, and a college. But it also supported one of the most notorious red-light districts in the country. The "good" citizenry lived on the bluff and the infamous generally lived in the valley.

Mayor A.J. Adams was the weld that held these diverse factions together. In fact, he not only united them; he had them living in harmony. No one ever knew for sure of his associations with the criminal factions, and no one dared inquire. It sufficed that everyone slept well at night and street crime was controlled by a trained police force commanded by the mayor's brother-in-law. The town had everything, and it had peace. The mayor saw to that.

Adams was a wiry, stooped-shouldered man in his mid-fifties. His face was drawn and often unsmiling, and his eyes darted from one point to another with a minimum of head movement. His speech was slow and deliberate, having a way of delivering his thoughts emphatically and without ambiguity. Yet, none of this made him seem unfriendly. Known as a Good Samaritan when called upon, he produced results for his constituents, regardless of their political leanings. One could understand his nonchalance for party lines when they learned he had been overwhelmingly elected Mayor of Riverport four separate terms. He seldom was opposed, on or off the ballot.

Hat in hand, he nodded to the doorman as he entered the Yacht Clubhouse. Two men just leaving, shook hands with him, exchanged brief greetings and turned away as he placed the hat on a cloakroom shelf and entered the dining room.

It was early for midday lunch, and the room was sparsely occupied. Clearly visible from the entrance and seated at a table in the far corner of the room sat Dr. Leonard Barstow. His eyes caught the mayor's as the latter moved toward him. They were accustomed to meeting here, and had spent many hours establishing every facet of city-company relationships. The outcome was critical to both parties, for they knew that the plant, soon to produce alcohol, would also soon be paying millions in taxes. This was big business, indeed.

'Good morning, Doctor," A.J. Adams said. "Have you been waiting long?

"Walked in just before you."

The mayor selected a chair at the doctor's side and asked, "Gittin' close to the big day?"

"That's why I called you. We've gotten the go-ahead from Wasserman and are ready to begin production."

"I expected as much. The editor of the *Riverport Times* told me you've placed an ad for production people," the mayor stated as he unfolded his napkin and laid it across his lap.

"Damn, there's not much happens around this town that escapes you, is there?" the doctor hissed as he examined the mayor's face.

"There better not be," Adams said.

The waiter, a tall, balding man, nodded as he came to their table. "Good morning, gentlemen," he smiled. "The usual?"

Both men nodded, and the waiter disappeared through swinging doors to the kitchen.

"Now look here, A.J.," the doctor started. "It is mandatory that you give us good police protection. Our security can handle the plant . . . but you have to keep those streets to the river open and peaceful. We sure as hell don't want the W.C.T.U. pickets out there blocking our new employees . . . in fact, I don't want to even *see* any of those old ladies."

The mayor permitted no one to call him "A.J." not even the goose that was about to lay the golden egg. "I assure you, 'L.B.', we have a plan for every contingency."

The doctor had never been referred to by his initials before. He got the point.

The mayor smiled and continued, "The 'Q' will set a row of hide cars along the spur. This will give us a boundary on the long side. Have your people use the Apple Street approach to the plant. It's a straight shot from the car line and into the parking lot. When your folks leave, have 'em go out through the stock yards to the state route."

"Hide cars and stock yards are not very fragrant to the nose . . ."

"And not very appealing to little old ladies wearing sachet," the mayor snorted.

The doctor chuckled. "And what of our employees? Do you believe they will not be offended by the odor?"

"After having their nostrils seared by vapors of 'alkie' for eight hours, I don't think they'll realize cows stink."

Both men laughed as the waiter set a cup containing Canadian Whiskey in front of each of them.

A veteran to public life, Mayor Adams was long identified by his unkempt graying hair, steel blue eyes, and weathered face, giving a forceful impression somehow denied by the arch of his right eyebrow and suggested smile. Slender as a reed, flexible as willow and tough as hedge, he smiled as he drank from the cup.

Melba's room in her uncle's house was on the second floor under a slanting roof, which required one to stoop when moving near the outer edges.

The ceiling and walls had been finished off with thin plywood from refrigerator boxes, and painted with a cheap casein paint that chalked off onto anything which brushed against it. A sheet hanging in the corner formed a closet. This was where Melba hung her wardrobe, consisting of one skirt, three dresses, and two blouses.

Orange crates covered with cloth served as a dressing table. A fabric shade fringed with faded material topped a lamp that was the only source of light in the room.

Aunt Pearl called to Melba from downstairs. "Melba, Hon, come to supper." Then, the older woman lumbered off from the foot of the stairs putting her great weight first on one foot, and then another, in a mechanical cadence that made the floorboards creak. Her apron was starched clean; the strings tied in a bow above her enormous butt. She wore her sandy-colored hair tightly braided around the top of her skull. In spite of her huge size, Aunt Pearl was fresh, clean, and distinctly feminine.

By contrast, this gigantic woman's husband was a mere wisp of a person. Uncle Shorty barely came to Pearl's shoulders and he was easily hidden from view whenever he stood behind her. His weight was less than one third of hers, but in spite of their divergence in size, Shorty was the ultimate authority in the house. No major decisions were made without his approval.

Melba entered the kitchen and sat with her aunt and uncle at the table. They bowed their heads and folded their hands as Shorty droned out a prayer of thanks to the Almighty. Pearl's bowed head caused her multiple chins to roll over her upper chest, making a strange profile. Her lower lip seemed to hang down as if to escape from her face.

Grace completed, Pearl passed a steaming bowl of hot food to Shorty, who dipped portions onto his plate and dispatched the bowl on to Melba. "How are you gettin' on in Riverport?" he asked.

"It's scary," Melba answered.

"How scary?" Uncle Shorty inquired.

"I mean the size of the town and the people. So many strange-looking people," she explained.

"Like the pits of Hades," Shorty thought out loud. "The whole damned world is goin' to Hell . . . men cursin', women drinkin', and kids smokin'. The last days are upon us. The Good Book tells us that!"

"That demon F.D.R. is goin' to become a dictator . . . you wait, he's takin' over . . . he brings back beer and liquor . . . pays people not to work, and farmers not to grow nothin'. He's the Devil's Disciple and he'll lead us to damnation!" With this, Uncle Shorty pounded the table, causing the dishes to rattle.

"Amen to that," Pearl mumbled.

"Lord, save us all," Shorty puffed as he started eating.

Melba cleaned her plate and sat with her hands in her lap, watching them stuff food in their mouths. At least eating kept them quiet.

On Friday, a letter came for Melba. Though it was in a plain envelope, she knew it where it had to be from – the distillery. She opened it and read that the personnel office wanted her to go to Dr. Frederick Wein's clinic Monday for a physical examination.

Melba had never had a physical. The very thought of an exam, even to get a job, frightened her. It crossed her mind to refuse, but she knew to do so would not be acceptable to the company. She simply had to go through with it.

Monday morning was hectic. Uncle Shorty had been late in going off to work at the brass foundry, and Melba got to the laundry late. The washing machine was kept on the side porch, and it was necessary to heat a boiler of water on the gas stove in the kitchen, and carry it by the bucketful to the machine.

Twin tubs of rinse water also had to be filled. The agitator beat back and forth thrashing the clothes and the water. When Pearl proclaimed the load finished the clothes were run through the wringers, dropping into the waiting rinse tub.

It was during this process that Melba got a hand caught between the wringers and before Pearl could release the roller, suffered a painfully bruised finger.

To get to Dr. Wein's clinic, Melba had to take a streetcar downtown. The throbbing of her injured hand took her mind off the nature of her mission.

Hanger straps, attached to the ceiling, swayed to and fro as the streetcar squealed lazily around a curve and started downhill to the business district.

Melba studied the faces of the other passengers. Most of them seemed preoccupied with their own thoughts and either read newspapers or stared blankly out the window at the bland surroundings. The first phase of her venture was uneventful.

She had no problem finding the clinic, which was located on the second floor of the Roxy Theater Building. A glass door next to the theater entrance bore the name of the clinic. Behind it, a narrow stairway led to a long corridor at the top. A woman wearing a nurse's cap sat at a desk, blocking further entrance.

"Hello," Melba greeted.

"Good morning," the nurse responded, smiling at the girl. "Do you have an appointment?" Melba handed her the letter from Wasserman. The nurse led her to a stall that looked like one of many voting booths. Each compartment had a short white curtain across the entrance. Melba wondered how the nurse knew which booths were unoccupied. She held the curtain aside and motioned Melba to enter the stall.

"Strip off to your 'teddy bears,'" she ordered. "Hang your clothes on the nail and sit on the chair. The doctor and I will be here in a few minutes."

With that, the nurse disappeared and the curtain dropped back to its original position. Melba looked cautiously around the inside of the small enclosure. White enamel paint covered everything. The air smelled of medical things, alcohol the most outstanding. She could hear footsteps at some distance as someone walked hurriedly across the wooden floor. She hung her clothes on the nail and folded her arms across her chest, cowering in a corner of the booth.

Time passed slowly. Finally, the curtain burst open and Dr. Wein and the nurse appeared. The doctor was wearing a white smock, which gave his squat body a rotund appearance. Encircling his bald head was a band that held a circular mirror above his brow.

He smiled briefly and asked, "Are you here for a physical?"

"Uh huh," Melba replied.

"Good," the doctor snapped as he poked a tongue depressor into her mouth; "Say 'ahh,'" he ordered.

"Ahhhhh yuk . . ."

"Still got those tonsils, I see. How'd you hang onto them so long?" Melba blinked as he removed the stick from her mouth.

"Are you from Riverport?" the doctor asked as he thumped her chest and again on each shoulder blade.

"No," Melba answered as the doctor looked inside her ears.

"Ever been married?"

"No."

"Had any children?"

Melba blushed and shook her head.

"Any problems with the menstrual cycle?"

Even more embarrassed, Melba looked at the floor and shook her head again.

"Sit down, cross your legs," he directed as he tapped below her knee with a rubber mallet. "Okay. Up on your feet. Close your eyes, arms extended, pivot right and left . . . that's it . . . now let's see you touch your toes . . . good girl . . . any medical problems? Then we are through. The nurse will finish the examination and complete some forms."

Melba was straightening her bra strap when Dr. Wein noticed her injured hand.

"Whoa! What's with this hand?" he asked as he looked closer.

"Caught it in a wringer," Melba mumbled.

"Nurse, this might need attention. Check on it before she leaves." He turned back to Melba and said, "A pleasure meeting you. Good luck." He disappeared beyond the white curtain.

Melba was shaking slightly as she dressed. Somehow, she felt violated. No one in her whole life had been as personal as these people. Now, she was committed to the processes of the working class. The worst was over.

The nurse finished the questionnaire and said, "Dress and go to the waiting room." Then the nurse disappeared beyond the white curtain. As she walked away from the booth, Melba was regaining her composure. She had decided to see this through.

When she got to the waiting room, she sat next to another girl. It was Francine.

"Hey, did you get hired?" Francine asked, her face beaming.

"Not yet, how about you?"

"One more hurdle . . . got a rug burn on my leg, and they want to make sure it's not the crud," Francine grumbled.

"So they're checking on you, too," Melba said.

"You got a rug burn?"

"No, a wringer burn," Melba explained, holding her hand up for observation.

"Wow, look at Papa Thumb and his four sons." Francine exclaimed, laughing.

Melba did not understand the joke, but she blushed in embarrassment.

Sorry," Francine said. "I was just thinking what a thrill that swollen middle finger could be . . ."

Melba bristled and put her hand out of sight.

"Oh, shit," Francine cursed, putting her arm on Melba's shoulder. "I'm so used to riffraff that I forget there are still ladies in this world. Will you accept my apology?"

Melba nodded.

"No, come on . . . a nod is not enough. Let me hear you say it. 'I accept your apology, Francine.'"

Melba chuckled at her insistence. "Okay, you are forgiven, Francine, but if you ever talk like that again around me, I'll give you a floor burn on your nose."

Francine sat upright and removed her arm from around Melba's shoulder. It was apparent that this kid was shy, but spunky . . . an attribute that fascinated Francine.

"Got a flat?" Francine inquired.

Melba shook her head.

"Wanna see mine?"

"Okay," Melba said.

"Wait for me downstairs. When the doc sees my gams, it will take a while to hurry him along. I'll be out as soon as I can."

Melba nodded as they called Francine's name and she was led into the nurse's office.

Melba was waiting at the bottom of the stairs when Francine came dashing out of the clinic.

"Did I tell you?" she asked, gesturing over her shoulder. "That ol' fart was right on cue. Acted just like I said he would. How'd he treat you?"

"The nurse looked at me." Melba confessed.

"Okay, let's git goin'. I'll show you around before we go to my digs. I'm gittin' to be an authority on Riverport an' I've only been here just this week. What'll it be? Booze? Men? Or both?"

"None for me, thanks," Melba said.

"You got some guy back home?"

"Naw, I've just got other things to git done before I git involved in *that*."

"It's number one in my book," Francine stated. "In fact, number two is so far down the list, I don't know what it is."

"Gettin' a job is number one with me."

"Oh, crap. I forgot to tell you. I got the doctor to show me the hired list, and you and are both on it."

"We got jobs?"

"Damned right!"

"Startin' when?"

"Monday, second shift," Francine replied.

"Swell, but why didn't you say so before? Are you sure?"

"It's an absolute fact. You'll get a letter telling you to get measured for a uniform at two-thirty next Monday. We got to wear tan smocks and hairnets. And they insist we wear low-heeled shoes. I'll wear high heels and change after I get to work."

"A job! What does it pay?"

"You're kiddin'."

"Am not. I never asked 'em what it paid."

"How's twenty-seven a week sound?"

"Every week?"

"Every week," Francine confirmed as she locked her arm into Melba's and the two young women darted around the corner.

Melba could not believe the 1932 Ford parked at the curb.

"You sure you didn't steal it?" she asked Francine.

"Do I look crazy?" Francine demanded. "It belongs to an old boyfriend who found it unsafe to drive around our home town. He loaned it to me until I get somethin' better."

"Somethin' better?" Melba asked. She was standing on the sidewalk, her hand on the door handle looking through the glass at the interior.

"Come on," Francine urged, as she opened the door and motioned for Melba to get in. "Let me show you some of the sights of Riverport, home of the rich and infamous . . ."

Melba shot a glance at Francine and got into the car.

"Up town is a place called the Bee Hive," Francine hummed. "Oh, Mona, it is just that . . . a beehive of action, and I'm already up for 'Queen Bee.' "

"It ain't a tavern is it?"

"Naw, Coke and hamburgers while the crowd waits for the street car."

Francine smiled as she shifted gears and wheeled down the street.

The Bee Hive was across from the court house on the most prominent corner in town. All windows on the street side, it appeared long and narrow. A marble topped counter ran the length of the room, and overhead was a table-laden balcony, equally long.

Inside, the noise was deafening. The patrons, mostly young people, shouted meaningless messages to one another and launched a blizzard of soda straws and paper planes at nondescript targets.

"Did you have anything like this in your home town?" Francine asked.

"Naw, nothin' like this. Are we safe?"

"Safe? They are the ones in danger. We could chew 'em up and spit 'em out if they rubbed us the wrong way. Here, sit down here and order up. My treat."

Melba would recount this moment for generations. She was perched rigidly on a counter stool looking up at the overhead menu when a soda jerk wearing a white envelope cap cocked absurdly over one eye came face-to-face with her.

"What'll it be, Miss?" he asked.

Melba dropped her eyes to meet his, and as she was to recount to her great-grandchildren, it was love at first sight.

Melba swallowed hard, and flushed. Goose bumps crept across her lower arms, her lips twitched, and her mouth went dry. It was love.

"Coke," she stammered.

"Me, too," Francine called from somewhere in the crowd.

"Cherry?" David Merriwether asked, staring at her face.

"She sure is . . ." Francine called from the throng.

Dave blushed and Melba turned crimson, looking down at the floor.

"Don't take it so hard. I hear that old joke a hundred times a day on this job," he said, squeezing her hand for reassurance. "Wanna switch to chocolate?"

She nodded and he left to get the drinks.

"What is it?" Francine asked, putting her hand on Melba's shoulder.

"It must be the air in here. I feel a little dizzy," Melba lied.

"You need a cigarette?" Francine inquired, pulling out a pack of Lucky Strikes.

"Naw, thanks. I don't smoke."

Dave was back with the Cokes and set them on the counter in front of the girls.

"You new around here?" he asked Melba.

She nodded.

"Where you from?"

"Logan."

"She your sister?" he asked, nodding toward Francine.

"Friend," Melba replied.

"I git off in twenty minutes. Can you stick around?"

"Oh, I don't know . . ."

"Sure can," Francine interrupted.

"Good, got to work the other end of the counter now. Stay right here," he instructed as he readjusted his cap and walked away.

"Why did you say we'd stay?" Melba asked.

"'Cause I'm not done with my cigarette, and they cost me fifteen cents a pack," Francine smiled as she blew smoke toward the ceiling.

Half an hour later, they left the Bee Hive with Dave walking between them. He had no auto of his own, and like Melba, he was fascinated with Francine's Ford.

Francine was amused at his reaction, and she let him drive, seating Melba next to him.

"Where to?" he asked, massaging the round knob atop the stick shift.

"Up Cook Street to the top of the hill. I'm going to show you two where I live," Francine instructed.

"Hang on!" he hollered as the car bucked from the curb and out into traffic.

Francine's flat consisted of two rooms and a bath on the second floor of an old mansion which had been divided into ten separate apartments. The house was fronted by a large porch, which nearly encircled the entire building. The entrance, a large oak door flanked by windowpanes of beveled glass, opened into a large vestibule and high-ceilinged hall. It was dark and musty inside. The stairs, while elegant and wide, were dimly lighted by an unshaded light bulb hanging on a wire from the ceiling.

Francine's living room looked out across the porch roof at a view of the city and river valley below. High ceilings and long windows gave the room a cold appearance. The grotesque, faded wallpaper did not improve this. The furniture was old but practical, and seemed to have an affinity for dust.

Humble as it was, it seemed a palace to Melba and Dave. They entered the apartment in awe, looking about in disbelief.

"You smoke?" Francine asked as she offered her cigarettes to Dave.

"No, thanks," he returned.

"Drink?" Francine offered.

"No, not now," came the answer.

"What do you do for fun?" Francine asked as she checked the seam of her hose.

"Enjoy life, naturally," he responded.

"You do natural things?"

Melba blushed for Dave. She could tell that Francine was making fun of him and somehow felt protective.

"No, I do what comes naturally," he smiled.

"I'll drink to that," the hostess smirked as she pulled a beer from the icebox and examined his lanky rawboned form.

He stood stooped shouldered holding Melba's sweater over one arm, and his jacket over the other.

"Are you two going to just stand there in the middle of the room?"

They looked about, pondering where to sit. They settled on the studio couch.

"Where do you sleep in this place?" Melba asked, noticing no bed.

"You're sitting on it," Francine said. Melba and Dave looked uneasy.

"Jeez," Francine exclaimed, placing the palm of her hand on her forehead. "You act like you think my sack is contaminated. Relax, loosen up."

Melba sighed and David cleared his throat. Francine put the bottle to her lips and swallowed long gulps of beer.

"Nice place you got here," Melba commented.

"Yeah, real nice," Dave said.

"It'll do until we get some of those Wasserman paychecks in our hot little hands," Francine said as she walked to the window, and stood staring down at the city below. "Then, look out big city, I'm going to turn you upside down."

The prestige of the federal government had reached an all time high. Admiral Byrd had radioed from Little America, John L. Lewis and Huey Long were contained, and Al Capone was in jail. The government had never before been so authoritative.

This reputation was exemplified by the personality of the newly appointed Treasury Agent, Alcohol Tax Division, assigned to Riverport. With infinite wisdom, Washington dispatched Benjamin Howard Bentley to head the gaugers to measure and tax the production of the distillery.

As he stepped from the train, a cloud of steam hissed out from under the coach, accompanied by the clang of the couplers. Destiny had set the stage to herald his arrival.

He was a wiry, slightly stooped man dressed in a wool suit smelling of mothballs. His white Panama hat and black and white oxfords were a contrast to the rest of him. His bulldog face was stern and unsmiling. He examined the crowd on the station platform and picked up his suitcase. His mannerisms seemed uncoordinated, but as the top "T" man in town, he was not to be underestimated. He had come to do a job, and to make his permanent home in Riverport.

Cabbies lined up along the platform, calling out for fares. Bentley ignored them and approached a trainman.

"Where is the Niagara Hotel?" he asked.

"Right downtown," came the answer.

"How far from here?"

"About six blocks toward the business district."

"Thank you," Bentley grumbled as he gripped his suitcase by the worn handle and took off with great strides past the taxis and across the tracks toward town.

Among the autos parked at the depot was a white Cord. From within, Dr. Barstow and McKenna watched the new arrival push through the crowd and charge across the tracks.

"Tough son of a bitch," the doctor said. "They say he goes by the book and cannot be coerced – but I've never met a government man who didn't have a price. I don't think this one is an exception."

"He was one of the primary witnesses for the government in the Capone case," McKenna noted. "Looks like he's gonna hoof it to the hotel."

"Right through the red-light district," the doctor said. "Let's watch and see what reaction he has to those 'sporting houses.'"

"If he lives up to his reputation, he'll probably close 'em as he goes by."

Barstow moved the car to the end of the platform so they could watch Bentley's progress toward town.

There were no houses of ill repute on the street he had chosen, but each cross street and alley bristled with prostitution. The houses were mostly small frame buildings with front porches. Competition was keen, and each house displayed their best-shaped harlot behind cheesecloth in the doorway. Red lights within the house provided illumination for her silhouette. Coins were rapped against the window glass, and the women's voices called out in the night to lure trade to their house.

Bentley was not wearing blinders. The first side street caught his attention. He stopped walking and stood staring in disbelief. After a short pause, he looked around to see if anyone was watching him. He put his suitcase down and pulling a notebook from his pocket wrote something in it. He put the notebook back in his pocket, picked up his suitcase, and continued on his way.

"What do you make of that?" McKenna asked.

"Whatever it was, he wrote it down so he won't forget it," the doctor said. "Go visit Madam Byrd tomorrow. We must take her a bottle of her favorite 'Canadian'," he added as he started the engine to drive away. "We may have found Achilles' heel."

CHAPTER THREE

THE PITCH, THE PARRY, AND THE PICKET

Church on Sunday was an all day event for Pearl and Shorty. First, there was Sunday school. Melba sat with them while a red-faced man wearing a toupee led the group through a verse of the Bible. Then, they listened while he explained his version of what they would read. And then they prayed. They put coins into an envelope and held hands before adjourning to the basement for milk and tea.

After the refreshments, it was back to the sanctuary for regular church services. They prayed again, stood to sing, took communion, and listened to the sermon.

After this, they went to the basement to set the tables for the noon meal. Melba and Pearl helped fix the food, and Shorty sat with the minister and several other men discussing church business.

There was a constant stream of new faces entering the room. Melba was introduced to each of them, but when the day was over, she could not remember more than one or two. She was glad to go home, where she retreated to her room.

On Monday Melba was up early and had done the wash by the time Aunt Pearl had finished the breakfast dishes. Grumbling about the Roosevelt Administration, Uncle Shorty grabbed his lunch bucket and left for work.

Pearl dried her hands as she approached Melba.

"Bless you, child. How come you did things so early?" she asked.

"I'm going to work on a new job," Melba answered.

"You got work?"

"It ain't much," Melba lied. "I've got a waitress job downtown at the Bee Hive."

"Praise the Lord. Everything in its own time," Pearl exclaimed. "What hours will you be workin'?"

"Afternoons and evenings, but I've got to get some shoes first," the girl explained.

Melba hated telling such falsehoods to Aunt Pearl, but she knew the truth would put an end to the distillery job, and Melba wanted nothing to come between her and twenty-seven dollars per week.

"Shall I fix lunch for you to take along?" Pearl asked.

"Naw, they have food there."

"I wish you'd told us this last night. Your Uncle Shorty would be proud that you got work already."

"When I went to bed, he was listenin' to the President's speech," Melba explained. Actually, they had both been so engrossed in the radio speech that she could not have gotten their attention had she tried.

Not wanting to get too entangled in the conversation and the lie she had told, she hung the last of the clothes on the line and went upstairs to her room.

Shortly afterwards, Francine drove up in front of the house and walked to the porch. Melba saw her from the bedroom window and raced to the stairs. She was glad Francine did not have a cigarette in her mouth – the rest of her appearance would be shocking enough for Pearl. The bright red skirt, high heels, rouged cheeks and painted lips were not unnoticed. It would have been better if Melba had arranged to meet her friend at the corner.

"Hi," Francine called out through the screen door. "Anybody home?"

"In here," Aunt Pearl answered. "Come in. Are you Melba's friend?"

"Yes, I'm Francine Ryan," she said with a broad smile.

"Melba," Aunt Pearl called toward the stairway. "Your friend is here to see you."

Melba was already bouncing down the steps, nodding at Francine as she descended.

"Hi there," Melba said.

"Ready to go for a fitting?" Francine asked.

"Fitting?" Aunt Pearl inquired.

"Oh yeah," Melba said, turning toward Francine. "I told Aunt Pearl about my job at the Bee Hive. I forgot to tell her we've got to be fitted for uniforms," she explained, winking at Francine.

"Bee Hive?" Francine started. "Oh yeah, we both got jobs at the Bee Hive."

"That's a busy place down there," the older woman observed. "Don't you girls take up with any 'slickers.'"

"Naw, not us," Melba assured, smiling at Francine as they crossed the porch and stepped down to the sidewalk.

"Bye, Aunt Pearl," Francine shouted from the curb.

Aunt Pearl waved from the bay window as they drove away. She wished Shorty was here to tell her what to think of this friend of Melba's.

"I thought you'd come by closer to noon." Melba remarked.

"Too excited. We've got things to do and see," Francine answered. "We ought to find the best route to Jacob Wasserman's plant. Looks like we'll be comin' and goin' every day."

"I didn't tell you about my Aunt Pearl," Melba explained. "She and her husband are very straight-laced. If they ever find out I'm workin' in an alcohol factory, they'd disown me."

"I saw the problem the minute I met her," Francine admitted. "Where'd you like to go today?"

It did not surprise Francine that Melba wanted to go to the Bee Hive, and it was not unexpected that she sat at the counter across from David Merriwether.

"Mornin', Melba," he greeted, adjusting his cap on his oily hair. "Coke?"

"Orange Crush."

"How about you?" he asked Francine.

"Same here."

"Comin' up."

Melba watched Dave as he walked away, and Francine watched a white Cord as it turned the corner. She had never seen such a beautiful auto. Someday, she'd get one for herself.

On Dave's break, Melba strolled with him down to River Park. It was too cool to sit on a bench, so they slowly walked along the water's edge.

"I get paid Friday. Could we take in a movie?" he asked.

"Before three or after midnight?" she inquired.

"Why then?"

"Because I'm going to work second shift starting tonight."

"Where?"

"At Wasserman's – but if my aunt or uncle inquire, I'm workin' at the Bee Hive," she warned.

"They don't know where you're gonna be workin'?"

"I can't let them know the truth just yet," she answered. Melba shuddered and Dave opened his jacket and wrapped it around her.

"What's that?" she asked, pointing to a red mark on his neck.

"Got splashed by hot grease at the grill," he answered.

"Looks like a hickey to me," she said.

"Hot grease," he reassured her.

"Did you ever do this before?"

"Do what?"

"Walk along here with your arm around a girl?"

"Not this week."

She stiffened and moved away. "What a prude!" he exclaimed.

"I'm not just another skirt, you know."

"No, and I never said you were."

They stopped walking and stood facing each other. He bent down and kissed her. Her eyes seemed bluer than ever, and her lips were warm and moist.

She shuddered again but not from the cold. His muscular body could be felt through their clothing, and she got dizzy.

It was 2 p.m. when Francine parked the car, and with Melba in tow, walked down Apple Street toward the distillery. The plant loomed larger and more alive as they approached. A row of empty boxcars blocked the view to the right, and row of old commercial buildings bordered the street on the left. This seemed to frame the big red buildings ahead. A plume of steam escaped from the top of the tallest building. From where Melba saw it, it appeared that people flowed into the place at ground level and escaped skyward in a jet of steam. Melba trembled, and followed Francine through the gate.

Once inside, things changed. The drone of voices seemed less intense. The paved streets connected the buildings like a concrete spine.

The women presented their papers to a clerk at a table. She gave each of them a numbered badge and name tag and directed them to the bottling house.

A short flight of steps led up to a battery of time clocks and card cases. All of these cards were fresh and new. Still vigorously chewing gum, Francine changed from heels to flats. They approached the card case.

Melba found their cards and explained to Francine that because their badge numbers were consecutive, their cards would always be next to each other.

When Melba inserted her card, the clang of the time clock seemed authoritative as it stamped the time and date. For five decades from this date forward, the tug of war between women and the corporate giant would be a daily battle.

The women changed from street clothes to uniforms in a locker room. Melba tightened hers at the waist by pulling the belt. Francine had brought extra safety pins, and made her smock form fitting. Once done, Francine checked her appearance in the mirror, brushed her hair, smoothed her lipstick, and examined the seams in her hose.

On the floor above, behind swinging glass doors, a large open room bristled with rows of conveyors transporting bottles to machines that filled and capped them. The sound was intense – everything in the room generated noise. The women along the assembly lines shouted to one another to be heard.

A supervisor greeted the new arrivals and gave a brief explanation of the process. She assigned Melba and Francine to visually inspect the passing bottles for flaws or cracks. The woman then disappeared down the line.

Melba's temples throbbed from the excitement. Francine looked about the room as if casing a bank before a heist. She turned to Melba, popped her gum, winked and went to work watching the passing flow of bottles.

It was a long shift, and after it was over, the women changed back into their street clothes and punched out. Outside the building, it was dark. The lights along the company street marked the route to the exit gate by the parking lot and stockyards. The air was heavy with smells in the damp atmosphere. Melba felt as if she had been flushed through a sewer pipe. Two other women who worked with them, walked along as they passed through the gate. They introduced themselves as Marge and Helen, and when Francine learned they had no transportation she gave them a ride.

Their destination was the Bee Hive. They were disappointed when they arrived. The business district was dark and closed.

The clock atop the courthouse reminded them that it was long after midnight. The last streetcar had disappeared down Cook Street.

On the Courthouse Square, a lone figure sat at the base of the Civil War monument. Melba recognized Dave and jumped from the car to go to him.

"Are you a vagrant?" she asked as she approached him.

"No, I'm just sittin' here waitin' for a carload of girls to come along and pick me up," he said. "I'll git her home," he called to Francine and the others.

"Are you sure?" Francine called back.

"Sure as can be," he said.

"See you tomorrow," Melba shouted over her shoulder as she locked her arm through his. They disappeared from sight as they strolled off into the darkness.

"Be careful, Pumpkin," Francine mumbled as she put the Ford in gear and drove off with her two coworkers.

A.J. Adams demanded that every prostitute in the city be examined by Dr. Wein once a week. Bud McKenna knew that Mrs. Byrd took her girls downtown to 'vote' on Monday night. Because business was usually slow then. This is why Bud picked this time to talk to her.

The alley off Main looked a lot like a European street. The buildings connected one to the other and the cobblestone pavement was narrow and winding.

Bud waited in the car until Mrs. Byrd and her girls returned. He gave them time to get into the house, and then he made his entrance. The house had been a private residence somewhere in the distant past. There was an entrance hall and staircase. He found the madam just inside the front door in a large sitting room.

She was a huge woman, over three hundred pounds, and she stood nearly as tall as Bud. It was rumored that she had had a twin sister, and in their younger days, they were known for their great beauty. No one knew if they were always involved in prostitution, or if this was something Mrs. Byrd got into in her later years. She appeared to be in her mid fifties. When she sat down in her oversized rocker at the front window, a gush of air retreated from the cushion.

"What brings you to my cat house?" she asked a nervous Bud who stood in the doorway, hat in hand.

"Got a deal for you," he answered as he placed a paper bag containing two bottles of Canadian on her lap.

She glanced into the bag and smiled.

"Two jugs! It must be one hell of a deal," she exclaimed.

"Biggest one yet," he assured her.

"If your boss wants *me* to go to bed with him, the deal is off," she joked.

"Be serious. He's after a particular john. If he doesn't come here on his own, we will have to bait him."

"If it's A.J., he's after, forget it," she warned, turning to the window and rapping on the glass at a passing pedestrian.

"More important than that," Bud announced.

"John L. Lewis? He wants my girls to lure John L. Lewis?"

"Come on, get serious."

"So, I'm serious. Who we gonna screw?"

Bud dropped the local newspaper into her lap.

"There's a picture of the new federal tax collector on page six. Doc thinks he might be attracted to the sportin' life. If he is, sooner or later, he's goin' to come to your place. If you make any contact with Ben Howard Bentley, it's worth big bucks to call at once!"

"And if he doesn't stop in?"

"Then we pick one of your most dependable girls and go to him."

"For which?"

"For which Doc takes care of all your little problems," Bud answered, dropping an envelope into her lap. "Pick out one of your classiest girls and be ready. Whether we seduce him here or on his own turf, just be ready."

Bud snapped the brim of his hat and departed.

Mrs. Byrd rocked in her chair as she watched him drive away.

"Now they want me to fuck the United States Government," she murmured.

Things went smoother at the distillery the second day. There was no slow down in the parking lot, or at the gate. Melba changed clothes and read the bulletin board while Francine primped. They found their time cards and punched in. Some of the faces seemed familiar from the day before. Conversation and laughter filled the air as they climbed the stairs to the bottling room.

When they pushed through the doors, they were met with silence. None of the conveyors or machines was operating. The lines had stopped. Two men wearing tanker coveralls stood astride line three, trying to free the conveyors, which had jammed.

Francine got a shrill whistle as she passed the men. Shouts of protest came from the women. "Let him git to work, so he can git this line runnin'," a husky voiced blonde shouted from the far end of the room.

"Yeah," the other women agreed. "Play with him on your own time, honey," an older woman advised.

The man smiled and went back to work. Francine popped her gum and swiveled off to her station.

The conveyor started with a jolt. The endless belt transported cases of bottles from the floor level up to the ceiling and through the wall.

Empty bottles entered the room from one end, passed through the bottling machine and emerged filled with amber whiskey, then filed before a row of women who placed them into cardboard boxes, glued them shut and sent them via conveyor to the shipping department.

It was only the second day for Francine, but she already felt the monotony. One thing that particularly bored her was the picture of a bearded Jacob Wasserman in profile on the label of each bottle.

"Ugly ol' bastard," she said aloud.

"Did you say something?" Melba called out above the roar of machinery.

"Ugly S.O.B.," Francine answered, pointing toward a label passing by. "If I had a face like that ol' hawk, I'd drink whiskey night and day."

"Shhhh," Melba hissed, looking about to see if Francine had been overhead.

A floor lady supervising the line approached Francine. "Anything wrong?" she asked.

Francine pointed again at Wasserman's picture. "Did you ever meet him?"

"That's my old man," the woman joked. "If you think he's somethin', you should see our brats!"

Laughter came from the women on the line.

Melba watched from the corner of her eye. She wished Francine would settle down.

"It's enough to make you drink," Francine called back, gesturing as if she was drinking from a bottle.

"Keep 'em movin'," the supervisor said as she walked on.

At first, the workers were full of excitement and vitality. As the shift wore on, and the clatter of machines and bottles continued, the spirit faded. Glances of despair were enhanced as fatigue took over. Only Francine seemed to maintain her energy.

A bell sounded. The lines whirred to a stop, and the women relaxed and stepped back from the assembly lines.

Melba flinched from the quiet and followed Francine and the others as they left to go to the cafeteria.

"Jeez, the noise," Francine commented between pops from her gum. "I thought this break would never come."

"It's a drag," Melba agreed.

They pushed through the double doors and descended to the first floor cafeteria.

"Coffee?" a woman behind the counter asked.

"If that's the strongest you got," Francine answered, putting her gum under the edge of the counter as she passed. Melba frowned at her disregard, and turned away.

How's it goin'?" inquired the floor lady as she came up behind them in the line.

"It'll do until I git your job," Francine smiled.

"I'm Jesse Woodrow," the supervisor said. "I'm a recall from the old Condor Distillery."

"Was that here?" Melba asked.

"In town, but not right on this spot," Jesse explained. Carrying coffee (and milk for Melba), the women went to a table and sat down.

"How'd you git to be supervisor?" Francine asked.

"Just luck and hard work, I guess," Jesse smiled.

"Or marry Jacob Wasserman," Melba jibed.

The women laughed in unison.

"You kids hang together around here until you learn the ropes," Jesse advised.

"We can handle it," Francine assured.

"Think so, heh?" Jesse grinned, putting her hand on Francine's back. "See that line of barrel jockeys along the back wall?"

Francine lit a cigarette and turned to look. The room was a sea of women seated at tables, but along the walls stood a continuous row of men, all wearing dark green coveralls.

"Jeez, when did they get here?" Francine asked.

"They were here when you came in. They're the biggest collection of studs in the state – they stand along those walls at lunch and break, acting like they are here to smoke a cigarette. They really are visually stripping and screwing every woman who comes through those doors."

"Whee, we've been gang-banged," Francine purred.

"Francine!" Melba protested.

"Oh, I'm Francine. This is Melba," she said to Jesse.

They nodded to each other.

"Remember, any problems, come to 'Aunt' Jesse. I've done it all, and my advice is free. That's what it's worth."

"Okay," Francine agreed as she made a visual examination of the perimeter of men.

When the break was over, the women filed toward the cafeteria exit. Francine stood out in the crowd. It may have been her nonchalant swagger, or the haughty tilt of her head, but the men noticed and reacted. Several of them pushed into line behind her and talked to her as the throng moved upstairs to the bottling room. Melba was too far away to catch any of the conversation, but she blushed at Francine's forwardness.

Once at the work site, Melba straightened her uniform and prepared for the assembly line to start, while Francine brushed her hair and cracked her gum. The lines started again with a jolt, and again the noise was deafening.

As the shift dragged on, Melba became more aware of the smell of whiskey.

"We could get drunk just breathin' in here," she shouted to Francine.

"Whas thet?" Francine slurred, acting drunk. "I'm Miss Wasserman an' I stay drunk because my ol' man is so *ugly!*"

"You wish!" Melba called back.

"My ol' man's uglier than yore ol' man," Francine continued as a defective bottle passed her station.

Melba saw the 'leaker' and darted for it. She moved under the line where the filled cases moved through the wall to shipping. It was here that the conveyor jammed and cases started rolling and tumbling.

Francine caught the movement in the corner of her eye and pushed Melba aside as cases came crashing to the floor. Melba steadied herself on the worktable and stared at Francine, then the falling cases and broken bottles.

"What was that all about?" Melba demanded.

"Look up!" Francine shouted, pointing toward the dancing cases.

"Jeez," Melba exclaimed as she dodged more cases falling to the floor.

"Get back!" Jesse shouted as she came rushing up. "Damn it, those cases could kill you!" She waved her hands in the air and someone threw the switch and stopped the conveyor.

Melba clung to Francine, shaking with fright. The line stopped, and cases ceased dropping from above. The floor was a sea of broken glass, whiskey and 'cardboard boxes.

Francine felt moisture around her feet and looked down at her saturated shoes.

"Oh, God!" she exclaimed, "My feet are soaking in eighty proof corn liquor, and my mouth is dry as cotton!"

"What happened?" Melba asked.

'The conveyor jammed overhead," Jesse explained, "You've got to keep your eyes open around here. There's lots of 'bugs' in this system, yet."

"Did you get hit?" Francine asked.

"I don't think so . . ." Melba stammered, looking down her wet legs. "All that whiskey and glass . . . what a loss, what a shame."

Francine," Jess interrupted. "Take her to first aid."

Francine's eyes followed Jesse's pointing finger to the back of Melba's legs where scratches had started to ooze blood.

"What is it?" Melba asked, turning to look behind her.

"Don't look, it's just some scratches," Francine said as she pulled her friend away from the assembly line.

The aid station was located in the guard office at the main gate. Hazel Mathews, a registered nurse was in charge when the two young women entered. She quickly appraised the, situation and went to work.

Melba lay on her stomach while the nurse treated the scratches.

"They burn," Melba cried.

"It's the whiskey," Hazel answered.

"They really burn," Melba repeated.

"Let's take a look at you," Hazel said to Francine.

"I'm okay," Francine protested.

"Up on the examination table," Hazel ordered, patting the leather-padded fixture with her hand.

Francine crawled atop the table and lay on her stomach.

"Oh, oh, you got nicked with some of the glass, too," Hazel observed. "I did?"

"Hold still. Have you had a tetanus shot lately?" Melba and Francine stared at each other.

"Well?" Hazel demanded.

"Never. Not me," Melba stammered.

"I'm immune," Francine lied.

"We are unable to give that shot here. I'll make arrangements for a guard to run you down to Dr. Wein's office," Hazel said.

"Do we *have* to?" Melba whined.

"Yes, you do!" Hazel snapped as she helped the women to their feet. Hazel made a telephone call, and a guard drove to the door in a station wagon bearing the silhouette and name of Jacob Wasserman. Before the two victims could make a second appeal, they were driven off toward town.

The women of the W.C.T.U. met at the G.A.R. hall, downtown. This meeting was particularly spirited. A plan of action was unfolded to the thirty-five members of the Riverport Chapter.

"We must take a stand," their leader shrieked from the podium.

"Yes!" the women shouted back.

"We cannot turn our faces from this dreadful business thrust upon our fair city."

"Yeah," again.

"We will bear our placards on high at the very portals of this place of iniquity!"

"Yeah!"

"A bus awaits us in front of the hall. Bring your signs, ladies."

"Let's shut down the dump!" came a shout from Aunt Pearl as she picked up her protest sign and headed for the exit.

The day had gotten cloudy, and the steam from the distillery seemed to hug the ground. Add to this, the stench of the hide cars and the smell of the stockyards, at best, made breathing difficult.

Bud McKenna watched from the second floor of the administration building. Dr. Barstow hooked his little finger under the mouthpiece and put the receiver to his ear as he gave the operator a telephone number.

"A.J.?" the doctor asked. "We've got trouble on Apple Street. A bus full of W.C.T.U. people is unloading across the tracks from our plant."

"A bunch of fat old broads," Bud mumbled.

"Get your cops down here and move in," the doctor demanded. "And no press. Do you hear? Tell your friends at the *Riverport Times* that if they give this any space, we pull our advertising. Got that? Thank you, Mayor," the doctor set the telephone down and joined Bud at the window.

"They look like bandits," Bud noted. "They look like female bandits with those scarves over their noses. They must not like the air."

"Listen, Joe," Barstow said, turning to the plant guard as he entered the room. The doctor's voice lowered to a soft whisper, unheard by the others in the room as he gave detailed instructions, pointing toward the stockyards. The guard nodded agreement and left the room.

The W.C.T.U. formed their line of assault and raised their protest signs.

They created a circular march pattern in front of the main gate. Bud and Barstow could hear their shouts above the sounds of industry.

A railroad brakeman stepped from between the freight cars and waved his arm overhead. From the rail yards, a steam whistle responded and a locomotive struggled forward, pulling loaded stock cars onto the track along the distillery fence. The bell on the engine clanged and steam hissed from the pistons. A switchman stepped onto the running boards at the front as the train chugged in the direction of the pickets.

Aunt Pearl saw it coming, and took a determined stance, her sign held aloft like a victorious goddess of war. She set her jaw, stood next to the track and glared at the approaching locomotive.

The company station wagon bearing Melba and Francine returned to the plant, and crossed the tracks between Aunt Pearl and the train.

As it came within feet of Pearl, her eyes fell upon the face of Melba, and she shrieked her disgust. Melba tried to hide, but she had been recognized.

Pearl chased the station wagon to the gate, thrashing it with her protest sign.

From the second-floor window, Dr. Barstow waved his handkerchief toward the stockyards and stepped back from the window.

Two men in dark green coveralls darted from the distillery into the stockyards, opening the pens as they went. First, there was a cracking noise, and then the sound of hooves on the earth. An escaping herd of steers bolted from the yards. Corralled on one side by the distillery fence and on the other by the moving train, they ran toward Apple Street and Aunt Pearl!

Pearl was now confronted by an approaching locomotive and a drove of frightened animals coming her way.

Melba tried to watch over her shoulder as the station wagon entered the company property and stopped before the first building.

It seemed Aunt Pearl would be trampled by the steers or crushed by the train. She elected to deal with the animals. Raising her sign high in the air, she brought it down across the nose of the lead steer. As it moved away, she fell in the opposite direction, with the agility of a ballet dancer, into the outstretched arm of the brakeman on the running board of the engine. She stood alongside the trainman, thrust out her fat chin and shuddered in triumph. Posing victoriously on her perch at the front of the train, she rode past the distillery and out of sight. The whistle wailed as the train picked up speed and went its way.

Melba breathed a sigh of relief and slumped down in her seat.

The pickets stood gawking in disbelief. They dropped their signs, returned to the bus, and disappeared up Apple Street just as five carloads of police arrived at the scene.

Melba sat in the company car and cried, Francine held her head and mumbled, "Jeez, did you see that? Your Aunt Pearl rode off on that freight train!"

CHAPTER FOUR

THE MEETING, THE MOVE, THE MEDIA

Melba dreaded going home when the shift was over. Even if Aunt Pearl had survived the train ride, there was no doubt that she had recognized Melba in the company station wagon. By now she would have informed Uncle Shorty and both of them would be waiting for her. The thought of confronting them under such circumstances was just too much.

"Can you drop me at the Bee Hive?" Melba asked as she got into the car.

"Any place you say, kiddo," Francine answered as she started the engine. "Will Dave be waitin' for you?"

"He said he would," Melba mumbled. "He doesn't know what a ratty day I've had. I've got to talk to him."

Francine looked at her friend from the corner of her eye as she drove the car onto Apple Street. "Will he make up for it?"

"Naw, I just want to be with him. He's my refuge, I guess."

" . . . You can count on him *that* much?"

"That's right," Melba answered, brushing the hair from her face.

Francine could smell Evening in Paris perfume. This told her that the meeting with Dave was important.

Dave was seated at the base of the Civil War Monument when they arrived at the courthouse.

Wire wheels and chrome made the Ford noticeable. The fact that there was very little traffic at that hour made it even more outstanding. But in case that was not enough, Francine beeped the horn and flashed the lights as she headed to the curb near Dave.

"Quiet," Dave shouted as he stood up. "You want to wake all the pigeons?"

"Just the 'bums' on the square," Francine shouted back from the car.

Melba jumped out and ran to Dave.

"Hi, Pumpkin," he greeted. "How'd it go at the whiskey factory tonight?"

His question caused her to review the day and its consequences, and she broke into tears.

"Hey, what the heck," he exclaimed. "What's this all about?"

"I had a bad day," Melba cried.

Francine sat in her car and waited.

Melba explained the day's events. He examined the scratches on the back of her legs, and they walked back to Francine's car.

"Looks like she better have reinforcements when she gets home," he said to Francine. "You got time?"

"Sure, Francine answered. "You comin' along?"

"The more the merrier," he answered as he followed Melba into the back seat.

Not one of them really wanted to confront Aunt Pearl and Uncle Shorty, but each of them knew it must be done.

As they approached the house, they saw an old truck parked in front.

"Oh, jeez," Melba exclaimed.

"What?" Francine inquired.

"My folks are here." Melba stated.

"What?"

"My folks are here." She repeated.

"Your folks?" Dave inquired.

"Oh, Mona, I'm really in for it now," Melba wailed.

Francine parked the car and the three of them got out. Their minds were racing as they approached the house.

Melba entered first. Francine and Dave reluctantly followed.

Her parents sat in the living room with Pearl and Shorty. No one stood up when Melba and her friends entered the room.

"Mom, Dad . . . what a surprise!" Melba started.

She hugged her mother, and patted her father's shoulder. "I didn't know you were coming to Riverport! Oh, let me introduce my friends, Francine and Dave. They work with me."

Dave and Francine nodded to the four solemn adults. They got no response.

"We've got personal business to talk about," Harold Starks began. "Ask your friends to let us talk in private."

"We don't have to talk in private. They are close friends. Say what you will," Melba said.

"This is family," Harold frowned.

"We'll wait outside," Dave said as he turned to leave.

"Don't go away!" Melba pleaded.

"Just to the porch. No farther than out here on the porch," Dave assured her.

He turned to leave the room with Francine right behind him.

Melba sat on the divan next to her mother. The room fell quiet.

After a brief period, Shorty stood and paced the floor in front of the others. His short legs and small feet gave him the appearance of a mechanical doll. He hooked his thumbs under his suspenders and paced some more. First he would stare at the floor, and then the ceiling. He seemed to be building himself into some sort of frenzy.

When he started to talk, he quoted the scriptures concerning sin. He expressed his opinion about alcohol. He did not condone its use, and he was adamantly against its manufacture. He listed the pitfalls of those who drank.

From here, he sang out the virtues of the home and family. Then he boasted of the purity of his own home. His voice got higher in pitch as he went on. At last, in a grand finale, he turned toward Melba and roared accusations that she had attempted to vilify his abode.

Lacey squeezed her daughter's hand. Harold rose and stood between Melba and Shorty.

The voices softened, and it was agreed that Melba would leave the house immediately. She stepped to the front door and beckoned Francine.

"Can you haul me and my stuff downtown to the YWCA?" Melba asked.

" . . . You gonna go for a swim?" Francine inquired.

"Naw, I'm movin'," Melba answered.

Dave came to her and put his hand on her shoulder. "You been told to git in the middle of the night?" he asked.

"Bag and baggage," Melba responded.

Man, they don't give no quarter, do they?"

"They are very set in their ways. I'll not give up my job at the distillery to oblige them. I'd sleep in the park before that," Melba stated.

"I'll take you wherever you want to go," Francine offered.

Lacey stepped alongside Melba and hooked her arm through Melba's. "Where will you go?" she asked.

"I'm goin' to move to the 'Y'," Melba explained.

"Wait, hold on," Francine interrupted. "Why don't you move in with me? I've got room, and you could sleep on the couch."

Melba listened for a complaint from her mother. She heard nothing. "Okay, it's a deal . . . . For five bucks a week?"

"Deal," Francine agreed as they shook on it.

"I'll help you move," Dave offered.

It took them few trips upstairs to gather Melba's worldly possessions. Dave and Harold took time to admire Francine's Ford and to talk of autos in general.

Melba went back to the house and hugged a rigid Aunt Pearl.

Harold and Lacey climbed into their truck and departed. Francine drove the rest of the gathering away in the Ford, leaving Aunt Pearl and Uncle Shorty still sitting in their living room.

When Harold and Lacey crossed Apple Street, he nodded toward the big red buildings, looming out of the darkness.

"That's the distillery," he mumbled.

Lacey searched the scene with her eyes.

"Twenty-seven bucks a week!" Harold exclaimed. "I wonder if they could use me?"

Lacey snorted in response, and the old truck rumbled off toward Logan.

The mayor had not forgotten that yesterday Dr. Barstow had called him 'A.J.'. He would get even for that affront.

Newspaper photographers leaned against the red brick wall of the rack house. Men in blue tanker coveralls rolled wooden whiskey barrels out into the sunlight.

"Have you met the government man?" an aide asked the mayor. "Not formally," the mayor responded. "Will you see that we are introduced before the 'Canadian' gets here?"

"Gotcha," the other man promised as he pushed through the gathering of aldermen and city dignitaries, and disappeared.

The approach of Benjamin Howard Bentley needed no accolade.

His height put him head and shoulders above the crowd. The solemn look on his ruddy bulldog face was a contrast to the excitement shared by the others in the gathering. He moved slowly but determinedly toward the center of the group. His eyes seemed stuck on the whiskey barrels as they rolled into the sunlight. His very presence seemed to put the stamp of authority on the occasion and the murmur of the crowd died out as Bentley and the mayor were introduced. Two government gaugers armed with pencils and clipboards talked to the barrel jockeys and made notes on their records.

"The local news wants a photo when the company pays you their first tax check," the aide advised.

"Won't be the first," the mayor corrected.

"I'm not much on ceremony," Bentley said.

"I'm rather used to it," the mayor said, smiling.

"Over here," Dr. Barstow called as he pointed toward the barrels.

"Dr. Barstow," the mayor greeted.

"Good morning, mayor."

"Have you met Mr. Bentley?" the mayor asked as he pulled them up close on either side of himself.

The press moved about for different angles and flashed the trio with their cameras.

Bentley and Barstow nodded to each other, and looked on while the gaugers measured the whiskey by volume and made their notes.

The press continued to take notes and scurry around.

Dr. Barstow posed with the check, as if handing it to Bentley. A.J. Adams, still in the middle, grinned for the picture, clutching the arms of the other two men. It looked as if the mayor had orchestrated the entire scene. He had.

Except for the conveyor belts, everything at the distillery began to work perfectly. Francine even learned to find her time card without Melba's help. In just a few weeks, the work had become routine. Friendships with other workers were established, and some cliques were formed. Usually the basis for such associations stemmed from residence. Many of the employees shared rides from outlying areas, and some of the workers were neighbors or former schoolmates.

Generally the women shared a spirit of companionship. They had distinguished themselves by becoming what the community called simply "the girls." No one could foresee that this name would stick forever.

Each week new faces arrived to work at the whiskey factory. Jesse Woodrow appointed Francine crew leader on the bottling line, and Melba was assigned to a group on the ground floor rescuing tax stamps from broken bottles.

The women always sat together at lunch and on the breaks. The cafeteria became a place of refuge. Even the perimeter of staring men became an acceptable part of the scene, and almost seemed fitting.

"Where'd you get that hickey?" Jesse asked as Francine set her tray on the table.

"I was out with your ol' man," Francine shot back. "He says he's goin' to make me a supervisor, like you."

"That's my boy Jacob," Jesse said, and they all laughed as they sat down.

"How much sleep did you get last night?" Melba asked Francine.

"Sleep? Who slept?"

"You hadn't gotten home when Dave left. I was worried that somethin' had happened to you," Melba explained.

"I was invited to a party at a private club," Francine explained. "Wish you'd seen it . . . man, there was *real* waiters and *live* music!"

"Sounds like the Riverport Club," Jesse noted.

" . . . And where else?" Francine boasted.

"Dare we ask who took you to such elaborate surroundings?" Melba inquired.

"You'll find out soon enough. What time did Dave leave last night?" Melba blushed, and the women all laughed.

"I'm goin' to start chargin' him rent," Francine joked.

Jesse lit a cigarette and blew the smoke toward the ceiling. "How about us havin' a party?" she asked. "I'd like you kids to meet my *real* old man, and I can meet these guys who keep my girls up all night long."

"Sounds good to me," Melba answered.

"Always ready to party," Francine chimed in.

"Next weekend okay?" Jesse asked.

"All right, but not Friday night," Francine warned.

"Why not Friday?" Jesse inquired.

"I'm goin' to meet some special visitors from Canada at the club," Francine explained.

"Holy smoke, who you runnin' with?" Jesse asked as they all stared at Francine.

"Big shots, nothin' but big shots!" She bragged as they resumed eating.

The next day, Jesse was transferred to first shift, and she was permitted to take Melba and Francine with her.

"My ol' man is not goin' to like me workin' first shift," Jesse complained.

"Why not?" Melba asked.

"'cause with me bein' home in the evening, he won't be able to go out with the boys," she explained.

"And I thought it was *his* influence that got us moved up," Francine mused.

"Well, it won't screw up the party. We will still get together at my place Saturday night, right?" Jesse asked.

"Right," Melba answered.

"Francine?" Jesse inquired.

"Oh, I forgot . . . Roddie Dixon from home will be in town," Francine mumbled,

"So bring him to the party!" Jesse exclaimed.

"Well, I could, but I'll have to see if he wants to come," she answered.

"Don't ask him . . . tell him! We'll make him feel at home."

"What's he like to do?"

"Mostly, he likes to park and make out."

" . . . Tell him he has to wait until after the party."

"If I wasn't usin' his car, I'd tell him to go pee up a rope," Francine retorted.

With this, they all returned to their workstations. The noise of the conveyor made further conversation impossible.

The first shift was a perplexing change. The workers were unfamiliar and older. They seemed to lack the spirit which prevailed on the second shift.

Starting work at 7 a.m. was not easy, but getting off at 3:30 p.m. was even more confusing. When they left the plant, it was daylight, and the outside world seemed starkly realistic. The only good thing about this for Melba was that she could see more of David Merriwether.

Their first real date came when they went to the Palace Theater to see a show. Melba had never before seen such a big theater. It not only was large and splendid, but it was beautifully decorated. This was an instant fascination for her. They sat in the balcony where the height made her uneasy, until Dave put his arm around her.

The show opened with six acts of vaudeville on stage. A huge organ rose from the orchestra pit, the organist played music which filled the theater and the curtain went up to singers, acrobats, and comics. The organ disappeared into the orchestra pit and the movie screen descended. There were several short films, previews, a comedy, and the Pathe News before the feature. A crowing cock introduced the newsreel, which opened with a battery of microphones across the chest of F.D.R. The President, in his reassuring but forceful manner, gave hope to a struggling nation. The scene changed to a tavern where workmen held their glasses high as the commentator told of legalized drinking. The audience applauded, shouted and whistled. Melba noticed that most of them were about her age, and probably had never tasted liquor.

The newsreel continued with a scene in England and a close-up of Prime Minister Chamberlain, umbrella in hand, disembarking from an airplane and reassuring the waiting throng that Adolf Hitler had promised "peace in our time."

Again, the crowd in the theater roared.

Melba did not understand all of this, but she felt safe with Dave's arm around her.

It was less than a week before the party. Melba was washing her only pair of silk stockings in the wash basin, while Dave tinkered with the radio. He picked up a Chicago station, and they listened to the Amos and Andy Show.

"Where's Francine tonight?" he asked.

"She didn't say. Somethin's taken a lot of her time," Melba responded.

"It must be some guy. Don't you know who he is?"

"She won't talk about it, but I think it's someone important. He takes her to the Riverport Club."

"Wow," Dave exclaimed. "That's the high-rent district."

"I hope she's careful," Melba said as she hung her stockings to dry.

Monday night was "Voting Night" in the red-light district. Mrs. Byrd's car dropped four prostitutes at Dr. Wein's office and proceeded to City Hall. The mayor's office was the only room lighted. Mrs. Byrd squeezed her great bulk from the tiny elevator and shuffled into A.J.'s cluttered suite.

The mayor was alone at his roll-top desk, wearing a green eyeshade and celluloid collar. His shirt was heavily starched. Sleeve garters kept his cuffs from getting in the way. To Mrs. Byrd, he looked more like a poker player than a mayor. As she entered, he stood and offered a large chair next to his desk.

"Glad you came," he said.

"Did I have a choice?" she asked as she eased herself into the chair.

"Don't be so wry. We are old friends, remember?"

"Sorry, I just get edgy around any place that has a police station on the first floor."

"Tonight you are here through my auspices. You have nothing to fear."

"I've got to pick up four of my girls at Doc's office. Can we get on with it?"

"Okay," he said as he lit a cigar and pushed his chair back onto the shadows. "What's new in your end of town?"

"New? In what way?" she asked.

"New faces. New johns. New operations."

"New faces . . . just one at my place."

"Who is she?"

"A little brunette came to town on a bus and called me from the depot . . . worked as a call girl in a hotel in New Orleans. Never been 'housed' before."

"And you put her to work?"

"Not 'til Doc sees her tonight."

"What about your customers? Have you noticed anybody new?"

"Nope, same old country boys and married men we see all the time."

"What about the Strickler Brothers? Someone says they're back in town."

"Not at my place. They'd know better than to show up at my place after what they tore up last time . . . and *no, the new girl is not with them.*"

"How can you be so sure? Did you see her come in on the bus?"

"I didn't, but the cabby who brought her to my house says she came in on the bus *alone.*"

"Why would you hire a call girl who has never worked in a house before? Would you be savin' her for something, or somebody special?" he asked, moving back into the light.

"Maybe I'm goin' ritzy. Maybe I'm branchin' out," Mrs. Byrd snapped as she rose to her feet.

" . . . And maybe I'd better know more about this broad from New Orleans," the mayor said. "Send her up here when the Doc's through with her. What name did she give you?"

"Toni DeChalet," the madam answered.

"Toni DeChalet your rosy red ass!" the mayor snorted. "Bring her to me. I'll get her back to your 'house' by noon tomorrow."

Mrs. Byrd waved her handkerchief and lumbered off to the elevator.

"Everybody wants to get into the act," she mumbled as she descended to the lobby. "Don't anybody pay for anything anymore?" she questioned as she left the building.

The Riverport Club was nearly empty, as was the norm for Monday night. Off in a corner of the dining room sat Francine with Bud McKenna.

"Won't your wife wonder why you're out so late?" Francine asked.

"She's used to my putting a lot of extra hours at the plant," Bud explained.

"What if she calls for you there?"

"Security will cover for me," he assured her as he drank from his glass.

"When do I meet these special friends you've been talkin' about?" she inquired.

"As soon as I know you can be trusted," he answered.

"Trusted for what? Not to call your wife, or Dr. Barstow, or what?"

"I just want to be sure that you are mature enough to handle it."

"I'll show you how to 'handle it,' she said as she slipped her shoe off, and ran her foot up the inside of his pant leg.

"How safe is your place?" he asked.

"Melba is there, but she will be asleep by now. You can come and go in the dark."

"She won't know who I am?"

"Are you kiddin'? She won't even know you are there!"

Bud called the waiter, and signed the check.

"I guess we are goin' to my place then," she asserted as she put her shoe on and grabbed a handful of flowers from the centerpiece.

"Right," Bud agreed as they left the club.

When Francine and Bud crept into the darkened apartment, Melba and Dave lay very still on the couch.

For a Monday night a lot was happening. Dave proved he had no control, Francine proved she was mature, and Toni proved that she was better than an ordinary whore.

Dr. Barstow sat in his Cord and watched Mrs. Byrd's house of passion. Benjamin Howard Bentley made notes in a notebook as he peeked through the window of the whorehouse. Usually, Mondays were a bore in Riverport.

Jesse Woodrow and her husband, Clark, lived in a modest bungalow squeezed between other houses which looked much the same. Clark was a truck driver for a salvage company. He was better looking than Melba and Francine had imagined, and they liked him from the start.

It was Saturday night and the house party had started.

Dave escorted Melba, and by a quirk of circumstance, Roddie Dixon showed up with Francine. There were several other couples already at the party when the foursome arrived. Melba had made a casserole and Francine carried the flowers she had pilfered the night before.

Jesse had gone to a lot of effort. The dining room table was loaded with dishes, mostly the product of her labor. Melba followed Jesse to the kitchen, while Francine checked her appearance in the hall mirror.

"Nice of you to bring the dish," Jesse was saying as she reached up to get glasses from a high shelf. "I want to get these, and then meet this special 'guy' of yours."

"Anything I can do?" Melba asked.

"Just relax and enjoy," Jesse smiled back.

Melba stepped closer to take some of the glasses, when she looked up at the shelves of the cupboard.

"What in the world . . ." Melba exclaimed. "What are all those bottles doing here?"

Three of the shelves were stocked with products of the Jacob Wasserman Distilling Company.

"Support your local distillery," Jesse joked. "I've got at least one copy of every product we put out. See the airline miniatures?" she asked as she handed one of the tiny bottles to Melba.

"How did you get all of these?" Melba asked.

'One at a time," Jesse responded as she carried a tray to the dining room.

Melba stood staring at the array of labels. It was the first time she had seen so many different sized bottles all bearing the gruesome silhouette of that ugly old man.

"He looks downright wicked," she thought to herself as she followed Jesse from the room. It never occurred to her that the bottles might be stolen.

There was a crowd around Francine. She had bet one of the guests that she could roll a cigarette, and now she stood in the middle of the group holding a tobacco pouch by the drawstring in her teeth. She held a cigarette paper between her fingers. Tobacco spilled from the paper as she nervously tried to roll it. Finally, she completed the task and licked the seam with her tongue. Triumphantly, she raised the cigarette above her head for all to see. A shout of praise went up from the guests. One of the men struck a match and held it out to her. Francine put the cigarette in her mouth and inhaled. Melba was shocked. She had never seen her smoke in public before.

Drinks were poured and passed. The drinking got heavy.

Clark, with Dave's help, rolled the rug back to the wall exposing the wooden floor. Someone started the record player and they began to dance.

Roddie was having a serious conversation with Francine. He held her close, and kept a firm grip on her buttocks. She was smiling as she talked to him, but it was not getting much of his attention.

She handed him a drink from the table, but he refused to loosen his grip to take the glass. She held the drink to his mouth, and he drank without loosening his hold on her.

Melba gave Dave a knowing look. Dave shrugged, and they danced off to a quiet corner.

Clark made it a point to mix, dancing with every woman at the party. His warm smile and smooth manner made them feel accepted.

Time passed quickly. Voices seemed to get louder in proportion to the amount of liquor consumed. The conversation between Roddie and Francine became more intense, even when she broke free and selected something to eat from the table.

It was nearly midnight when Francine approached Melba and Dave. "Hey guys, this is kinda awkward, but could you get a ride home with someone? Roddie is in a snit and I've got to get him out of here before he makes a scene."

"We'll get 'em home," Jesse assured Francine. "Is he alright?" She nodded toward Roddie.

"Demanding. Just demanding," Francine answered as she stuck a thumb under a shoulder strap and straightened it. "See you tomorrow?"

"Be careful," Melba warned as Francine grabbed Roddie and departed.

Roddie drove the car as if he was angry at it. He made it lurch when he shifted gears, and when he turned the steering wheel; he did so in rash, abrupt jerks. It was obvious that the liquor had not tempered his mood.

"You tryin' to wreck that clutch?" Francine asked as he jammed the gears while turning a corner.

"*My* clutch," he reminded.

"My *neck*," she shot back.

Roddie drove over the bridge and parked on a levee across the river from Riverport. The lights of the town reflected on the water. The brightest light was the big red sign on top of the high wines building at the Jacob Wasserman Distillery.

Francine leaned back onto Roddie and studied the whiskey factory. It looked different from here. It was almost majestic in the silent night. The second shift had already punched out, and the parking lot was empty.

Roddie pulled her skirt up and thrust his hand down into her panties. She did not move. She had just noticed a light on in Bud McKenna's office.

CHAPTER FIVE

THE GIFT, THE GANG, THE EMBARGO

The election of 1932 had resulted in great national change. By 1934, this change was becoming evident. The "wets" had won over the "drys." The Democrats had come to office on a landslide over the Republicans. Both the unemployed worker and the beleaguered farmer looked to the new administration for direction. The programs of Franklin Delano Roosevelt added a new list of acronyms to the vocabulary of the average man. There was the N.R.A., the W.P.A., the C.C.C . . . . and there was renewed patriotism. It was cunning genius on the part of the Wasserman organization to announce the grand opening of their new distillery would be on July 4, 1934. Independence Day seemed to be a fitting day to prove that Prohibition was dead and a person could legally drink alcohol if he so desired.

Riverport's natural resources were not the only reason that this location was chosen for the Jacob Wasserman Distillery. It wasn't just because pre-Prohibition distilleries had been there, either.

It was mostly because of U.S. Representative Oscar Keel.

The congressman had been involved in the distillery business before the advent of the Eighteenth Amendment, and had developed a deep interest in the gains to be had by making alcohol, legally.

This is why he worked so hard to pass the Twenty-First Amendment. For his efforts, Canadian friends were so pleased that they invited the congressman to Riverport while they officially opened their new facility.

Few people caught the significance when he was named to the Wasserman board of directors.

The assembled dignitaries enjoyed an elegant luncheon in the main building. Congressman Keel, Mayor Adams, and Dr. Barstow made speeches. The general contractor, who had constructed the plant, presented a brass plaque to the chairman. The menu was akin to a medieval feast. The refreshments came straight from the bottling house.

After lunch, the guards opened the gates to the public. A crowd of curious citizens entered the plant and assembled before a platform in front of the Administration Building. Several hundred people listened to short speeches from the principal delegates and a band played patriotic anthems. (The music was both American and Canadian.) The crowd then shuttled off on guided tours of the plant, while the dignitaries removed themselves from the hot sun into the cool comfort of the boardroom.

"Bud," Dr. Barstow whispered into his assistant's ear. "Is security keeping an eye on those people coming onto the property?"

"We've got our people with each group," Bud reported. "Everything's going okay."

"Any W.C.T.U.?" the doctor asked.

"Naw, it's too hot for those old ladies to be out there today," Bud assured.

"What about those presentations from the employees?"

"The girls are waiting outside."

"Good, then let's get on with it before the congressman gets drunk," Dr. Barstow instructed as he turned to address the group. "Gentlemen," he called. "May I have your attention, please. Two of our employees are outside waiting to present a gift from the workers to those who were instrumental in putting this great facility together. Let them enter and be heard."

Two uniformed guards opened the mammoth doors at the end of the room to reveal Francine and Jesse waiting to enter.

Both women were dressed in ruffled white summer dresses, adorned with garlands of sweet peas and baby breath. (Bud had decided against using roses because of the possible reference to a competitor's product.)

The women stepped into the room, one to each side. Following them, a white-smocked steward came pushing a small cart. Each box contained a fifth of Jacob Wasserman Bourbon, and each box bore a small brass tag commemorating the event.

Francine and Jesse were introduced to the Canadians and each of the local big shots as they moved around the room. Each man they met was presented one of the varnished boxes. Each guest was pleased to see the label on his bottle read, "Specially bottled by the Jacob Wasserman Distilling Company for . . . . (The guest's name)." It was a surprising personal touch. Having the employees make the presentation was good labor relations. Francine and Jesse made a lasting impression on management. They were invited to join the directors. They were still with them when the group went into the patio to watch a fireworks display over the darkened river. It was a day to remember.

Francine didn't come home all that night, with no explanation to Melba. Talking later to his wife, Bud McKenna blamed his absence on the visitors from Canada.

With Francine gone, Melba and Dave had the apartment to themselves for the whole evening. Melba served a meal of roast beef, potatoes, and cold beer.

Because of the July heat wave, the apartment was extremely warm. After sundown, they sat on canvas chairs on the porch roof. Large trees surrounding the house helped shade the house in the daytime, but seemed to block the breeze after dark. The air was still and suffocating. By midnight it was still in the eighties, and because of the heat, they took off their last remaining clothes. Dave ran his hands over her damp body, studying each curve with intense interest.

"You know, I shouldn't let you do this," she said, peering up at him.

"Sorry, but I can't behave when I'm around you," he confessed.

"I want to be with you all the time," she said.

"We are spending more and more time together – do you think we should get a place of our own?"

"Are you proposing marriage?"

"Well?"

"If you want to tie the knot, ask for me on bended knee," she demanded.

"Oh, come on."

"On bended knee, buster," she said, pointing to a spot on the roof in front of her.

"Okay, okay," he agreed as he went down on one knee in front of her. "Will you please marry me so we can stop sneaking around?"

"Why?"

"Because I love you," he said, holding his arms out at a wide angle.

"Oh Dave, of course I'll marry you. When?"

"Let's borrow the car from Francine and Roddie, and do it next weekend," he suggested.

"Of course," she said, nodding her head. "Francine can be our witness."

"I hope she comes home before then," he smiled as he put his arms around Melba and pulled her close.

The Strickler Brothers had come to Riverport from another part of the state. In some ways, it was Riverport's misfortune that they came at all. There were five of them. They were mature, grown men who had been tavern owners and farmers in their previous experience. The authorities could not agree on what it was that turned them abruptly to a life of crime, but whatever it was, it made its impact on the City of Riverport.

Those in the know agreed that much of their early criminal activity had to do with bootlegging. This is how they operated taverns during Prohibition. Once the government made alcohol legal, most of the profit went out of the liquor business. The Stricklers considered the sale of legal booze to be too small for their type of operation. For this reason, they looked to other pursuits to create a high return on their time and efforts. Prostitution looked like a good prospect. They tried to muscle in on the established houses, but they soon found that people like Mrs. Byrd had that market sewed up. They did get one good idea from their confrontations with the madam. They noticed that jukeboxes were a necessary fixture in the front room of all the busy whorehouses. So they got into the music business, eventually branching out into taverns, restaurants, hotels and almost any place where people get together. The success of the music boxes financed their entry into slot machines and tip-boards. By the time the distillery had its open house, the Stricklers were in the big bucks from these new endeavors. They were big enough to war with rivals in Chicago and St. Louis. In fact, in Riverport they were to their world what the Canadians were to the whiskey business, except that they did not necessarily intend to stay within the bounds of the law. Both groups came under the wary eye of A.J. Adams.

The two factions might not have ever crossed paths, except that a jukebox owned by the Stricklers was installed in the distillery lunchroom, and Bud McKenna had it removed. It was not a great loss of income; it was the principle of the thing. Arlo Strickler called a meeting that night in the gangsters' "board room" in the rear of an arcade on Fort Street.

All of the brothers arrived and went to the meeting room. Arlo studied the faces of his brothers. There was an uncanny family resemblance about each of them. They were all stocky, blond haired gorillas of German parentage. It was admitted by all, that Arlo was by far the most intelligent, and Heinie the most dangerous. The others fit into the family picture somewhere between these two extremes.

"We been evicted by a local outfit," Arlo started out. "It is one of our absolute rules that *nobody* refuse to avail themselves of our music. If the people wanta hear our records, it is their right, an' our pleasure to make our music available."

"So why the meeting'?" Heinie asked. "Why call us together for something simple. You coulda just called me on the phone, an' tomorrow the place would be under new management."

"'Cause it ain't just no ordinary place, and we can't put it under new management," Arlo protested.

"Can't think of no place that we couldn't handle for business purposes. Where is it? The post office?" Heinie asked.

"It's that goddamned distillery," Arlo shouted. "They got the guts to have our machine pulled after we had it in an' makin' music!"

"How we gonna come down on them?" Heinie asked as the other brothers turned to Arlo.

"Through the ranks," Arlo shouted, pounding on the table with his fist. "Like a kidney punch in a street fight! We get 'em where they ain't lookin'."

"You mean we attack 'em from the river?"

"No, no, you dummers, we're gonna organize their workers into a union!"

"We don't know nothin' about no unions," one of the quiet brothers protested.

"We didn't know nothin' about music boxes either, but look at us now! We're goin' to St. Louis tomorrow an' bringin' back a experienced union organizer. I promise you, in six months we'll have this Jacob Wasserman by the balls!"

The brothers to the man sat in silence and stared at Arlo. This caper seemed a little too complex for their imaginations.

At the same time, another organization was meeting in the G.A.R. Hall just two blocks away. Aunt Pearl sat on the rostrum looking proud and determined while the expanded attendance of the W.C.T.U. plotted their strategy against the same opponent, the distillery.

Since their ill-fated attempt at picketing, the membership had explored other tactics. And while the first onslaught had been just short of a complete fiasco, Aunt Pearl had emerged as somewhat of a champion. She took the new attention in stride and sat in silent superiority holding sway over her sisters, haggling on the floor of the meeting room.

"Let's have order in the hall," the chair called, rapping her gavel on the dais. "Come now, ladies."

The women went to their chairs and sat down.

"In keeping with the authority of my office in event of a material need, I appointed a committee to explore our next action to eliminate the disgusting distillery from our midst. We will now have a report from Bernice Kaplan, committee chairman."

A dowdy middle-aged woman, heavily powdered about the face and overly rouged about the cheeks and lips, stood before the group, fondling a roll of papers in her hand.

"This committee," she began, "has exhausted every legal means of accomplishing our objectives, and has recommended to the body of this fine organization that they fight fire with fire. By a vote of five to one, we have decided to call upon our farming friends to boycott the distillery by refusing to sell grain for their evil purposes. The grain arrives at an elevator outside of the company property. We suggest that this group stop farm trucks from delivering any further grain to this plant. We can stop the distillery from making alcohol by cutting off their supply of material."

The membership went wild in response to the plan. Women cheered and rattled their chairs on the floor. Aunt Pearl clapped her fat hands together, thus indicating her approval of the tactic – at least it was not as risky as riding a switch engine. The membership agreed to meet at the hall early the next morning to start their stranglehold on the corporate giant.

Melba rode the streetcar to work the next morning. She had gotten used to Francine's absence, but this was the first time she did not make it home in time to go to work. Fortunately there were other distillery workers using the same means of transportation and it helped stave off the feeling of abandonment.

Melba had punched in and dressed in a clean smock, when Francine came dashing into the locker room.

"Did you punch me in?" Francine asked.

"Nope, I didn't know if you would show up today," Melba answered.

"Jeez, now I gotta go back to the time clock," Francine protested as she disappeared down the hall.

Jesse was just locking her locker as Melba passed.

"She burnin' the candle at both ends?" Jesse asked.

"Why ask me? You were with her, weren't you?"

"Up to a point. When the stewards brought the empty carts back, I came with 'em."

"And Francine?"

"She stayed with the big shots."

"It must have been quite a party," Melba mused as she walked to her workstation.

Francine thought the first break would never come. Her head pounded, her knees were weak, and her stomach threatened to reject its contents at any moment. If this was not enough, she was so fatigued that she could hardly function.

During the break, she did not go to the cafeteria with Melba and the others. She crawled under the conveyor line, and fell sound asleep. Before the break was over, Hazel Mathews, the company nurse found her and escorted her to the first aid room.

"The front office called to say you did well for the company yesterday and you should sleep it off on their time. Lay down on one of those cots in the office, and I'll wake you in time to punch out."

Francine did not answer. She went straight to the cot and dropped.

When the shift was over, Francine was waiting for Melba at the time clock.

"Hi, Pumpkin," she greeted Melba.

"Hi, yourself. How'd you make it through the day?" Melba asked.

"No sweat," Francine answered through a yawn.

They walked out of the plant to the car. Once inside, Melba could no longer keep her secret.

"Have I got news for you!" Melba started.

"Don't tell me Aunt Pearl wants to move in with us!" Francine joked.

"Dave and I are going to get married next weekend," Melba blurted out.

It was the first time all day that Francine forgot that she had a headache.

"You are going to do WHAT?" Francine shouted as she shifted gears.

"Married, you know, tie the knot . . . *get married* . . . like 'until death do us part' . . ."

Francine searched Melba's face waiting for the contradiction.

"Is this on the level?" Francine inquired.

"Right as rain," Melba assured her. "You and Dave . . . married?"

"Of course, why not?"

"But you haven't known him long enough . . . . Don't you think you should wait a while?"

"We know all we need to know about each other, and we will be married this weekend," Melba said emphatically. "Could you stick around tonight to help me plan things out?"

"Sure . . . sure, Pumpkin, I got no plans tonight."

The Strickler brothers had what was known as a "90" series Buick limousine. This specially built auto was usually owned by morticians, who used it to transport the bereaved behind the hearse. It accommodated seven if you used the jump seats. The five brothers and a former carny, recently turned union organizer, named Bits Casso, rode in this car as it approached Riverport. Heinie Strickler was at the wheel, driving as if the police were in hot pursuit.

"When we get to Frieda's, pull over," Arlo ordered from the back seat. "I need a drink, and Bits will change cars. No need for anyone in town to see us together."

"Gotcha," Heinie grunted.

"How do I contact you in person?" Bits asked.

"Ain't no way," Arlo growled. "But if it's really important, come here to Frieda's an' tell her you want a bottle of Old Country Schnapps. She'll get in touch while you wait at the bar."

"All the rest is up to me?" Bits asked.

"Like shootin' fish in a barrel," Arlo said. You got a flat, a hall across from the distillery, cold cash, and a great new union, 'The Amalgamated Brotherhood of Distillery Workers.' You hire your own goons an' we sit back an' watch ya organize Jacob Wasserman's whiskey factory. When it's a union shop we'll tell you what we want."

"That's one hell of an order," Bits mumbled. "You just take care of your end."

Arlo glared back. He did not like being threatened by anyone, particularly someone he considered "bought."

Heinie pulled into the parking lot at Frieda's and backed the Buick in alongside the wall of the building. Arlo was thus able to depart the car and enter the building in less than two steps.

One of the lesser brothers walked Bits to a nondescript auto, handed him the keys, and pointed the way to Riverport. Bits looked neither right or left as he pulled onto the highway and drove off. The A.B. of D.W. Union was on its way to town.

Down in Riverport, under the cover of night, Benjamin Howard Bentley sat in a diner sipping coffee and making pencil marks in a notebook next to his saucer. So far this night he had made entries on six "houses" operated by Mrs. Byrd.

Dr. Barstow sat in his Cord down the street watching Bentley's strange behavior. Could this man actually be frequenting the red-light district in line of duty? The doctor had lost enough sleep. He started the engine, and drove away. It was too late to go home and try to get some rest and it was too early to go to the plant. So its curious owner guided the Cord through the streets of the town.

The courthouse sat ominously quiet and deserted. A newspaper truck had pulled up across the street, and the driver was throwing bundles of papers onto the sidewalk. The headline was larger than usual and told of unrest in Europe. Hitler had killed three hundred Germans trying to leave the fatherland.

The Cord turned toward Apple Street and the plant. There was no obvious activity at the distillery.

The lights were on, but no one could be seen. The doctor knew his auto was too distinctive, and would be recognized by the guards, so he did not drive into the illuminated parking lot. Instead, he headed down the dirt road leading to the granary. Before he got to the truck scale, he came to a wide spot in the narrow road and he pulled in and stopped. The area was open like an abandoned battlefield. Large pieces of concrete and mounds of dirt bordered both sides of the road. This had been a dump or fill, raised in elevation to keep the river back. From this point, he could see the plant, but the taller buildings blocked the view of his office. He saw the company station wagon drive down Apple Street and enter the plant. In a few short minutes, he saw Bud McKenna's car pull away from the Administration Building and depart toward town. Dr. Barstow looked at his watch. It was 3 a.m.

The grain elevator next to the distillery was a separate but connected part of the total operation. Like the distillery, it was perched on the edge of the river, but unlike the plant guards and fence did not surround it.

The grain had been produced and stored on local farms. At dawn, loaded farm trucks started to line up on the dirt roadway leading to the granary. Attracted by the premium prices offered by the distillery, the farmers brought it here for sale. Rigid inspection and accurate measure were mandatory steps in the purchasing process. For this reason, the line moved very slowly.

The bus carrying the W.C.T.U. pulled up parallel to the line of trucks. Matronly women dressed in white blouses, black skirts, and flat straw hats stepped from the bus and went to work. The women scattered among the farmers. Handbills telling the effects of the demon rum were distributed and the women made speeches pleading with the drivers to pull away and boycott this elevator. The women even predicted the wrath of God on these humble farmers if they allowed the fruits of their labors to be used for alcohol.

Two large blond men wearing bib overalls operated one of the trucks sitting in line. There was nothing to distinguish them from any of the others. While they were not full time farmers, they still kept their hand in, in spite of their other lucrative business ventures. Partly for business, and partly for curiosity, Arlo and Heinie Strickler had come to the elevator to sell their corn.

Aunt Pearl approached them, leaflets in hand.

Arlo liked Pearl the minute he saw her. She was big and powerful and resembled his own dear, departed mother. She even walked like his mama and made many gestures characteristic of Frau Strickler.

She had no problem getting their attention. They were already fascinated by her appearance. They listened to her speech. They seemed to have never considered the physical damage done by alcohol consumption. They had never before been asked to think of the widows and orphans created by its use. If there was anything they feared, it was death, and the leaflet headed by a picture of the grim reaper brought the point home to them.

The feeling of mutuality between Pearl and the Stricklers was understandable. She fantasized that had she had children of her own, they would have looked like the Stricklers.

She accepted them at face value and became interested in their farm. They, in turn, listened to her talk of religion. Before the meeting was over they would have purged the line of trucks just for Pearl, and in fact, they did.

Arlo was smart enough to see that the W.C.T.U. strategy could hurt Wasserman's operation, and as he saw it, he would not lose anything by cooperating. Arlo told Heinie to put their truck perpendicular to the roadway, and while he did, Arlo walked the line telling the others to turn back.

Most of the farmers recognized him, and not wanting to get involved, they did his bidding. One by one, the trucks maneuvered around and left.

Aunt Pearl was joyous. She threw her fat arms around Arlo and then Heinie and hugged them. The women of the W.C.T.U. considered the day a success, and they got back into the bus and departed. The Stricklers sat in the cab of their truck and wondered what they had gotten into.

Francine kept her promise, and stayed home to make plans for the wedding.

Melba's firm conviction to the matter convinced the unbelieving Francine that this was serious business.

The apartment was torrid. Riverport was suffering a heat wave. A small electric fan whirred away at the scorching heat, sending puffs of hot air around the living room.

Francine came out of her clothing and poured a glass of ice tea. The ice clattered in the tumbler as she squatted on the floor in front of the fan.

"So, where do we start, Pumpkin?" she asked Melba.

"All day I've been putting this together in my mind," Melba started. "It won't be much, but it will be somethin'. Dave is more nervous than I am."

With a towel, Melba brushed sweat from her face. "He wanted to just go to a J.P. and tie the knot, but I want it in the church."

Francine paused. "You got a church?" she asked, rattling the ice cubes in her glass.

"I got church connections," Melba replied. "You forget I'm acquainted with Aunt Pearl's church. As good Christians, I'm sure they would not deny my request to be married there . . ."

"She'd throw you out just like she threw you out of her house."

"Not if I include her and Shorty in the plans," Melba remarked.

"Include them? How?"

"Aunt Pearl plays the organ, and Uncle Shorty could handle the traffic."

"Traffic? How many people are you planning on?" Francine asked, sitting upright.

"Just family and friends, but it will give him something to do . . . and they can hardly deny me such a request.

"Will Dave approve such a plan?"

"He will, and he has."

"Where do I come in?" Francine asked warily.

"Bridesmaid, of course. You are the number one gal . . . next to the bride, of course. Want to have Roddie down for the wedding?"

"Roddie . . . Jeez, I never thought of asking him down for this."

"I'll call Roddie," Francine agreed. "We'll have to have cold beer to keep him out of our hair. Are you goin' to have a reception?"

"Jesse said if we need anything . . . to give her a whistle." Melba suggested. "I'm goin to see if she would handle that end of it . . . maybe at her house."

"So who's the best man goin' to be?" Francine asked.

"Dave's brother, Julius, is his first choice. Of course, the family doesn't know me, and he may balk. We'll try to get his side involved."

"And your side?"

"Mom and Dad will be there, of course. Nobody knows where my brother Boyd is . . . somewhere out West. He won't be there . . . and that's it!"

"Guests? Who's on the guest list?"

"I'll have Jesse invite the women from work. Dave will invite his friends from the Busy Bee . . . but just to the reception. The wedding will be necessarily small."

"Jeez, Melba . . . if every woman on the line at work comes and brings a guy, you'll have more people than you can handle."

"I'll leave that up to Jesse. Will you get together with her and get things started? Dave and I have to go to the courthouse tomorrow for the license. We need a witness. How about you?"

"Witness to what?"

"To get the license . . . . You gotta have a witness."

"Jeez, Melba, this is gettin' pretty complicated . . . . Yes, of course, I'll be the witness, on one condition. When my time comes, you have to be *my* witness."

"Deal, so long as your time comes during the day. Don't call me in the middle of the night!"

"Funny girl," Francine chided as she threw ice at Melba.

Bits Casso was looking for an excuse to fill his newly rented union hall. He was out stumping for members when one of the women mentioned Melba's wedding. It fit perfectly. Most of the guests were employees of the Jacob Wasserman Distilling Company, and the occasion would be very timely.

Jesse agreed to have the wedding reception at the hall and Bits agreed to pay for the cake and refreshments.

Melba and Dave did not know that the Strickler gang indirectly sponsored their reception.

CHAPTER SIX

THE VENDETTA, A VISIT, AND THE VOWS

The next day the women of the W.C.T.U. took up positions along the dirt road leading to the grain elevator.

The farm trucks were met with scorn and chatter from the pickets.

Arlo and Heinie, wearing bib overalls, parked their auto on Apple Street and walked to the scene.

As they approached, they could see Pearl's bulk, leading the protest. There was much shouting and waving of arms.

"I told ya these farmers wouldn't stay away . . . look at the trucks!" Arlo grumbled to Heinie.

"Wouldja listen? I took care of it . . . they ain't goin' ta sell no grain today!" Heinie assured.

As the two men got to where Pearl was confronting the farmers, someone in the temperance group started to sing.

"Onward Christian soldiers . . . onward as to war . . ."

Pearl saw the Stricklers and threw an arm around each of them. As she did this, she joined in the song.

" . . . With the cross of Jesus . . ." she sang louder than all the rest.

Arlo frowned at Heinie, and both men joined in the song. Someone in the farmer's group threw a tomato, and it landed in the women's group. Shrieks of protest went up and clods of earth sailed back through the air.

Arlo and Heinie stood before Pearl to protect her. Missiles hurdled in both directions. At the peak of the fray, there was a loud boom and the first two trucks in line exploded. A large cloud of black smoke shot skyward, followed by a cloud of gray smoke and then a flame.

Drivers ran from the explosion. All eyes turned toward the holocaust. The rock throwing stopped and the protest signs fell to the earth.

"What in tarnation!" Arlo said, looking at Heinie.

"They musta drove over some dynamite," Heinie said, squinting his eyes and smiling at Arlo.

From the city came the sound of sirens as the fire department and the police headed toward the distillery.

The women were hurrying into their bus. Pearl wrapped her huge arm around her "boys" and pushed them aboard. The excited chatter drowned out any protest they might have made. Pearl was silent until she herded her charges into the long bench at the rear of the bus. They all sat down as the last of the women boarded and the bus started to move, It rocked, rolled and rumbled onto the road and moved away from the fire. When they reached the main road, they turned toward town and after getting under way met the emergency vehicles going to the scene.

Pearl reached into the picnic hamper and extracted a thermos of cold lemonade and a tray of oatmeal cookies. She offered the refreshments to the Stricklers. Heinie would have declined, had he not noticed the look on Arlo's face.

"Yeah, sure, thanks Pearl," he said as he filled his hands with cup and cookies.

Arlo nodded in agreement and did the same.

"I hope my two 'boys' didn't do nothin' ta blow up them trucks," she warned, as she busied herself with the food.

"Not us," Heinie said, swallowing the cold drink and looking at Arlo.

"Naw, not us . . ." Arlo agreed, staring at Heinie. "Can we get off before you git downtown?" he asked.

"You can if you promise to come to my place and meet Shorty," she replied.

When's this?" Arlo asked.

"Tomorrow night," she answered. "It's our anniversary and the whole neighborhood will be there."

"Oh . . ." Heinie stammered.

"Sure," Arlo promised. " . . . But just me and Heinie. The rest of our family has chores."

"Come about 7 p.m. I'll be lookin' for both of you," she said as she made them wince from her hug.

The mayor's office was charged with indignation. A.J. Adams stood in the midst of a group. The chief of police chewed on a cigar butt and dripped sweat on the desktop. The fire chief sat in a chair, holding a telephone receiver to his ear. He was getting a report from the fire scene. The newspaper reporters shouted questions at the three of them.

"Who bombed the trucks?" a reporter asked from his perch on the back of a chair, pad and pencil in hand.

"Is it gang warfare?" another asked.

"Quiet!" the mayor shouted. "Just get quiet in here! That's an old dump on the river bank down there. Maybe a discarded oil drum got too hot in this heat."

The reporters laughed. One of them cupped his hands to his mouth and called out. "Maybe someone popped their lunch bag on the fender."

"Or cracked a hot one after beans and beer!" another newsman joked.

More laughter and loud talk.

The fire chief was getting an update on the telephone. He talked, and listened, and turned to the mayor. "Fire's under control," he said. "Probable cause of the conflagration . . . dynamite . . . . No injuries."

"Dynamite?" the mayor shouted. "Where the hell did anybody get dynamite? Why they settin' it off down there?"

"We better talk this over," the police chief said, nodding towards the door.

Dr. Barstow came storming into the room. He charged past the crowd, and into an adjoining room. A.J. Adams and his department heads followed, closing the door behind them.

"What happened out there?" the doctor asked.

"Someone blew up two farm trucks down on the levee," A.J. answered.

"Are you aware that there is an attempt to create a grain boycott?" Barlow shot back.

" . . . We know that," the mayor acknowledged. "We cannot believe that a bunch of old women from the W.C.T.U. could know the first thing about explosives."

"What the hell, Adams, you know how mandatory it is that we not be disturbed. We've got millions invested on that river bank . . . with more on the way . . . are you going to tell me that you can't guarantee our safety from petty vandalism?"

"Nothing has happened to threaten you or your investment," the mayor asserted.

"It's too damned close for comfort!" Barlow shouted as he brought his fist down on the desktop.

"Get rid of the press," the mayor bid the police chief.

The chief left the room and confronted the reporters.

"Alright, lads," he called. "Let's break it up for now. As soon as we get a handle on this, we'll call your city desk. For now, we want you to leave the building."

A moan went up from the reporters, as they were herded from the room into the corridor.

"Cover-up!" shouted one newsman as he was pushed out.

Dr. Barstow sat breathing heavily, studying the face of A.J. Adams.

"Get a hold of yourself," the mayor said, as he bit off the end of a new cigar and spit into the cuspidor. "Nobody around here would blow up a couple old trucks just to intimidate your people. I'm sure we will find out it has no connection with your operation."

"We can't take that chance," Barstow replied indignantly. "If you can't squelch this crap, we'll have the Feds in here to do so. They will listen to the state's biggest taxpayer!"

"Hold on now," A.J. cajoled. "You are magnifying this out of proportion. Give us twenty-four hours, and I'll personally make a complete report to you."

"Damned right," Barstow agreed. "Twenty four hours, and it better be good!"

The mayor blew smoke toward the ceiling, held the door open and watched Barstow leave.

"You heard it," he said to his assistants. "Now get off your asses and get me some answers."

The chief of police and the fire chief left through the side door.

Dr. Barstow wasted no time in dispatching Bud McKenna to Mrs. Byrd's palace of passion.

It was early for the madam, and she was still in her private room. Bud had to wait in the front parlor.

Every time a new john came into the house, the girls lined up in the parlor for a ritualistic selection rite. It seemed that the girls who were most popular wore the least clothing. Maybe that was because they had the least time to get dressed.

The line up was full of contrast. There were short and tall, and slim and fat women. Most of them were in their thirties, and looked hardened. Bud thought two of them looked too young to be working in a cathouse.

Dusk came, and the trade under cover of darkness began to pick up.

Mrs. Byrd's maid announced, "Company, girls," each time new customers arrived.

Bud was beginning to get bored by the routine, and embarrassed by the delay.

"Hey Honey, you goin' to take one of us to bed?" one of the whores asked Bud.

"Not hardly," he answered.

"Then what the hell you doing in a fuckshop? You get your kicks outta gawkin' at us?" the woman demanded.

"He's here to see Ma," the maid interrupted.

"Probably a pimp," the whore hissed at Bud.

Bud stood up facing the woman. "I ain't no pimp and I resent your mouth!" he shouted. The parlor door slid open, and Mrs. Byrd stood in the opening.

"What's all the noise about?" she inquired.

Bud was red-faced and hissing.

"Lucy called this man a pimp, Miss Byrd," the maid explained.

"Why Lucy, you flatter him. He's really the 'house' boy for the biggest house in town. Right, Bud Boy?" Mrs. Byrd taunted.

"'House,' your ass," Bud growled.

"What then? Are all those broads virgins?"

"Are you purposely trying to piss me off?" Bud demanded.

"Of course not, honey, I like your little gifts too much to cause a rift between you and me. What brings you to 'Ma' Byrd?" she asked, motioning the girls to leave.

"Doc sent me because somebody is puttin' muscle on us at the plant. He wants to know who's new in town."

"We don't see many new faces down here," she began. "You might be interested to know that three nights runnin' we've had a guy in here throwin' money around like paper. He brags a lot, 'specially when he's in bed. The girls tell me he calls himself a union organizer from St. Louie, and he's got your plant in his sights."

"God damn!" Bud exclaimed. "What's he look like?"

"Tough lookin', big, tattooed, and just plain rough. He's got a jaw that juts out from a neck as big around as my leg."

"What's his name?" Bud asked.

"Don't know, but he is being bankrolled by someone 'cause every time he goes broke, he leaves for a couple hours, and then returns with fresh money."

"You got someone we can put on him?"

"Sure have, been savin' this little sweetheart for somethin' special. She comes high."

"Is she trustworthy?"

"She is that. Can your boss afford two hundred a week and expenses?"

"How about one hundred?" Bud replied.

"How about one fifty?"

"One twenty five and expenses. Don't let him know she's connected to you. Have her call you daily, and we'll pay the money to you as an advertising account."

"Startin' when?"

"Starting now."

"You don't let grass grow under your feet," she said as the doorbell rang, and the maid walked by to answer it.

"When somebody's doin' their talkin' with dynamite, we can't wait very long for answers," Bud said as he handed her an envelope and left.

Mrs. Byrd fanned herself with her handkerchief as she watched Bud get into his car.

"Tell Toni I want to see her," she said to the maid. "I gotta feelin' things are goin' to git a lot hotter before it cools off in Riverport."

The thirty-fifth anniversary of Pearl and Shorty Starks was an astoundingly lavish affair. The crowd was enormous. It was composed of their church family, real family, Shorty's friends from work, and their neighbors from all those years crowded into the house and yard. Movement was virtually impossible. From a distance, it was a sea of humanity.

Oriental lanterns hung in the front and rear yards. Autos were parked for blocks around their house and people came from all directions to congratulate this unusual couple.

Inside the house, Pearl sat in the center of a sofa, reaching out to friends as they filed past. Shorty stood at the side, smiling and shaking hands with the guests.

Arlo Strickler did not like crowds. Neither did Heinie. They had wronged so many people that they could not remember the faces of all their enemies. Further, they were generally anti-social. It could not be determined if being a gangster made them anti-social, or whether they were gangsters because of their hostility toward people. They both thought of turning back, but they *had* promised Pearl to come and meet Shorty. They cautiously entered the house and searched for Pearl in the crowd. Heinie carried two bottles of German wine as a gift. Arlo carried his hat in his hand.

When Pearl saw them she threw out both arms in welcome and with a beaming smile, she called them to her side.

"Oh! Look Shorty. Here's my two heroes," she purred. "Shorty, this is Heinie and Arlo Strickler. I've adopted them as my own. I just *love* these two young men."

"Hi," Shorty nodded, shaking hands.

"Hullo," Heinie mumbled, looking at Shorty and wondering how such a small man happened to be married to such a large woman.

"Congrats," Arlo said, handing the bottles from Heinie to Shorty.

Shorty hesitated, then took the bottles, wondering what to do with them.

"Ain't that sweet, Shorty?" Pearl observed. "They brought us wine for the communion. The Lord loveth a grateful giver," she recited, squeezing the hands of both Stricklers. "Lucille, take these two gentlemen to the buffet. I want them to enjoy themselves."

One of the church women led the Stricklers off to the dining room where they were lost from view.

When Melba and Dave arrived, both Pearl and Shorty seemed to catch themselves. They made welcoming gestures, and the two couples confronted each other. Pearl enveloped Melba in one of her famous bear hugs.

"Congratulations to both of you," Melba said, kissing Pearl on the cheek. "I love you," she added. Then, "Dave and I are getting married next weekend. Will you help us?"

Pearl clung to Melba and looked over her shoulder to Shorty's face.

"Him too," Melba whispered. "We need *both* of you, and your church."

Aunt Pearl studied Melba's face.

"You genuine sure?" she asked.

"No two ways about it," Melba smiled.

"Oh, Lord, child, of course you can count on us. The pastor is here in the house at this moment. We can work out all the details tonight!"

Melba kissed Pearl again, and hugged Uncle Shorty. Dave nervously shook hands with both of them.

Melba led Dave into the crowd to look for her parents.

Overlooking the distillery on the corner of Apple and Ninth streets was an old building that once housed a small grocery. It had large plate glass windows along the front, and one on the side street. The entrance was on the very corner of the building. Painted on the front glass were the letters "A.B. of D.W." This was the world headquarters for the new distillery workers' union.

Inside, a scarred glass counter and a row of wooden chairs separated the front from the office area.

Bits Cassno sat in his shirtsleeves before an old roll top desk. He cocked his chair back at an angle just short of tipping. Above his head hung a solitary, naked light bulb, dimly shining in the gloomy room.

He was reading a rolled newspaper and sucking on a broken toothpick as he swung one foot back and forth.

Toni DeChalet stepped to the entrance and walked in.

She had prepared her appearance with exacting detail. She got the reaction she expected.

Bits looked up from the paper. She was standing between him and the sunlight from the large show windows.

At first, he saw mostly silhouette. Her dress was thin, and she stood, feet apart facing him. The view was tantalizing. He could see her long, beautiful legs, curving hips, and small waist. Her shoulder length hair and snug torso caused the blood to surge to his head. He nearly lost his balance in the chair, making a clumsy recovery coming to his feet. The light behind her was too bright to see her face. He moved toward her.

"Good day, Sir," she greeted. "Would this be the union hall?"

"It is, if that's what you're lookin' for," Bits answered.

"Mah name is Toni DeChalet," she cooed. "Ah'm lookin' fo' the leadah of the new labah union."

"I'm the head man," Bits answered, moving around to get the light on her face. Now the light was behind him. Her face was exquisite. She had large brown eyes that dominated high cheekbones, full red lips and cleft chin. "What can I do for you?"

"Ah come to Riverport from down south to work at the distillery. An' they won't hire me because mah daddy is a union leadah in New Orleans . . . . so ah decided to come to y'awl for a job."

"What makes you think that's the reason they didn't put you on?" Bits asked.

"'Cause ah was hired fo' next Monday .... an they phoned down home an found out about mah daddy . . . an reversed their decision . . . now they don't want me."

"Imagine someone not wantin' you!" Bits said, looking her over. "Too bad we don't need some help here."

"Ah'm very talented in union work," she pleaded, leaning on his arm and exposing her cleavage.

"Don't need no women to build this union," he remarked, sliding his hand down over her rump.

"Not even a lil' ol' secretary?"

"No secretary . . . wait a minute. I've got a couple hours work on a reception here in the hall. Think you could play hostess?" he asked.

"Now what evah made y'awl think ah'm not a superior hostess?" she smiled, brushing against him. "Ah can handle that lil' ol' reception like a dream. Know what ah mean?" she asked.

"Yeah, I know what you mean," he agreed. "Let's make a list of what I want before it slips my mind."

He locked the door and hung the "closed" sign in the window.

It had not occurred to Dr. Barstow to check the whereabouts of Benjamin Howard Bentley during the day.

The federal tax income from the distillery had approached an average of one million dollars per month. The Treasury Department had established a regional office in Riverport to handle the collections. Bentley remained the top man.

With all the new responsibilities, it would have been understandable if Bentley had stayed on routine matters. It was an experience as a youth that caused him to frequent the red-light district in his unorthodox manner.

He had grown to early manhood in a small town in West Virginia where his parents operated a ma and pa type local grocery. They could foresee the limitations the isolated town might have on their son's future, so they saved enough money to send him to college in the East. What they had not counted on was that Ben had fallen in love with a local girl, Sally Pace.

Knowing he would not leave for college while she stayed home, Sally moved to Cincinnati to seek her fortune in the world while Ben got a formal education.

When she stopped writing, Ben went looking for her. The trail led across the river to the infamous red-light district of Covington, Kentucky. He spent an entire semester searching for her. He never learned why she went to Covington nor what became of her. Bentley never courted another woman and he never married. He had deep-seated hatred for red-light districts and everything they stood for.

Now, he was preoccupied with the red-light district of Riverport.

Had Dr. Barstow watched in the daytime, he might have noticed the Klene Towel Service delivery truck had an assistant driver helping with the deliveries to Mrs. Byrd's houses. Bentley dressed in a white uniform and black visor white topped cap similar to the regular driver. At each house, Bentley made the delivery and collected the dirty linen. After making the rounds, he would sit in the back of the van and make entries in his notebook. He was unaware that another laundry and dry cleaner made deliveries to a more elegant 'house' at the top of the hill. This establishment was also owned and operated by Mrs. Byrd, but it was too fancy for her tastes, and she seldom went there. 'Duke' Byrd, her illegitimate son, handled the operation.

Melba and Dave were going over the ads for apartments when Francine came home.

"Hi, Pumpkin. Hi, Dave," Francine called as she went to the icebox for a cold bottle of beer. "Is it hot, or is it hot?" she asked, popping the cap and gulping at the contents."

"It's hot," Dave agreed. "We're looking for a place in the ice house. Have you seen an old cave for rent?"

"Rent? Oh, for Pete's sake, you guys lookin' for a place?"

"Did you think we were goin' to celebrate our honeymoon with you?" Melba asked, smiling.

"I never thought about it," Francine mused. "If you move out, I'll be alone."

"No more often than you come home, I doubt that you'll miss us," Dave joked.

"I've got it," Francine said, her face suddenly coming alive. "Why don't you guys just stay here an' I'll look for a place to live? I've kinda got some plans in that regard."

"We couldn't do that," Melba complained.

"Will you listen?" Francine insisted. "I've got other plans and I won't need this place anyway."

"How soon would you have another place?" Melba asked.

"A week. Give me a week. I promise I'll be out in a week. Can't we overlap just a week?"

"I *do* like this place," Melba thought aloud.

"It is close to everything," Dave agreed.

"The rent is reasonable," Francine reminded them.

"Okay, it's a deal," Melba said, putting an arm around Francine and squeezing her.

"With that settled, I've got to buy a suit," Dave remarked, standing to leave.

"Francine and I have plenty to do. When you get your suit, be sure it will be altered and ready 'in time for the wedding," Melba instructed, as she kissed him on the cheek.

"Blue, right?" he asked. "You think I oughta git a blue suit. Ain't that what you said?"

"Yes Dave, to match your eyes," she said as she pushed him through the door. "Now let's git goin' on the loose ends," Melba said to Francine as she brushed her hair from her face.

Francine had promised to be at the union hall by 5 p.m. It was 6:30 when she wheeled up to the curb at Apple and Ninth.

Toni was sitting on the front stoop because it was too warm to sit around inside. Anyway, the place gave her the creeps when Bits was not around, and he had gone off to "confer" with his advisors.

"Hi there," Francine greeted as she stepped out of the car. The Motorola radio under the dash was playing a Rudy Vallee song. She turned back into the car to shut the radio off. "I'm Francine Ryan," she continued. "Are you Toni?"

"That's right, ma'am," Toni answered. "Are y'awl here to decorate?"

"I've got the stuff in a box," Francine explained as she tugged at a large box in the back seat. "I got crepe paper, and balloons."

" . . . . You got any string?"

" . . . Saw some around hyar today," Toni replied, as she stood and brushed the back of her skirt where she'd been sitting on the step. "What kind of string did y'awl have in mind?"

"Any kind will do, it's just for tying the streamers and the balloons," Francine explained.

"Let me help with that box," Toni offered. "Do y'awl mean that jest the two of us are goin' to decorate this entire hall fo' the weddin'?"

"I guess so. A friend of mine was goin' to help until he found out it was at the union hall, and he skinned out."

"Don't he like unions?"

"Don't 'speck, since he is management and he didn't wanna be seen around here."

"Well, ah declare, there must be some gentlemen somewhere out there. We'll just have to enlist them so they can enjoy the pleasure of our company," Toni joked. "Do y'awl have any ideas about how we should begin?"

"A couple of dolls like us shouldn't have to wait long before the guys offer a hand," Francine noted as the two of them carried the box into the hall.

An old stepladder was found behind the building. It creaked and swayed when Toni climbed on it. Francine grasped the bottom of the ladder trying to hold it steady.

They discovered that the walls and ceiling of the old room were dusty, but there was not time for general cleaning so the two young women wrapped their hair in towels for protection and used brooms to brush the dirt down. "Ah declare," Toni observed. "This place is just filthy. Mr. Casso better get a cleanin' person in hyar."

"We mustn't look a gift horse in the mouth," Francine cautioned. "He is donating the place for the reception."

"And well he should," Toni exclaimed from the top of the ladder. "Do y'awl have a husband, honey?"

"Not me," Francine asserted. "Men are a bunch of bastards as far as I'm concerned."

"But darlin', how would we fare without them?"

"I'd like to try. I've got one I don't need, and need one I don't have," Francine complained.

"Yo *are* married then, honey?"

"Not married, just obligated."

"Sometime I'll tell you my story," Toni said, as she tied the end of a streamer to a steam pipe.

Francine looked up at her and noticed that she wore no panties. "It must be a pip." she said, looking away.

"Sorrid, honey. Plain sorrid, but I'm still not what you could call a man-hater . . . a man user . . . of course . . . but ah cain't get around to hatin' the opposite sex."

"You'd hate 'em if you'd been 'had' as many times as I have," Francine assured her.

"Really, darlin'?"

"Really, babe."

The two women talked increasingly as they worked. In getting to know each other, they also were becoming friends. In spite of their opposing viewpoints about men, they had a lot in common.

They were still working when the shift changed at the distillery. Several men from the rack house were on their way home when they stopped in to help.

By midnight the hall was decorated. Exhausted, Francine sat cross-legged on the floor. Toni lay on her back next to the wall. Francine remembered she wore no underclothing and hoped she would not expose herself. One of the men folded a newspaper and fanned her. It was very warm in the building and they were thirsty.

"How about goin' up town for a couple of cold ones?" the first man asked.

"How about havin' one on the union?" Toni asked. "Ah'm sure Mr. Casso would like y'awl to have a refreshment on him."

"You got a cold one for each of us?" the second man asked, offering his hand to help Toni to her feet.

These circumstances lead up to the signing of the first members of the distillery union. These men from the rack house joined the A.B. of D.W. and later became the nucleus of a larger membership that played a significant part in the rise and fall of the Jacob Wasserman Distilling Company. During a heat wave in 1934, a lot was starting to happen.

The heat seemed even more intense on Sunday afternoon. There was no breeze. Only the scorching sun prevailed on the steaming streets of Riverport. The New Bible Church reflected the sun's rays from its white wooden exterior walls.

Just inside the open door, in the shade, stood Uncle Shorty waiting for the first guests to arrive. He was wearing a dark suit, white shirt, and bold necktie. A lodge pin sparkled on the lapel of the suit. His Cuban heels gave him unusual height, making him appear strange to the familiar eye.

Melba, Francine, Lacey and Pearl crowded into an anteroom off the vestibule. They helped Melba with her dress and veil. Francine brushed the bride's hair and checked her makeup.

At the opposite end of the church, Dave and his brother, Julius, waited for the music to begin and nervously paced the floor of a side room.

The guests, including the workers from the distillery, arrived and were seated. Jesse and Clark sat predominately toward the front.

Aunt Pearl stepped from the anteroom and nodded to Shorty. He closed the doors to the sanctuary as Pearl stepped to the keyboard of the organ and started to play "Oh, Promise Me."

Outside, Roddie Dixon took one last drink from his beer bottle, hid it behind a rain barrel, and stepped into the church.

The minister stood before the altar and waited for the prospective newlyweds.

The ceremony was necessarily short and simple. Melba and Dave exchanged vows with sweat running down their faces. They exchanged rings, kissed and departed the building in a hail of rice. The guests followed on their heels glad to get outside where the air was cooler. Aunt Pearl and Lacey hugged Melba and cried. Uncle Shorty faced the wall and blew his nose. Roddie Dixon went back to his beer bottle.

Roddie and Francine drove the bride and groom to the Union Hall. All the others, save the minister, Pearl and Shorty, followed.

Clark took photos of the bridal group with a box camera, and the party entered the hall.

Francine was right. The guests were so numerous that Jesse stepped in to control the situation. She formed lines before the wedding party so that each guest had an opportunity to offer the couple good wishes.

The newlyweds cut the cake, drank a toast, and stepped back for Jesse and her helpers to take over.

Before they departed, Melba tossed her bouquet into a group of anxious women. A loud cry went up along with much clutching for the flowers. In the midst of it all, Francine fainted and fell to the floor.

Melba turned back and ran to her. Jesse brought a glass of water.

"Francine," Melba called. "Oh, Francine, what happened?"

"I'll take care of her," Jesse offered.

"It's just too damned hot in here. She'll be okay. You kids go on."

Melba hesitated, but decided Jesse could handle it. She and Dave ran from the building into Harold Starks' waiting truck and left the guests behind.

The next day Bits Casso looked at the mess in his union hall. Then, he examined the names of the first members signed up. He smiled and pulled Toni to him.

"You did a damned good job here," he said. "Would you like to stick around with me on a regular basis?"

She had planned it that way. It was what she was sent to do. She would call later that night to tell Mrs. Byrd that her mission was successful.

CHAPTER SEVEN

THE HEAT, THE HALL
AND THE HANGOUT

The club was busy for a Monday night being one of the few places in Riverport that was air-cooled. Like the local movie houses it drew more patrons when the weather was hot.

Ordinarily Bud McKenna was not particular about where he sat in the club, but he had been forewarned by the tone of Francine's voice that this was not to be the usual dinner format. He reserved one of the private dining rooms. Except for the lack of a better description, it was hard to understand why these cubicles were called rooms. They were little more than enclosed booths lining the perimeter of the main dining room. Francine arrived just as he was being seated.

"Right on time!" she said as she dropped into a chair across from him. "Somehow, I expected you to be here late . . . or not at all," she continued.

"Why not at all?" he asked.

"Just a hunch," she answered.

"You seem to be tense," he said.

"That's an accurate observation," she mumbled, looking into the mirror on her compact as she fixed her lipstick.

They ordered and ate without significant conversation.

Bud sent for their favorite drinks, and sat studying her face.

"Something go wrong at home?" he asked.

"Sure, something went wrong alright," she snapped. "Yesterday I passed out at the wedding reception, and this morning I'm having morning sickness."

His eyes met hers.

"Do you think you're pregnant?"

"Well, it is a possibility. Girls have an inclination. I've been exposed," she said.

" . . . But you haven't seen a doctor?"

"Of course not . . . not on a weekend," she snapped. "You'd better help me out of this situation you've gotten me into."

"Lower your voice!" he warned. "It is probably due to your nerves, and is not what you think."

"What are we going to do?" she asked. "Do you know a good doctor? How about a place where we could get it fixed?"

"Hold it, we don't know yet if you *are* pregnant. Let's check that out first, and if you are in a family way, we will take steps accordingly." He put his arms around her and pulled her down onto his lap. She sat rigidly upright as he kissed her neck and ear. "Now, why don't you just calm down and let's enjoy this moment. We can't do a thing until tomorrow, and if you *are* pregnant, it won't matter if we make love or *not . . .*"

"If I am pregnant, you'd better get ready to hold my hand during the abortion!" she warned.

"I'll stand beside you," he assured as he started loosening her blouse. She turned toward him, and curled into his chest.

Francine and Bud were interrupted when the maître d' seated the mayor and the chief of police at a table on the other side of the partition. They were so close that Bud tried to quiet his breathing, lest it be heard.

The pungent odor of cigar smoke seeped through the cracks into the booth, causing Francine to gasp. Bud signaled her to be silent. She stifled a choke and eased back into her chair as she straightened her clothes.

The mayor blew smoke across the table and glared at his brother-in-law.

"We are on the edge of disaster," the mayor threatened. "We must keep on top of this thing. I want you to be tuned into every source of information from the street to City Hall, including every barfly, cabbie, and chippie in town. If Barstow gets any idea what we are up against . . . or that we can't control things, he'll call in the Feds and we lose all the way around. We can't enjoy our station in life if we lose control of the liquor people. Don't do anything to upset the balance we have enjoyed in the past."

"You want me to go out and pinch the Stricklers?" the chief asked.

"Hell, NO! They'd retaliate by bombing City Hall! Dammit, it's statements like that that worry me. Don't you do anything *unless I approve of it!*"

"How you goin' to throttle the Stricklers?" the chief inquired.

"By indirect methods," the mayor said. "First, we slow down the red-light district, and all the associated taverns. That will cut deeply into the jukebox revenue. We've got to squeeze them in the breadbasket."

"They'll shove back," the chief warned.

"Possibly, but it will divert their attention from Granary Road, and stop the intimidation of the grain producers."

Bud was sitting upright listening intently. Francine studied his face. She knew she was in the center of something big, but she couldn't decide how it might affect her.

Dr. Barstow appeared at the entrance to the dining room. He hurriedly looked about and nodded towards A.J. Adams.

"Stay long enough to say hello, and then get goin'." the mayor told the chief. "We don't want him to get upset."

The mayor stood, and extended his hand to the doctor. "Hello," he greeted, indicating the doctor to take a seat next to him.

"Good evening," the doctor responded.

"You know the chief of police," Adams said, nodding toward his brother-in-law.

"Yes, we've met," Barstow grunted. "I hope he has something to report."

"We've been comparing notes," Adams continued. "Things are looking good. I'll bring you up to date. The chief has to get back to work."

The chief stood, shook hands and departed.

"The usual," Adams instructed the waiter, and turned toward Barstow. "Are you having dinner?"

"Not now," Barstow hissed. "Let's get down to brass tacks. I've got a board to report to."

"Well, it's not all that bad," Adams soothed. "My sources tell me it was just a prank done by some country boys from down south. They didn't even have you in mind when they blew those trucks.

"I want the truth," the doctor demanded.

"We've got the two Johnny Rebs in the lockup at the station. They were still drunk when we brought them in . . . and had about half a case of dynamite."

"What would you have me believe was their motivation?" Barstow hissed.

"Just wild, rebellious southerners wanting to detonate some powder . . . picked on that dump by the river. The trucks just happened to get involved."

"Coincidence! Do you expect me to believe that it was only coincidence that the trucks were blown to kingdom come?"

"Don't take my word for it, Doctor. Come down to the station and ask them yourself."

"No thanks, I have no business with them *or* your jail. Can I expect this to be an end to the harassment?"

"It is . . . and to be sure, I'm beefing up the police patrol along Granary Road."

Bud and Francine sat close to the partition, listening.

"Just as added insurance," the doctor continued, "I'm suspending further shipments from the plant to your cousin's store."

"Oh, come on doctor, there is no need to get horsey with me," Adams complained. "These two dynamiters needn't slow up our retail supplies."

"When I'm sure I'm safe, I'll resume your shipments. Until then, your store will have to make routine orders through a bona fide distributor."

"Won't that draw attention to our sales?"

"I'll take care of the distributor's curiosity," Barstow assured as he raised his glass to drink.

Bud and Francine remained in their compartment until after A.J. Adams and Dr. Barstow had departed. The conspirators were not aware that the young couple had overheard the conversation.

Bits had been drinking all day Sunday. By Sunday night he was a mean drunk, giving much abuse to Toni. Inside the darkened hall, the heat was stifling. He sat on the stoop of the back door, stripped to the waist, feet extended into the alley.

Toni sat in a wooden chair just inside, staring at him from the darkness.

He took a long drag on a beer bottle, spilling part of the foamy contents down his bare chest. His head slumped forward and his body leaned into the jamb.

"Hey! How about another beer?" he slurred, waving the empty around in the air.

Toni sat motionless looking at him.

"Ho! Ya lil' shithead . . . git me a beer!"

She stood and reached for the bottle in his hand. Bits lost his balance, and fell towards her. As he went over he caught her at the ankles.

"Gotcha," he slurred as he pulled her feet out from under her.

Toni's rump hit the old wooden floor with a thud as she came to a sitting position across from him.

"Ha! I can see yore bare ass!" he exclaimed looking up her legs. "You got sweat all the way to your pee hole an' I'm gonna wring ya out."

She tried to pull her foot free of his grasp, but he had expected such a move and had put a viselike grip on her ankle.

"Resist me!" he snorted, rising to his hands and knees. "Go ahead, I like dames who resist!"

She tried to kick loose, but failed. He stood and pulled her feet up to his chest.

"Gotcha, mouse!" he slurred. "Gotcha for what ever I desire!"

Toni did not like being overpowered and she feared what this drunken sop might do to her. Screwing was her game, but she did not know what was forming in his inebriated mind.

"Ha," Bits grunted, holding her upside down like a skinned rabbit.

Toni's skirt fell toward the floor, leaving her naked lower body exposed to his view. She squirmed and twisted, but he held her aloft.

"Ha, I got me a woman with spunk!"

In spite of his drunken state, he was very strong. She writhed about suspended and helpless. She was trying to swing away from him when he put his bare foot on her hair, pinning her head to the floor. She bent her knees and kicked. He straightened his arms and spread her feet.

"Want loose do ya?" he laughed. "I'll let ya loose after I get done with ya."

The beer caused him to lose his balance and he fell to the floor across her. She tried to spring free, but he grabbed her by one shoulder and a leg.

"Ha, feisty lil' bitch . . . now you get it up the ass," he slurred as he grabbed at the buttons on his fly, holding her down with his other hand.

"You bastard!" she shouted. "Stop this crap right now!"

Bits slapped her across the face and rolled her over, bringing her bare butt up to his groin.

She reached out for balance, and in doing so, her hand discovered the discarded beer bottle. Grasping it by the neck, she arched her body and sprung up at him as he leaned forward.

She connected the beer bottle to his head, and with a sickening thud he dropped like a felled steer across her body.

Toni lay on the floor under his sweaty hulk, panting for breath. Her dress was up under her armpits. She wriggled one leg free and was scooting out from under Bits when she realized two men were standing above her looking down.

She froze in shocked silence.

The larger of the two smiled and stooped down.

"Here, let me help you up." he said.

"Who the hell are you?" she demanded. "What are you doing in here?"

"Is this the A.B. of D.W.?" he inquired.

The second man rolled Bits onto his back, stared at his bleeding head and whistled.

"How's it look?" the first man asked.

"Beautiful, just beautiful," was the reply.

Pulled to her feet, Toni straightened her skirt and replaced her shoes. The man kept a grip on her arm. At first, she thought it was to give her balance, but he did not release her after she straightened up.

"Let go," she demanded.

The man grinned a broad smile and held onto her.

"Come on," she complained. "What do I look like, a piece of luggage?"

"Put her in the trunk," he said as he shoved her into the arms of the other man.

Toni screamed. Both men grabbed her and wrestled her fighting 90 pounds in to the trunk of Bit's auto sitting in the alley. The lid slammed down and despair and darkness shrouded her.

From inside the trunk, she could hear the low mutterings of the two men. First they were talking near the car, and then they moved into the union hall. Soon she heard them snorting as they struggled to put Bit's unconscious form into the back seat. The car doors slammed and the engine started. The vehicle rocked and squeaked as it lumbered down the alley and into the street.

Once before in her life, Toni had ridden in the trunk of an auto. She recalled as a young girl being picked up on the road near her home in Louisiana. A man and a woman in a Lincoln had asked directions to the parish house, and when she approached they forced her into the trunk, and consequently a life of prostitution. She was doubly terrified this time.

The car picked up speed and moved onto a highway. As she bounced around, she groped around for some object that might serve as a weapon. The best she could find was a tire iron. This she clutched with both hands as she planned her defense.

It seemed like an eternity before the car stopped. When it did, the men stepped out and slammed the doors. She could hear them struggling with Bits' still form. There was silence and then the agonizing screams of Bits Casso!

At first, she was glad to know he was still alive, but the screams became so desperate that she feared he was being slaughtered.

Then there were no more screams. Just sobbing. She presumed it was Bits.

"Unions don't mix with the whiskey business," one of the men asserted. "If you don't want us comin' back on you, you better pull up stakes and git."

Toni bristled. The men were walking toward the trunk. She clutched her weapon.

The trunk lid flew open. One of the men stood over her, one hand on the lid, the other reaching out for her.

She jabbed the tire iron at his groin. It was a direct hit. He cursed and doubled over.

Toni popped out of the trunk swinging the heavy tire iron at her captors. The second man came to the rescue of his wounded confederate. She knew she would lose a physical fight, so she kicked off her shoes and ran into the nearby woods. The men chased her for a short distance and stopped. As she bolted through the underbrush, she could hear them far behind shouting curses and firing pistols into the air.

Tired to the point of collapse, she fell to the ground behind a log and listened.

She could hear the mutterings of the two men and the rattling of gas cans. There was the sound of the car engine and a crashing noise followed by the breaking of glass, and the *whoof!* of a sudden fire.

Toni peered over the log. She could see no one, but she could smell the black smoke rising in the air. She heard the crackling of fire and then saw the red flames.

In the light of the fire, she could see the two men standing between her and the burning auto. Bits lay on the ground in front of them.

The men called to her in the night.

"Come on out ya lil' whore, an' we'll take you back to town," one of them shouted in her direction.

"Hell, she's waded across the marsh by now," the second man speculated. "Let's git goin."

The first man rubbed his groin as he picked up Toni's shoes from the ground. He unbuttoned his pants and urinated into her shoes, throwing them back to the cinders. Both men laughed as they got into a waiting auto and drove away.

Toni listened to the noises of the departing car, and watched the crackling flame.

She wondered if they'd return. And what of Bits? Was he alive? Could she rescue him?

Slowly she rose to her feet, swatting at a horde of mosquitoes hovering about her. Her bare feet sank into the mud with each step as she clung first to one sapling, then another. She approached the fire with caution. Stopping at the edge of the undergrowth, she studied the scene. Bits was hardly recognizable. His face had been sandpapered and he was a bloody mess. She crawled to him and pulled him away from the heat.

Bits was alive but bleeding heavily from the sides of his face. Toni sat in the mud holding his head in her lap. In his delirium he mumbled strange things.

"Ain't enough pay, Arlo," he murmured. "Ain't enough in it for me to get busted up . . . want more from you Stricklers or I go back to St. Louis."

Toni's eyes welled up with tears. She had not been up north very long, but she knew who Arlo Strickler was, and she knew she would confront him as soon as Bits was safe.

The car was wrecked against a tree and burning. Some of the surrounding foliage had started to burn. She had to figure how to get him to safety.

In the distance, she heard the sirens of the Riverport Fire Department.

She prayed they were coming her way as she tugged on Bits' feet. She lost consciousness and slumped to the ground. Her next recollection was being carried by the firemen to an ambulance. She opened her eyes to determine that Bits was beside her, and she blacked out.

"Drinkin' an' drivin'," one of the firemen said as he sprayed water on the smoldering car. "Where'd they be if we didn't come along and pick up the pieces?"

"Fried to a crisp," another fireman answered as he scooped up her shoes and pitched them into the swamp. "Fried to a crisp."

A police car carrying the chief pulled up and stopped. He stared at the ruins of the auto.

"Any dynamite?" the chief asked.

"Just drunken drivin'!" the firemen answered.

The police car turned about and left the scene.

During the "dog days" of August each day seemed hotter than the one before.

The retreating night had not cooled the pavement of Apple Street where it approached the gates of the Jacob Wasserman Distilling Company. The air was stifling. It was Monday morning and Melba came to work with mixed emotions.

Already, working in the alcohol factory had become routine. She felt as if coming to work here was something she had been doing for years. Being Mrs. David Merriwether gave her new spirit. For the first time in her life, she had significance. She was important to someone and this fact gave her strength.

Mrs. David Merriwether, she thought as she pushed through the crowd of women toward the time clock. *I'm Mrs. David Merriwether, and I'm going to make that mean something special.*

The chatter of the women predominated the scene. Everyone seemed to be talking at the same time. Melba punched in and turned to come face to face with Jesse.

"Hi Pumpkin, how was the honeymoon?" the older woman asked.

Melba blushed and smiled. "Fine," she said looking down at her feet.

"Pretty tough comin' in to work?" Jesse asked.

"Naw, Dave had to work too."

"Better stick close to me today," Jesse advised. This bunch loves to kid a blushing bride, and your face turns red at the mention of the wedding."

Melba nodded and followed Jesse through the doors into the bottling room. The women were awaiting her entrance.

"Here comes the bride!" came a call from the group.

All eyes were on Melba. She crowded up closer behind Jesse as they moved toward her station on the conveyor line. For this reason, Melba did not see her workstation until she was upon it.

White tape from an adding machine had been used as ribbon and formed into a bower around her station. An empty case had been fashioned into a miniature bed and crude faces drawn on cardboard to depict a man and a woman in it.

Melba's face turned crimson. She put her hands to her face in embarrassment. The crowd roared with laughter, and then into a song starting with the wedding march and concluding with a barroom song about a wild night in Riverport.

The bottling line jerked into motion, and like a column of rigid soldiers the bottles moved forward. The first bottles to reach Melba's station had condoms shrouding their tops.

Melba broke into tears and wept on Jesse's shoulder.

Jesse, motioned for silence, and got it as only the clatter of machinery prevailed. She reassured the bride as everyone got back to work. Francine gave Melba a warm hug and kissed her cheek.

"Keep a stiff upper lip, Pumpkin," she said. "They're just envious. I'll see you at break time."

Melba concentrated on her work without looking up, as she slowly got control of her feelings.

Toni put Unquentine on Bits' face and bathed his body as she made him comfortable as possible . . . Toni was afraid the ruffians might return, and so they had checked into a second floor room in a cheap hotel near the union hall. She had gotten a small G.E. oscillating fan and put it into action near the bed. When she had done what she could, she kissed his hand and left the room. She would not be long. She had telephoned Frieda's and told them she was coming to meet the Stricklers. She was confident they would be there.

At first, she did not see anyone when she entered the tavern. The bright afternoon sun contrasted to the shadows inside the place. A noise in the far corner booth attracted her attention. As she focused her eyes, she saw several men sitting in the booth staring at her. Two other men stood next to the booth as if on guard.

"Strickler?" she called out. "Arlo Strickler, are you over there?"

"Over here," came the reply.

She moved toward the booth clutching her handbag to her stomach.

"That's far enough," a man's deep voice warned. "Who sent you to see Arlo Strickler?"

"Bits Casso sent me," she lied.

"Damn!" the man cursed.

"He's sick. Two men came yesterday and nearly killed him. He told me to come tell you. He says this wasn't in the deal. He says he wants protection, or he goes back to St. Louis."

"Who beat him up?" came the reply.

"I don't know, they were big men. They used sandpaper on his face and told him to take his union and stuff it up his ass."

"Huh," came a grunt from the dark. "And you, who are you?"

"I'm Toni, his girlfriend. I was with him when it happened."

"He gonna make it?"

"Yes, I'm takin' care of him."

"Tell him to put out some handbills to the distillery workers. Let them know what's happened. Pass them out at the gate. Get some union applications out. I think this will cause a rise in membership. Get that membership signed up!"

"What about protection?"

"Not to worry. You get union members, we'll keep you safe. Now, git your ass out of here and forget we ever talked!"

Toni hesitated, then turned and left the tavern. She had to get back to Bits. He needed her.

When Monday's shift was over, Francine drove Melba to the Bee Hive and excused herself while the newlyweds drooled over each other.

Francine used the pay phone to call Roddie Dixon in Tonica. When he answered the telephone, she could tell he had been drinking.

"Roddie?" she asked. "Roddie, is that you?"

"Yeah, who'd you expect?" he slurred.

"It's Francine, baby. Are you okay?"

"Hell yes. How's my car – ya didn't wreck it did ya?"

"No, it's okay. I've got somethin' to talk to you about."

"I'm gonna need my car back to drive myself to camp. I joined the Army! I'm in the Army now!"

"The Army!" she exclaimed. "Why did ya go an' do somethin' like that?"

"To see the world. I'm gonna travel far, far away."

"Listen baby, I've got to talk to you. Can you come down here tonight? It's *really* important."

"Damn right, I'll come get my car."

"Okay, baby, you come git your car, an' I'll talk to ya tonight." She heard him grunt and hang up. Francine carefully replaced the receiver on the hook. She was in deep thought as she left the Bee Hive.

The Ford was parked at the curb and Francine got in and started the engine. For a few minutes, she sat staring ahead deep in thought before she put it in gear and drove away.

Arlo Strickler sat at a table in the back room of the gang's meeting place. A single light bulb in a green glass shade shined down on him. He looked out from under his hat at his brothers sitting around the table. Only his eyes moved as he surveyed the scene.

"Wanna hear somethin' good?" he asked. "Wanna hear what's goin' on right under our nose?" He slammed his fist on the table. "Right here in *our town*, the goddamned distillery has an outlet for illegal booze!"

"Heinie bit the end off a cigar and asked, "What'cha mean?"

"I mean they got a system of bottlin' more booze' than the government taxes, and they sell it retail . . . one of their outlets is right here in Riverport!"

"Cute," Heinie commented.

The others moaned in disdain.

"Now we know how to hurt 'em," Arlo shouted. "They can't make too much complaint if their secret outlet goes up in smoke!"

"Gotcha," was the response. "Let's set off some fireworks!" the men shouted.

Arlo pulled his hat down over his brow and filed out the back door. The others followed.

Happy Hooligan was the attendant on the highway drawbridge. People had called him that for so many years that no one could recall his real name.

When a boat came along on the river, it was his job to raise the bridge. This seldom happened, and most of his time was spent sitting in the shade of his shanty watching the water flow underneath or waving at an occasional motorist crossing the span.

He was regarded by some as a dullard. Some thought his sluggish mind was due to a head injury suffered while working for the city. It was this reason that prompted the city fathers to give him a lifetime job tending the bridge.

When things confused Happy, he called his sister Mary for an explanation. The sight of four limousines full of men crossing the bridge from Riverport qualified as confusing. This is how the party line was alerted to the movement of the Stricklers, and how their target was ready for them when they arrived.

The liquor outlet fronted by the mayor's cousin appeared to be neglected. There were no cars parked in front, and no visible activity inside. The lights were lit in the windows and a red neon light on the roof buzzed in the hot night air. Otherwise, all was quiet.

The roadway in front of the building was a two-lane concrete pavement, which carried no traffic other than the Strickler limousines. The cars slowed to a stop as the occupants surveyed the scene.

"Where's everybody?" Heinie asked.

Arlo was in the car behind. Heinie looked back for direction. Arlo shoved the muzzle of his Thompson submachine gun out the window and told his driver to lead the others past the scene. Some of the gang climbed out onto the running boards for better firing positions.

The defenders inside the building lay on their stomachs on the floor, expecting the Stricklers to enter through the door.

The drivers shifted gears, and the autos jerked forward.

"I don't like the looks of this," Arlo muttered out of the corner of his mouth. "It's just too quiet around here. Keep on your toes. Once we start to shoot, keep movin'. Now let's git goin.'"

The cars started moving faster. Heinie was the first to fire his weapon. He shattered the large front window and sprayed the roof for good measure. After that, it was impossible to determine who shot what. Bullets hit the building and the surrounding area like hail. Boards fell from the roof. Bricks flew out of the walls, and glass spewed in all directions.

Not a shot was fired from the defenders. They covered their heads and endured the barrage. The whole ordeal took less than two minutes, and the Stricklers were gone.

Smoke from the broken light fixtures and dust from falling plaster filled the interior with a gray cast. For several seconds after the assault broken glass and fixtures tottered and dropped. The damage was enormous, but not one person had been injured.

The mayor's cousin crawled from under a table; brushed himself off and went to the phone.

"We been hit by the Stricklers," he said into the mouthpiece.

"It don't look good, but nobody got it." He nodded twice as he listened to the person on the other end of the line. "Yeah, yeah, we'll stay where we are until you get here."

As the Stricklers were returning to Happy Hooligan's bridge, over in Bridgeport a solitary man wearing dark clothes walked up the alley behind their headquarters. He broke a rear window and threw five sticks of dynamite into the building. With all the cool of a sign painter, he sauntered from the alley and disappeared.

The Stricklers were just crossing the bridge when the night lit up with the flash from the explosion. There remained only a large hole in the ground where their building had stood.

The war was on!

CHAPTER EIGHT

A TURKEY, A TRANSFER AND THE TEST

Melba set out to make the apartment become a home.

One thing she did not like about the building was the dark and dusty stairwell leading up to the apartment. The landlord refused to replace the light on the second floor landing, and Melba had done so, attaching a lampshade to the lonely light bulb hanging above. This made things more visible, but accentuated the condition of the walls and ceiling.

David tried to ignore her prodding, but when he came home to find her standing on a chair at the top of the stairs, he gave in.

"Hey, what's going on?" he asked.

"Oh, David, look at the dirt," she exclaimed holding out a handful of blackened wall cleaner.

"Yuck, why you doin' that?"

"I'm tryin' to make the place look nicer," she pouted.

"Well, don't fall off that chair, it's a long way to the bottom of those stairs."

"Will you help?"

"Oh, alright. Let me have some of that stuff. What is it anyway?"

"It's wallpaper cleaner. Work it up soft like a big ball of bubble gum and then pull it along the surface. See how it takes the dirt off the wall?"

David held some of the cleaner in his hand. He sniffed it cautiously and then took her place on the chair.

"Here goes," he sighed as he took a long stroke down the wall.

"Just our side of the hall," Melba warned as he approached the corner.

"Why?"

"'Cause that's all the cleaner I bought and we don't have enough to do the whole hallway."

David shrugged his shoulders and attacked the wall as if speed was a necessity.

"It looks better already," Melba reassured as she stood back to admire his efforts. "It makes the entrance to our apartment look special."

David nodded agreement and kept working.

When the hall was cleaned to their satisfaction, they went into the apartment to eat supper. Getting the cleaner off their hands took special effort. They stood at the sink with the water running while they scratched at the sticky dirt.

"Care to hear the latest news?"

"You got news?" she asked, kissing him on the cheek.

"Yeah, the guy from the apprentice school was in again today. He says that if I can get Uncle Bill to endorse me, I can get into the carpenter's apprentice program."

"Oh, David," Melba exclaimed, putting her soapy hands around the back of his neck and embracing him. "Think what that would mean to us if you got into that school!

"I've gotta get the endorsement . . ."

"You'll get it. I know you will. What do carpenters earn?"

"I'd only make twenty-five cents an hour while learning . . . but a couple bucks per hour if I was finished with the course."

"Wow! That's big money!" she speculated, keeping her hold around his neck.

"Yeah, we could rent a place with *clean* walls," he laughed.

"You're not happy with this place?" she asked, looking up at him.

"Happy? I'm crazy with this place," he joked as he gave her a long kiss.

The heat wave extended from summer into fall and into the last weeks of October.

Melba and Dave cooled off at night on the porch roof staring at the overhanging elm tree and talking about their future.

Francine had not missed the Ford after Roddie repossessed it. She spent more time away from home and friends. Melba never asked her where she was staying. It was presumed that she and Bud had established a lovers' hideaway somewhere. Her pregnancy was beginning to be obvious to everyone except the company. The Jacob Wasserman Company promoted her twice since she started with them. This was another reason Melba seldom saw her, even at work.

At the end of November, the company gave each active worker a dressed turkey. Melba was so excited about this unexpected windfall that she telephoned her parents and asked them to come to Riverport for Thanksgiving. But when the threat of bad driving conditions made the venture hazardous, it was agreed that Melba and Dave would bring the turkey and come to Logan by train.

Taking the train back home, she remembered riding the train on her first trip to Riverport.

Thinking back, she was amazed that she had made the trip alone. She had never been away from her parents or into a large city before that time. That night on the train with the drunk was very frightening.

She studied Dave's face as he looked out the window. It was difficult to believe that this guy sitting next to her had so changed her life. Now she had a home, a job and a husband! She had come a long way since she left her parents.

At Logan, she saw the truck parked at the depot before she saw her father waiting on the platform.

She ran to her parents and threw her arms around her mother. Dave shook hands with Harold and Lacey hugged Melba. They could not all fit into the truck, and Dave rode in the back so Melba and her parents could talk on the way. When they got home Lacey poured coffee.

"We'll have lunch now – it will be hours before dinner," Lacey explained as she put dishes on the table. They sat down and studied each other.

"How's your work?" Harold asked Dave.

"Good. I'm an apprentice carpenter and will have my certificate in little over a year," Dave said.

"Praise be to God," Lacey mumbled as she passed the food.

"Wish I coulda got into somethin' like that at your age," the older man asserted. "Once the war was over, the army sent us home to take whatever licks society wanted to pass out. There wasn't much to be had."

"I'm lucky, and I realize it," Dave agreed, squeezing Melba's hand under the table. "Between the two of us we should be able to move up in life."

Lacey studied Melba's face. Her daughter seemed happy. Lacey wondered if the good times this couple expected would materialize.

"Can I help with the cookin'?" Melba asked.

Both women stood and turned to the sink. The men moved to the front room to sit by the stove.

As they worked in the kitchen, Melba felt dizzy. It must be the excitement of being home again, she thought.

The distillery was now producing peak quantities of bottled goods and working three shifts a day. More than one thousand women worked there, and they averaged thirteen-hundred to fourteen-hundred dollars per year. The plant made twenty-four separate products that they shipped to every port in the world. In addition, the distillery paid millions of dollars in taxes to the federal government. It had become a big operation.

The directors in Canada were pleased with the successes of the Riverport Plant. Dr. Barstow was rewarded with stock, and Bud McKenna was promoted and recalled to Canada. Francine learned this information while sitting at the dinner table in the club. They had finished eating and the conversation had somehow dissolved into silence.

"I'm going back to Canada," Bud announced. "The company has called me back to the home office."

She wanted to cry, but she did not move. Pain swept through her body. The shock and humiliation of the news dominated her for an instant, and then she recouped.

"That will make your family very happy," she said.

"You mean my wife," he corrected.

"Yes, your wife," she agreed.

"Look, I'm not running out, you know."

"Of course not."

"I've made plans for you and the baby. You are to send your time cards to me in Canada. I will see to it that you receive your full pay right through the birth. When you can come back, your job will be waiting."

"How sweet," she whispered, glaring at him.

"Come on, now let's not have a scene," he pleaded.

Francine jumped to her feet and ran from the club. Bud sat staring at the exit as if he thought she might reappear. Somewhere back in the kitchen someone dropped a tray of china. Their meeting seemed to be over.

Losing the Ford was almost as big an inconvenience as losing Bud, now that both were gone. Francine did not intend to become a pedestrian.

Almost overnight she established a friendship with a squat, cigar-smoking used-car dealer who had a place of business near the distillery. She would borrow cars from his inventory in exchange for an occasional clandestine rendezvous when his wife was out of town. Fortunately, his wife liked staying at home, and Francine was not often called upon to return his favors. Really, it was better than having Roddie's car. This way, she had variety. And when given a choice, she often selected the most ridiculous vehicle on the lot.

This is how she happened to be driving a LaSalle town sedan when she pulled up in front of the hotel where Toni and Bits were living. Toni did not recognize Francine until she pulled off her hat and allowed her hair to cascade to her shoulders. Toni leaned from the window and waved.

Bits was sleeping, and the women decided to go sit in the car.

"What is this?" Toni asked as she climbed into the rear seat.

"A doozie," Francine answered, slamming the door and sitting up front in the chauffeur's seat. Toni was talking inside the passenger compartment, but the window was closed between them and Francine could not hear her. She reached over and pulled the glass open.

"Where to, 'madam'?" she inquired.

"Y'awl gonna sit up there?" Toni asked.

"I'm your driver, ma'am," Francine joked, as she pulled her hat down over her brows. "Where to?"

"N'awlins, James. Take me below th' Mason Dixie Line!"

"Yes ma'am," Francine responded, turning to the steering wheel and starting the engine.

"Hyar now! Ah was merely funnin'," Toni complained, sticking her head through the open partition. "Let's stop at the union hall to check on some things."

"Yes, ma'am," Francine agreed as she cut the corner short, causing the rear wheel of the long car to bounce up and over the curb. "Sorry, ma'am."

Toni put the brass speaking tube to her lips and gave Francine the raspberry for her clumsiness. Both women laughed as the car moved toward Apple Street.

To describe the union hall as deserted was an understatement. When Toni opened the front door, the air seemed to come from a tomb.

"Lordee, it smells like Hades in this ol' buildin'." Toni complained.

" . . . And it looks like it." Francine agreed. "It's a house of horrors with those pictures of Bit's bleedin' face on all those posters."

"Yes, but membership is soarin', in defiance of those goons sent by the company."

"Can't the union afford a better place?"

"Fo' the time bein' all our meetin' will be' held in the Labor Temple. That way those blackguards can't destroy us by destroyin' our meetin' place."

"If you don't need this place, why not close it up?"

"Sentiment, ah reckon! Bits and I had some of our most romantic experiences in this gloomy building. Your friend Melba celebrated her wedding reception here. Sentiment and a legal address fo' the union, that's what keeps the place open."

Francine stared at the smoke stained metal ceiling and the dingy walls. The large front windows were only clean where the sign painter had rubbed them off before painting on the name of the union. The floors were dusty and creaked when she walked. Considering the new growth, the union needed a better hall. When she thought of growth, she thought of her personal problem.

"I think I'm pregnant!" Francine said.

"Y' *think* yore pregnant! Don't y'awl know?" Toni asked.

"I'm sure," Francine answered, her eyes filling with tears.

Toni came to her friend and put her arm around her.

"Bless ma soul," Toni started. "Jest th' other day ah thought y'awl were gettin' a lil' porky. How far along are you?"

"Probably six months."

'Six months! Honey, we best start shopping fo' baby things!"

"I didn't plan to carry it this long."

"Have y'awl done anything?"

"You bet, I took urget, and that didn't work. Then, I tried to strain myself. I lifted cases of half pints one whole day, and all I got was a sore back. I even drank turpentine; and couldn't jar it. I tell you, this baby's comin' full-term."

"What about your job? How will y'awl git along?" Toni asked.

"Jacob Wasserman will see to it that I get paid. You wouldn't believe who's responsible for my condition. Gettin' paid is the least of my problems."

"Y'awl must have the daddy by the testicles," Toni exclaimed.

"By the ass would be more like it," Francine asserted.

Both women laughed and hugged each other. Arms around one another, they strolled from the building to the sedan.

Melba had cooked corned beef and cabbage with bread pudding for Dave's birthday. She had bought him some phonograph records and they had planned to stay home and listen to them.

Someone knocked on the door just as they had finished eating. Dave opened it to see a smiling young man in an Army uniform.

"Roddie?" Dave asked. "Roddie Dixon, is that you?"

"Hi Dave. Hi Melba," Roddie responded, removing his khaki cap as he stepped into the room. "Is Francine here?"

"Roddie," Melba exclaimed. "How you've changed. Where is your hair?"

Roddie brushed his palm across his close cropped head. "Army barber," he said. "Can't shoot the rifle with hair in my eyes. Where's Francine?"

"We took over here," Dave explained. "She moved into a place up by the park. We'd better call her to tell her you are in town. Did she know you were coming?"

"Didn't know it myself," Roddie said. I finished basic training, and got transferred to Camp Robinson. They gave me a leave while I'm makin' the move. I'm a P.F.C., see," he said, raising his upper arm to their view.

"Sit down for coffee and we'll go get her after we eat," Melba insisted.

"Naw, thanks, I'm kinda in a hurry to see her . . . if you know what I mean."

"Sit down while I go downstairs to get her address," Melba suggested.

Dave took him by the arm and led him to a chair in the living room. Melba dashed downstairs to the landlady's apartment.

She was relieved to find someone home and even further pleased to use the telephone.

"Francine!" Melba cried when the phone ceased ringing, "Francine, are you there?"

"Uh huh," came the answer.

"Francine, if that's you, you better straighten up. This is Melba and Roddie Dixon is at our place and he's lookin' for you!"

"What?" came the answer. "He went into the Army!"

"Yes, dear, and he's home on furlough in uniform and funny haircut, lookin' for you!"

"Keep him there. I'll get dressed and be right over. Keep him over there!"

"Sure thing," Melba promised, hanging up and returning to the stairs.

Roddie's unexpected return caused a great deal of change.

Francine could not let him see the love nest established and abandoned by Bud. Dense as he was, he would know it was above her means and ask uncomfortable questions. Her first inclination was to tell Roddie to get lost, but the fact that he had come to her on his first leave made her feel guilty about thoughts of casting him off.

Men in uniform were taking on new prestige, too, and for the first time in his life, Roddie was admired. Ill-fitting as it was, the uniform had a certain air of authority about it. He was particularly pleased with the attention he received from girls. To Francine, it was not just the uniform – for some other reason, Roddie took on a new dimension. He had risen above the old hometown spoiled-brat image. He had become a force to be reckoned with, and for all her faults, Francine could not ignore a man with potential.

For the duration of his furlough Francine spent every minute with Roddie. Melba and Dave allowed them to share the apartment. Crowded conditions not withstanding, it worked out for everyone. Melba watched the budding romance between the two. She hoped it would lead to something good. Dave was just happy about having friends around.

Before he departed for Camp Robinson, Roddie Dixon married Francine Ryan. Melba and Dave stood up with them. The justice who performed the service feared that the bride's water might break before the ceremony was finished.

They honeymooned in Little Rock, Arkansas, where Roddie had been assigned to an infantry division. After Roddie's unit moved out to Hawaii, she returned to Riverport and took up residence with the Merriwethers.

It was 2 a.m. February 14th, 1935, when Dave was awakened by Melba's voice.

"David, we need you honey, come here." He rolled over in bed to find he was alone.

Melba called again from the living room. "David, darlin', I need you in here!"

Drunk with sleep, he threw off the covers and staggered into the front room.

Melba was holding Francine's head and shoulders on her lap.

Francine was kicking and thrashing about on the sofa. A solitary table lamp illuminated the room.

"What's goin' on?" Dave asked.

"We're into labor here. A blessed event is about to happen here in our home!" Melba exclaimed with pride. "Francine is havin' her baby!"

Dave nearly fell to the floor. He clutched the doorjamb and leaned into it for support.

"A baby!" he cried. "Here? Now?"

"Quickly, darlin', we must get ready. Run to the corner pay phone and call Aunt Pearl. Tell her we need all the things she can bring. There's no time to dilly-dally, David . . . MOVE!"

Dave spun around and disappeared down the stairway.

"Ugh!" Francine grimaced, contorted in labor.

"There now Francine, help is on the way and I'm here to see you through. Just take a deep breath and squeeze my hand!"

Francine grasped Melba's hand and shuddered.

Within the hour, Aunt Pearl was on the scene. Loaded with sheets, pails, clothes and bottles, she assaulted the stairs wheezing her great bulk up each flight to the top. Uncle Shorty helped carry things in from the car and then sat down in the hall way.

By sunrise, the birth was complete. Melba laid the little girl down alongside of Francine and beamed down at both of them. Aunt Pearl reclined in a chair, fanning herself for air.

Francine smiled and touched the baby. "Oh, Melba isn't she just the sweetest?" she whispered.

"The sweetest ever," Melba agreed. "You'd better get some sleep, Hon."

"She's my valentine," Francine murmured as she studied the baby's face. I'll name her Valentine. We'll call her Val for short."

"Val Dixon," Melba smiled. "That's a good name. Now get some rest."

Francine hugged the baby and closed her eyes.

Federal tax was charged on each barrel of spirits. The wooden barrels were rolled on a run from the rack houses to large tanks above the bottling lines. Government gaugers recorded the number of barrels and taxed the distillery accordingly. The barrels were stopped in place by use of wooden wedges as they entered the tank room.

Management had gotten more than concerned about spillage at this point in the process. Production was also a problem. They wanted the barrels moved with dispatch, but without loss of product and tax.

The foreman of the tank room and his two aides were summoned to the office of Dr. Barstow.

"We have to keep this alcohol off the floor," the doctor said. "The record shows too many barrels lost already."

"It's those damned gaugers!" the first worker started. "They got to see each barrel. We don't bottle from the barrel. We bottle from the tank. I suggest that you git them to tax us by the tank."

"We don't *get* them to do anything!" the doctor shot back.

"Well, I mean, suggest to them."

"That is not a solution," Barstow said. "'We must develop ways to transport the barrels from the rack house to the bottling lines without loss!'"

"Maybe we should distill the alcohol in the tanks," the second workman said, smiling.

"That is also not a solution," the doctor snapped. "Put up additional runs. I want more barrels to the tank room!"

"That is dangerous," the foreman said. "A workman could be crushed by the rolling barrels in such a limited space."

"The workmen will just have to stay sober," the doctor said. "I'll have a crew out there in an hour. Just stay on your toes!"

The men grumbled as they left the office. Management was putting them in a dangerous situation.

From the start, the workmen complained about the increased activity in the tank room. Before the new run was a week old, one of the workers had an accident. He caught his hand between two barrels. It was like the ball return at a bowling alley. The first barrel in line stopped, and the next barrels came crashing against it. The workmen had a hold of the first barrel when this happened.

Nurse Hazel Mathews knew she had a serious case when she saw the wound. She sent for a plant guard and the company station wagon. She tended to the workmen en route to the Riverport Hospital.

Word got out in the plant that an employee had lost a hand. In the tank room the men shut off the process and walked out, leaving the government gaugers staring at their clipboards.

On the way downstairs they entered the bottling room where the women, already shaken by the news, stopped the lines to hear about the accident.

The mood went from pity for the injured to anger at a tyrannical employer.

"What do they care about our health and safety?" cried a near-hysterical woman.

"To hell with their attitude," cried another.

Jesse dashed to her station and rang the bell to resume work.

The women turned on her with shouts and threats.

"Go to hell. Go to hell." chanted the women.

"Strike!" someone gave a cry from the line. "Strike! Strike! Strike!" they chanted as they started to mill around the room. The women turned to the exit and burst through into the hall.

Atop the boiler house, the steam whistle blasted four sharp notes followed by a long constant one. The plant guards raced to the bottling house and arrived in time to meet the women coming down the stairs.

There was the mixture of uniforms as the two groups struggled. The greater number prevailed. The women burst from the building into the company street.

The wrap-around uniforms worn by the women had proven too restrictive and not sturdy. Some of the women lost their uniforms in the melee. Those that did not come into the street semi-clad soon discarded their company work clothes and threw them into the air. Now almost all the women were outside the building in their teddy bears and stockings.

Marching up the street toward the administration building, the group now numbered in the hundreds, chanting for a strike. By the time they arrived at the administration building, they were mostly disrobed. Shouting and screaming, they gathered in front of the office.

When Dr. Barstow appeared at the top of the steps, the shouting intensified.

He raised his hand to silence the women. When that did not work. He pulled a pistol from his pocket and fired it into the air.

Silence came instantly.

"Thank you, ladies," he said. "I would appreciate it if you would cover yourselves. For those of you who have lost your clothing, the guards will hand out new uniforms. If we can find them," he said, chuckling.

The ice was broken and the women laughed.

As the crowd milled about before the administration building, Bits Casso came charging down Apple Street to the main gate. The guards refused his entrance. The employees could see this and they again started to chant.

"Union! Union!" they shouted. "We got a union! Hurray for the A.B. of D.W.!"

Dr. Barstow ignored them as he directed his ruffled guards to form on the perimeter of the scene.

"I will meet with your union man in the guard house if you will all return to your work stations," he offered.

The women stood around talking. Finally, in small groups they returned to the bottling house and entered.

Barstow met with Casso only briefly. When no one was watching, Bits was escorted off the property.

Melba was amazed how things had changed since Val arrived. The apartment had been completely taken over by her presence. There were baby bottles to be sterilized, diapers to be washed, and burping and bathing to be done. Every room contained items having to do with the baby.

Francine had been slow to regain her strength. David thought she was faking to get attention, but Melba knew it was real. Aunt Pearl came to the apartment every morning to help with the baby. Melba delegated many of the details to her because she had been called back to work at the distillery.

Francine got a letter every month from Canada. Her check was always on time.

It troubled Melba and Pearl that Francine seemed to avoid Val at every opportunity.

It all came to a head one Thursday afternoon when Francine announced she was going to travel.

"Travel where?" Melba asked.

"Parts unknown," Francine answered over her shoulder as she collected her clothing. "I'm goin' to hit the bricks, kid. You can have my checks and cash them. What you don't spend on Val, you can blow on yourself. Maybe you can get yourself a better place to live."

"We don't want a better place to live, and we don't want you to run off and leave your child!" she sobbed.

"I'm not tuned for motherhood," Francine explained. "I'd poop out on Val sooner or later, and it's a good time to get out now."

"You sound permanent."

"Naw, just 'til I get it outta my system. I'll write once a week. Let me know if you move."

"How?" Melba cried. "How will we get in touch if we don't have the faintest idea where you are?"

"I said I'd keep in touch."

"I'm not sure we can take care of two babies," Melba groaned.

"Two babies?" Francine asked, as she turned to face her friend.

"You mean you haven't noticed?"

"Pumpkin, are you pregnant?"

"Of *course* I'm pregnant. I expect to deliver in August!"

"Oh sweetie," Francine exclaimed, throwing her arms around Melba and hugging her.

The two women sat on the window box and talked in low tones, stopping occasionally to squeeze hands or hug one another.

Before Dave came home from work, Francine carried her suitcases to a waiting taxi and left town.

The sun rose to warm the dew-laden sod. A crow flew from a hedgerow like the departure of winter, calling out to awaken the earth. The day turned bright. The air was fresh and clear.

The boards on the barn wall absorbed the sunlight and seemed to breathe in the coming of spring.

Arlo Strickler, wearing a large-brimmed straw hat and bibbed overalls stepped from the house and threw a bucket of slop into the pig trough.

Heinie would not get up because he had been out most of the night breaking the legs of farmers who sold grain to the distillery.

Arlo had to do the chores without Heinie's help. There was livestock to feed and water and stove wood to fetch.

Arlo had done it all when he started toward the woodshed. Crossing the barnyard, he noticed a thistle growing next to the fence. He kicked it loose with his boot and stopped to pick it up. If there was any growing thing Arlo hated, it was thistle. As he straightened up, two men stepped from the woodshed, guns in hand.

Pete Mandel, one of the Strickler mob, commonly slept in the barn. He had awakened and was standing, watching Arlo through the barn door.

Arlo came face to face with the intruders. "Who the hell . . ."

A burst of gunfire cut him off. Arlo slumped forward and fell to the mud.

"You bastards!" Pete screamed, grabbing a shotgun and firing from within the barn.

Heinie awoke at the first burst and came running from the house in his underwear. On his way, he had picked up a machine gun.

"Heinie!" Pete shouted. "They're in the woodshed!"

Heinie saw Arlo lying on his face. He fired a burst and ran for cover at the corner of the barn.

Shots from within the shed splintered wood on the house and barn.

Arlo raised up on one arm and looked back at Heinie.

"Blast those bastards," he said, falling back on his face, still clutching the thistle.

The two men in the shed darted to a protected place behind the smokehouse. One of them was coughing and wheezing. A motor started, and an auto pulled away and headed for the field. The two men jumped onto the running boards as it passed them. Pete and Heinie fired every round they had, but the target disappeared down the road. Then they turned to look at Arlo. He was dead.

The shooting was headline news. An extra edition came out and newsboys hawked the paper at every major intersection. It was ironic that the paper reported Arlo Strickler had died because of a hunting accident.

Aunt Pearl scheduled services at her church. Emotions ran high. The gang was seething for vengeance. The city fathers feared open warfare. The distillery doubled plant protection, and Aunt Pearl was overcome with grief. She sat in vigil all night by the casket, not noticing the arms carried by the men stationed about the church.

The next day was as spring-like as its predecessor was. Only, the funeral made it somber.

A nervous minister made token remarks about the deceased, read a short passage about the hereafter and droned a brief prayer. Aunt Pearl, tears in her eyes, stood in the choir loft and sang, "Let me walk a little way with thee . . ." The mourners filed past the casket (some not wishing to look upon the body), and into a row of limousines. The hearse was loaded and the strange processional made its way to the cemetery. Long rows of black cars filled with grim men in big hats were followed at the rear by Pearl and Shorty's little blue Essex.

Things had taken a turn for the worse.

CHAPTER NINE

THE DEAL, THE DECISION, THE DELIVERY

A.J. Adams bit the end off a new cigar and spit it through the open window. The chief of police stood before his desk, rigid with anticipation.

"Well now, who knocked off Arlo Strickler?" the mayor demanded.

"Professional job, Mr. Mayor," the chief explained. "Probably came in from Chicago and went right back up there."

"Professional?" the mayor asked. "Professionals in *my* town?"

"It was all too smooth to be any of the lunkheads around here."

"Mobsters from Chicago would have to be around town several days before a hit like that. I thought we were on the alert to any strangers coming into Riverport!"

The chief walked over to the window and looked out. He could see the entire business district of Riverport from this office on the third floor of the city hall. Traffic on the bridge was about normal for this time of day. Smoke from a railroad engine at the train station revealed a second route in and out of this town. There was a surprising amount of activity in the red-light district where cars and pedestrians came and went in a slow methodical pace.

"Mrs. Byrd was supposed to call us if any new mugs hit town," the chief said, without turning toward his brother in law.

"She was supposed to call *me* personally," the mayor snapped. "I've not had one damned peep out of her."

"Some of the 'girls' would have known about big-city professionals. I can't suppose these killers were so well disciplined that they wouldn't take a trick or two while they were gettin' set up," the chief offered.

"Maybe they had their ladies with them. Maybe they didn't *have* to get laid by Mrs. Byrd's small-town whores."

"Come on, Mayor. When did you ever see that type travel with broads?"

"I can't suppose they came in with women, but it's not inconceivable they knew some bimbos here before they arrived?" Adams theorized.

" . . . And?" the policeman asked.

"And made themselves at home while they were casing the Stricklers! Don't you suppose they could have even had a 'plant' right here in town all along?" the mayor shouted, standing and walking up face to face with the chief.

This made the chief feel uneasy. He did not like being this close to the dynamic A.J. Adams. He had never seen the older man fight, but he had always supposed that the mayor could handle himself. The chief was being intimidated and he did not like it.

"Now you get your rosy red ass out there for an unmarked car and drive me down to the infamous cathouse of ol' lady Byrd. I want to see her eye to eye. Either we're following a blind lead, or one of our sources is not playin' straight with us. In either case, I've got some news for our fat friend. She's about to take a trip!"

The chief turned and left the office. As soon as he was out of earshot, the mayor picked up his telephone and called Dr. Barstow.

"Hello doctor," the mayor said. "Just in case you haven't heard, we are on the edge of a war zone. Some silly ass put the finger on Arlo Strickler and his whole organization is out on the streets lookin' for revenge."

"What does this have to do with me?" the doctor asked.

"Who ever pulled this job had big bucks. It costs money to bring in outside guns to pull a caper like this and disappear like a wisp of smoke. I'm just notifying those who didn't see eye to eye with the Stricklers and also had enough resources to handle the kind of action that has gone down here. You are tops on that list, my friend. I have my sources, and it won't take me long to know who the culprit is."

"Here now. Are you accusing me of involvement in this sordid crime?" the doctor demanded.

"No, I'm just trying to protect a friend who may have done a stupid thing and put this community at risk of a shootout that will make Chateau Thierry look like a skeet shoot."

"I don't like your insinuations," Barstow hissed. "You have no license whatsoever to make such a call on me."

"I'll show you what I have a license to do, if I discover you and your people had anything to do with setting off this fuse! You're the one who always wants things handled with pacification. Shooting Arlo Strickler was the dumbest move that could have been made!"

"I'm sure I speak for my entire organization when I say that we had nothing to do with this petty assassination. Now, be gone with you. I'll take your insinuations up with my superiors before this day is through."

"Double the guard on that alcohol factory, Doctor. You have no idea the forces we deal with. Heinie Strickler is a raging bull, and he'd just as soon charge your china shop as any." With this last admonition, the mayor hung up and went to the waiting auto. His next confrontation would be with Mrs. Byrd.

Toni had received three letters in five months from Francine. She had just gotten the third one and sat down to read.

Francine was in California. She had become a camp follower and was living in a small room near the Army base where Roddie was stationed.

"California is much different than the Midwest," she wrote. "There is not a lot of difference in temperature this time of the year, but the trees and bushes are strange-looking, and this part of the state has no lawns like we see back home. Once in a while, we see palm trees, but these are transplanted from Mexico." Toni leaned back into her chair and turned the page.

"Roddie works hard and hopes to become a gunnery officer. He has earned one stripe and a little more pay. The new stripe permits him to wear a campaign hat which he is proud to do. His hair has grown out and while he must keep it very short, it doesn't look as bad as it did on his first furlough. You should be here to see all the men in this Army post! They all notice me every where I go. Roddie says he can tell where I am by listening to the wolf whistles. Some of these boys have the cutest lines, I just get a kick out of listening to their pitches. Yesterday, a sergeant in the P.X. asked me if I would hold it against him if he told me I had a good shape. I'd heard the line before, but he was so cute about it that it made me giggle."

Toni heard Bits come in. She folded the letter and went to meet him.

"How's the picket line?" She asked, popping the cap on a beer and handing it to him.

"Same old faces. Can't get those bastards from shipping to help out," he answered, taking the beer and swallowing half of it in one gulp. "In fact, I'm not too sure but that the guys from the rack houses are gettin' yellow." He grunted as he kicked his shoes off and dropped into a chair in front of the fan. "Did anyone leave a message for me?"

"No, I've been here ever since I left you down on Apple Street. I got a letter from Francine, but there is nothing else. What was it you expected?"

"A letter from Mama," he answered sarcastically. "Another day, and Mama hasn't written." He wondered what was going on in the Strickler camp, but he was not going to ask Heinie to meet him at Frieda's. Bits had been told to increase the picketing and that was tough enough without more manpower. The men from the barrel house were the most cooperative about picketing and he had to get some of the other employees involved in the program.

The mayor sat erect, looking straight ahead as the chief guided the auto down Water Street. It was a bright, warm day. Many of the houses had windows open. Errant curtains waved in the sunlight. Some of the open windows revealed semi-naked prostitutes peering from inside. Occasionally one of the more aggressive women would stick her head out to talk to a man passing on the sidewalk. Gestures and body language made it evident that the subject was an invitation to enter the premises. Barter was discussed, and each man either stepped to the porch or continued on to another house.

All of the activity seemed oblivious to the occupants of the approaching auto.

As they neared Mrs. Byrd's Palace of Pleasure, the madam was leaning from a window talking to an acquaintance. She recognized A.J. Adams' stiff-necked posture and disappeared inside, closing the window and pulling the curtains.

She was too late. The mayor had seen her. He jumped from the car. Followed by his brother-in-law, he approached her front door.

Mrs. Byrd did not immediately respond to the bell or his rapping. A.J. Adams was fuming.

"Harry," he said to the chief. "Break the damned thing off its hinges!"

"Just turn the knob and walk in," the chief said, and did just that.

"It's just like church," Mrs. Byrd cooed from her large rocker as the two men entered the parlor. "My doors are never locked to the needy, just the greedy," she chuckled.

"I'll show you greedy!" the mayor hissed. He waved his hat at the whores standing around in the room. "Git, the whole lot of you!"

The women filed from the parlor and disappeared.

The chief stood behind the mayor. He gave a hand signal to Mrs. Byrd to keep cool. She saw the signal and sat back in her chair.

"Never saw you so rash before, Mayor. Is something bothering you?"

"Of course something bothers me. You operate this street only because I say you can. In exchange, I was to know what was happening . . . who's in town and who's gonna snuff who!"

"Yore mad about Arlo gittin' it?" she asked in surprise.

"No. I'm mad because some big-time hoods can come into my town, stay for a couple of days, do a job and *disappear* like I didn't have control of this burg!"

"How you figure they was in town from the big time?" she inquired.

"How else could such a job go down?" A.J. Adams shouted. "Anybody livin' around here woulda been too scared to have gone for Arlo, much less shoot it out with him on his home place!"

"So why you shoutin' at me?" she asked, folding her arms across and leaning forward on her elbows. "You think I shot Arlo Strickler?"

"No, but I think you're damned uncooperative, and I've come down here in person to tell you this street is closed!"

"Now Mr. Mayor – "

"No compromise. You are closed!" Turning toward the chief, he demanded, "Do you hear what I'm saying?"

"Now look here, Mayor, isn't this a little drastic?" the chief pleaded.

"If you can't handle it I'll do the job myself," A.J. Adams warned.

"I'll take care of it," the chief assured him, holding his hands up in resignation.

"The paddy wagon will be here in thirty minutes to round up anybody caught in this neighborhood," the mayor said as he grabbed at the doorknob to leave.

As the door opened, he came face to face with two men wearing laundry uniforms, carrying bundles of linens.

"Take it back," Adams shouted. "This place is closed."

Benjamin Howard Bentley stared at the mayor in disbelief. It had never crossed his mind that he might run into Adams at Mrs. Byrd's bawdy house.

"You can't close this place," Bentley said. The mayor was going to ruin everything.

"And why can't I?" the mayor demanded.

"Because you *can't!*" Bentley shouted.

Adams and the chief were both bewildered. "Come out to the truck," Bentley pleaded.

Adams and the chief stared at each other and followed Bentley to the laundry truck. Bentley entered the large, enclosed van and the mayor and chief followed.

"You've intruded on a serious federal case here," Bentley announced.

"What possible interest do you have with the red-light district?" Adams asked.

"We've worked on this case for many weeks. You screw us up and we'll file charges against you, mayor or no mayor."

"What the hell is goin' on here?" Adams asked.

"You heard me, you can't close these places down just when we're gettin' the goods on them."

"The goods for what? The Mann Act?" he wondered aloud.

"Tax evasion," Bentley answered. "When we wrap it up, we hope we don't see you involved."

The chief shuddered and looked away.

"I've got a war on my hands!" Adams said. "I've got to close her down until peace prevails."

"Okay, one week. One week from today we resume our work, and there had better not be any tip-off, understand?"

"One week!" the mayor agreed as he climbed from the truck.

Dr. Barstow was still fuming about the mayor's telephone call when he called his superiors in Canada.

"Barstow here," he began. "We're facing deep problems at this location." He listened and then continued. "We were unable to pinpoint the source of creosote in our barrels, except that it had to happen before they arrived at the distillery. We have fifty thousand gallons of tainted alcohol. It is still possible to market it as fuel. We thought the crux of our problem had been eliminated, but the local mayor predicts an uncontrollable crime wave."

Dr. Barstow listened intently and acknowledged his instructions. He hung up and walked to the window of his office.

Down on Apple Street union pickets were forming up to halt traffic into the plant.

"That damned union is next!" he muttered to himself.

For the next three days, A.J. Adams had his hands full.

A stolen truck went out of control and took out the bridge tender's shack before going into the river. Happy Hooligan was crushed in the rubble. The coroner held an inquest, and for lack of evidence declared it an accidental death.

The workers at the distillery had started picketing for safer working conditions, and fistfights had broken out at the gates to the plant. This required twenty-four-hour police presence on Apple Street, a heavy tax on such a small force.

The Canadian Connection was demanding more. The mayor was debating whether to call in the National Guard, which would be an admission on his part that he could not handle the situation.

A.J. Adams decided he would control things his way. He was not one for compromise.

It seemed everything that could happen, had happened.

Then the mayor's nephew, who ran the liquor store across the river, was found on the fairway of the Country Club with a bullet through the back of his head.

The local newspaper labeled it an armed robbery and presented a story of stick-up and kidnap. The only thing accurate in the report was the fact that a large sum of money was missing.

Heinie Strickler was indeed a raging bull, and Riverport was a china shop. Glass crashed on all sides. Adams could not pacify him because he could not finger the assassins. He could not restrain him because the city lacked the force to do so. Somehow, the situation had to be resolved.

It was at this time that an unexpected event interceded.

As an employee of the distillery and a union member, Melba had mixed emotions. A strike had not been called, but pickets were blocking the routes to the plant.

She was sympathetic to the causes of her fellow workers, but she was also loyal to the Jacob Wasserman Company. Going to work each day flanked on each side by shouting pickets was unnerving. She dreaded the walk down Apple Street. When fights broke out between company guards and union pickets she was frightened and appalled. She did not want to take a stand and did not want to risk getting hurt. Her pregnancy was developing and she already had maternal feelings for her baby. Each day, it seemed things became more intense.

On a dark night in July, Toni and Bits came home after a full day of union activity. Bits drove the car into a parking place, and Toni got out to walk to the door.

"I'll get a couple of cold beers and meet you on the steps," she said as she turned to leave.

"Bring two for me, and some pretzels," he instructed as he turned off the lights. Bits was locking the car when two men stepped from the shadows of the alley and opened up with shots in their direction. Bits dropped instinctively to the ground. Toni dropped to the ground, dead.

The assailants disappeared as mysteriously as they had appeared. Bits crawled to Toni and lay sobbing on her bleeding body.

A.J. Adams was at home when he got the call. He crushed his cigar into the ashtray on his smoking stand and called his brother-in-law.

"Harry!" he barked. "The routine's the same. Those two bastards are still runnin' loose in this town!"

"Looks like you're right," the chief agreed. "We've put up a dragnet around the town – that should stop 'em from leavin.'"

"Stop anybody who tries," the mayor demanded.

"We'll get 'em for sure this time," the chief assured as he turned to the work at hand.

A.J. Adams made an immediate call to Dr. Barstow.

"Hello," Barstow said into the telephone.

"Dr. Barstow, this is the mayor. We've had another killing. This time it is the woman friend of that union organizer."

"My God!" Barstow groaned. "What union man?"

"Bits Casso," Adams answered. "The thugs missed their mark this time and shot the wrong person. I think we've got 'em bottled up."

"Thank you, Mayor, but why the special report to me?"

"Because I want you to call your plant and make sure none of the second shift knows about this until we get them out of the plant and up Apple Street."

"I see your point," the doctor agreed.

At midnight, Melba and her coworkers punched out and filed out of the bottling house. Company guards usually inspected purses and lunch boxes for stolen bottles, but they did not do so this night. The workers left the plant without incident. Apple Street was lined with police cars, sitting ominously silent with the officers standing in rows alongside them.

Halfway to the car line, a male worker stumbled and pushed against a policeman. A scuffle resulted, and in an instant a near-riot developed. Melba was shoved into the thick of it, then rescued by Jesse, who was walking with her.

"You okay, kid?" Jesse asked.

"I don't know," Melba answered, groping for a place to sit. "I feel kinda faint."

Jesse motioned to another woman for help and they supported Melba to the car line where they sat on the curb.

Like rolling surf crashing on the shore, word of Toni's murder came down the street. Apple Street was a sea of humanity coming from the distillery.

"Murder!" a man shouted. "The company has resorted to murder!"

In spite of her discomfort, Melba had heard what was being said. She clutched at her stomach and cried, "Oh, Sweet Jesus, help me!"

What happened from that point on was a blur in her memory. Jesse got help from some of the workers. One of them went for Dave and he met her at the hospital. She remembered being taken through a corridor on a rolling table. She saw nurses and interns looking down upon her as busy preparations were made. David stood nervously at her side.

"Oh, David," she cried. "Those men pushed me down as I was coming from work."

"It's alright, honey," Dave whispered. "They say our baby is on its way. We're in good hands. We're in the hospital. Let me hold your hand. I'm here, now."

She grimaced as she writhed in labor.

The crowd had grown on Apple Street. Hundreds now milled around at the main entrance to the distillery. It was not difficult for Bits Casso to go unnoticed as he worked his way toward the plant. He carried a glass jug of liquid and had a coil of rope over his shoulder. When he got to the railroad tracks, he turned away from the plant entrance and walked toward the stockyards.

Plant security reported a trespasser over the fence behind Rack House No. 10. A search of the premises revealed no one. The guards directed their attention back to Apple Street, where the fire department was turning hoses on the crowd.

The noises of the conflict and the hiss of water against the street and walls were deadened by the roar of a mighty flash of flame which jumped skyward from Rack House No. 10. The guards, the firemen, and the workers stood in shocked silence looking upward at the huge tongue of flame. Then, in unison, the entire crowd followed the fire trucks through the gate and toward the fire. The heat was intense. It seared their faces and they fell back, away from the building. Explosions could be heard inside the large red brick structure. Then there was an enormous internal quake as one of the floors fell, spewing the heavy whiskey barrels down on the level below. The earth trembled. The men shuddered and fell back. It seemed the whole plant would soon be shrouded in flame. The light of fire was clearly visible sixty miles away. The plant sewers belched whiskey into the river, killing wildlife and fish for a hundred miles.

At 2 that morning, Melba and Dave became the proud parents of a daughter. She was named Lacey Starks Merriwether.

David was allowed to enter the room where Melba lay holding the child in her arms.

"Good morning, honey," he smiled down as he kissed her on the brow. "Who's that you've got ahold of there?"

"Isn't she sweet?" Melba asked, holding the blanket back so he could see the baby's face.

"Sweetest there ever was," he agreed.

Melba noticed the red fire in the sky on the far side of town.

"What's that, a fire?" she asked.

"Yeah, a fire down by the river," he answered.

"What's burning, David?"

"I'm not sure, Pumpkin. You get some sleep. Everybody out there is alright."

She smiled and turned toward the baby, closed her eyes, and slept.

It took three days to control the fire. Miraculously, the only loss was the rack house and its contents. Hundreds of barrels of aging alcohol had gone up in vapor. There was no missing firefighters or company personnel. There were unsubstantiated reports that the first firefighters on the scene saw a man running up the stairs in the burning building. The ruins were too charred to produce any evidence of a fatality.

By the end of summer, the company recognized the union and signed a contract with it. Bits Casso was not there to participate. Rumor had it that he was so grieved by Toni's death and fearful for his life that he left town the night of her murder and was never heard from again. The Canadian Connection would not speculate on any of these events. The company announced two new whiskey products aimed at the lower-income consumer. One was named "River Home."

CHAPTER TEN

THE HOME FRONT, THE WAR FRONT AND CHRISTMAS

Melba was in the hospital for nearly a week. Finally, the doctor told her she could go home. Aunt Pearl and Uncle Shorty drove Dave down to the hospital to pick up the new mother and baby. It cost Dave $118 to pay the bill. Fortunately, he got some help from one of the carpenters at work, and he was able to settle the entire account. A nurse wheeled mother and child to the entrance. Dave and Pearl carried a variety of potted plants and baby paraphernalia along side Melba. Uncle Shorty had pulled the car up near the doorway and stood grinning as the family approached.

"Isn't she the sweetest baby?" Pearl asked as they stepped from the building. "We haven't heard one peep out of her since she was fed."

"She's my little angel," Melba cooed as she nuzzled the baby's cheek.

"Do you get the impression we are not much needed?" Dave asked Shorty.

"It's a big day for all of us. Praise the Lord," Shorty called out as he held the car door open.

"Praise the Lord," Pearl echoed.

"Praise the Lord," Dave whispered as he helped Melba.

The nurse handed the baby to Melba, tucked the blanket around the child, offered her congratulations and disappeared back into the building.

"Her first auto ride," Dave said as they pulled away.

"Her first day outside the hospital," Melba said, snuggling up under Dave's protective arm.

"Parents. You and me. Parents!" Dave smiled. "Makes you feel proud."

Pearl had not been idle while Melba was in the hospital. She had somehow managed to push her great bulk about the small apartment cleaning and making preparations all the while tending to Val. The landlady who made her home on the first floor volunteered to watch Val while the others went to pick up Melba. She held Val in her arms at the top of the stairs, watching as the happy group came home.

"Oh, she's so pretty," the landlady commented.

Melba folded the blanket back to give everyone a good look at the child.

"Little Lacey," Pearl commented. "That's what we'll call her, little Lacey."

Val made a gurgling noise and clapped her chubby hands as if to confirm the announcement. Everyone laughed as they moved into the apartment.

From that day forward, the apartment seemed to contain little that didn't center around the two babies. There were bottles to be cleaned and boiled. Bottles to be filled and chilled and warmed and tested. There were nipples to be cleaned, and squeezed and sucked. Diapers hung in the bathroom, the front room, the hallway and out on the porch roof. The floors were hidden under cribs and rockers and scattered shoes, stockings and rattles. Bath pans, wash rags, bottles of oil, cans of powder, Ivory soap and rubber ducks obscured the kitchen sink.

Aunt Pearl came every morning and stayed until late afternoon when Shorty picked her upon his way home from work. The big woman never paused except to feed the babies while Melba dozed.

Lacey was a fat baby from the start, and soon looked nearly as large as the petite but older Val. People would inquire whether the girls were sisters.

Melba's parents came on the weekend to visit. They always went home before dark, because the old truck was not dependable on the road.

David always dreaded Harold's coming because they had so little to talk about. Life had not made Melba's father any less bitter, and he reflected a morbid attitude in everything he did and said. They did find common ground when it was learned that they both were fans of the St. Louis Cardinals.

"I got to talk to Pepper Martin at Sportsman's Park once," Harold boasted.

"You were in St. Louis?" Dave asked.

"Yep, some of us from the pottery went down on the interurban."

"Did Lacey go along?"

"Naw," Harold answered. "Just a bunch of guys went. We got drunk down there and went to a kooch show."

"Striptease?" Dave inquired.

"Yep, got drunk at the game and went to the burlesque afterwards."

"Who won the game?"

"St. Louis, of course."

"I've never been to a game," Dave said. "Maybe sometime we could take the train and go down."

"Not with two babies to tend to," the cynical Harold replied.

"Well, just maybe," Dave said as he got up and moved to another chair.

For their anniversary, Dave took Melba to the Busy Bee. They toasted each other with Orange Crush and then went to a movie. The feature was a Shirley Temple show called "Bright Eyes." The news from the Pathe cameras told of "Kingfish" Huey Long's crackdown on New Orleans, questioned whether Bruno Hauptman was indeed guilty, and made casual reference to the growing Nazi Party in Germany. Melba was tired when they left the theater. Aunt Pearl was asleep on the couch when they got home, and Uncle Shorty was listening to a religious service on the radio. He woke Pearl, and they kissed the babies and groaned down the stairs and out to their car. Melba could not believe she had been married to David one whole year. So much had happened! To keep from waking the babies, they made love on the floor and slept in front of the fan.

Francine's letters to Toni were returned, with no explanation from the Post Office. After the third letter came back, Francine went to a pay phone and called Jesse.

"Hello, Jesse?" Francine asked above the humming and crackling in the line. "This is Francine Dixon."

"Who?" Jesse inquired hesitatively.

"Francine Dixon . . . Ryan . . . from the distillery. Remember Francine Ryan from the distillery?"

"Francine!" Jesse shouted. "Where are you?"

"I'm callin' from California. How is everything in Riverport?"

"Boomin', babe. How's everything out West?"

"Unbelievable. Is the plant workin' steady?" Francine asked.

"We're doin' about four days a week. Startin' four new lines next month," was the answer.

"How about Melba. Is she workin'?" Francine asked.

"Sure is, after she had her baby. You know she had a baby, don't you?"

"Oh, Jeez, I forgot she was pregnant. What did she have?"

"A little girl. Named her Lacey after her mother. Don't you want to know about anybody else?"

"Yeah. I just can't face the fact I ran off and left my baby. Tell me about Val," Francine said as she started to sob.

"Fit as a fiddle. Gettin' cuter every day. You ought to be here to enjoy that lil' doll," Jesse reminded.

"Oh, cut it out, Jesse. This is long distance and I can't go into all that from a pay phone."

"Do what you want. It ain't easy on Melba and her husband now that they've got a kid of their own, you know."

"Yeah. Yeah. I can go to church out here if I want to hear a sermon. Tell me, why are my letters to Toni bein' returned unopened? Did she and her guy move?"

"You didn't know?" Jesse asked. "You didn't know she was killed?"

"*Killed?* Killed how?"

"By gangsters. Shot by gangsters. Late one night several weeks ago. She died instantly – plugged full of holes. Oh, Francine, it was awful. We've had a war goin' on back here. We had strikes and rioting in the streets. Toni was shot. Melba was pushed down and had her baby early. Bits disappeared and a rack house went up in smoke."

"Oh, Lord," Francine exclaimed.

"It's beginnin' to calm down, though. We got a union now." Jesse could hear sobbing on the other end. "Francine? You there, babe?"

"I'm comin' home," came the answer, followed by the click of the switchhook.

As predicted, the distillery increased production and added four bottling lines. New women, mostly housewives, began to appear at the time clock. For the most part, they were white and in their early twenties. None of them had ever worked in industry before and it took a lot to acclimate them to the ways of whiskey production. With the fresh new faces (and bodies) to see, the barrel jockeys jammed together along the walls of the cafeteria. Interaction between the two groups started to develop and complications came with it. Up to this time, divorce was taboo. Now, hardly a day went by without the word coming up in factory gossip.

As one woman put it, "Comin' to work in the bottlin' house was like kickin' off your panties and walkin' into a stud barn."

Melba remained aloof, ignoring the promiscuity that surrounded her. Soon, the older women did not gossip or talk of men while seated near her in the cafeteria. She became the nucleus of a group of women set apart from the others. At her table, the talk was of household problems and raising children. Even the buffoons in the tanker's coveralls recognized her respectability and avoided slurs in her presence.

Jesse never told Melba that Francine had called. Weeks went by, and when Francine did not appear, Jesse supposed her resolve to come home had been thwarted.

Fall came and A.J. Adams won re-election handily. The mayor relaxed and permitted the red-light district to reopen with new fervor. The U.S. district attorney told Bentley that his case to get Mrs. Byrd was not tight enough for a trial. The prosecutor could not believe that statistics on the number of towels used could convince a jury that the madam was holding out on her income tax. For the time being, Bentley concentrated on taxing whiskey gallons. When the distillery opened in

1934, the excise tax was two dollars a gallon. Now, the tax was twice that. The federal government collected millions of dollars each week from this solitary alcohol plant.

The Canadian Connection was called back to the home office for briefing. Management anticipated the threat of war. Historically, war did strange things to the production of spirits. It not only affected supplies, it increased demand. The Jacob Wasserman Company wanted to prepare for future contingencies, and advised Dr. Barstow to double production.

Franklin Delano Roosevelt expressed his displeasure over the confusion over Thanksgiving. The public could not agree which Thursday should he designate.

Congress would finally settle the matter by passing a law declaring the entire country would celebrate the holiday on the fourth Thursday of November.

Melba found a ticket attached to her time card. All of the other cards had the same.

"What's this for?" she asked Jesse.

"You get an autographed photo of ol' Jacob," Jesse joked.

"Good, it'll help keep the mice away."

"How's those bambinos?" Jesse asked.

"Lots of work. Poor David is such a dear, but it takes so much of our time. We haven't been anywhere since our anniversary. The stairs got to Aunt Pearl, and she can't hardly help anymore. Val is startin' to walk, and you know how that will change things. David worries about the second floor. Crawlin' she is hard enough to watch, but walkin' we'll have to put a gate on the stairwell. Do you know, to this day, we've heard nothing from Francine. Do you suppose she's alright?"

Jesse felt like a heel for staying silent. "I'm sure she's just fine."

When the shift was over, the workers found a large truck parked at the gate, its rear doors standing open.

Half a dozen barrel jockeys, supervised by plant guards, exchanged the tickets on the time cards for Thanksgiving turkeys.

Melba was delighted with hers. It was a large dressed bird, and she clung to it with both hands as she boarded a streetcar to ride home.

Aunt Pearl needed no prodding to cook the Thanksgiving dinner, and the six of them ate heartily. Uncle Shorty and Val pulled on the wishbone until it slipped from Val's grip and Melba gave her a helping hand.

Roddie Dixon made the promotion to gunnery officer and got his orders to embark for Hawaii early in December. Francine was tiring of the camp life and was drawn to return to Riverport. She embraced Roddie at the dock and waved goodbye. In the pit of his stomach, Roddie knew he would never see her again. She packed up her simple belongings and caught the Santa Fe for Chicago. The depot was decorated with Christmas lights. She had forgotten that Christmas was almost upon her. She shopped at the newsstand for a gift for Val. She really had no idea what to get.

The mayor had summoned Mrs. Byrd to City Hall. She arrived in mid-afternoon and puffed her bulk up three steps to the lobby.

A.J. Adams was reading a letter, head down, eyes shaded by his green visor. The elevator groaned to a stop on the third floor and trembled as Mrs. Byrd stepped off.

When the madam entered his office, he greeted her without looking up.

"Come in my fine friend," he beckoned. "You got here just in time for tea."

"This mama needs somethin' stronger than tea," she complained.

"How about a little brandy?" Adams asked as he pulled a bottle from his desk drawer.

"I'd rather have a shot of schnapps," she complained.

"What's your favorite brand, Jacob Wasserman?" he asked, raising his eyes to stare at her.

"It's as good as any."

"Maybe it is better than most because it doesn't cost you anything to drink it," Adams growled.

"Why wouldn't it cost me?" she asked.

"Because I have it on good authority that you get it delivered to your door by the distillery steward who comes to your place as if he was just one of the johns."

"We have a lot of curious customers," she said, smiling.

"Come clean, my friend, what's your connection to the distillery?"

"Their boys like to play with my girls," she lied.

"Let's not get cute. I still hold your fate in the palm of my hand. What's your association with the distillery?"

"What's this all about?" the woman asked, looking suspiciously about the room.

"It's about an old cohort of mine, who, it seems, has been playin' both sides of the street!"

"Nobody I know has been playin' both sides of the street. The whiskey people always did like a little screwin'. It shouldn't surprise you that they come to a whorehouse to get it."

"Them comin' down to your neighborhood for a fuck is like takin' a sandwich to a cafeteria. They got the only cathouse in the world with a neon sign on the roof!"

"Let's git down to brass tacks," she said, leaning toward him.

"Brass tacks, shit! You been workin' with them Canadians! I'm permitting you to operate, and you're playin' along with these bastards to my detriment!"

"No detriment. Just tryin' to get along with all you pimps," she hissed.

Silence fell on the room as the mayor sat glaring at her and snorting through the gray hairs in his nose.

She waved her hand in resignation. "I'm sorry," she apologized. "I didn't mean it that way. You got me pissed."

He sat glaring at her, breathing heavily. His eyes seemed to narrow, and it looked to her they glowed red.

Finally, he turned away from her and selected a new cigar from the box on his desk. She watched suspenseful as he bit off the end and spit it into a cuspidor. He struck a match on the side of his leg, and puffed on the stogy. A cloud of smoke surrounded his head as he drew on the cigar.

"Now, then," he started in a calm voice. "Let's start from the top and tell me everything you know."

She sat, looking down at her own folded hands wondering what it was he wanted her to tell. "Let's clear the air for both of us," she began.

"What am I to think about a protector who knows the Feds are checking on me and doesn't tip me off?"

"How do you come by that information?" he asked.

"I knew what was goin' on when you talked in that truck in front of my place that day. I knew they was countin' towels. I'd had the maid washin' towels at her place for a month just so they'd not get a clear picture of the real count. You talk about both sides of the street, I see you all over town! Now, let's hear some information from your mouth."

"Nothing came of it. They couldn't prove a case, but don't think they'll give up. That Bentley has some kinda vendetta about whorehouses. He'll be back."

Mrs. Byrd sighed heavily and wondered what possessed her to get involved in a business targeted by so many people. "Maybe there is a 'leak' right here in City Hall," she suggested.

Adams spun around towards her in his swivelchair. "Who hired the hit man we had around here last July?"

"The Canadians."

"Ah ha! And who were they really after?"

"It wasn't me, or I'd be gone," she said shaking her head. "They did more harm than good. I expect their 'client' knows now that it was a dumb move."

"Why the secrecy? Why didn't you tell me?"

"At the time, I didn't know who their 'mark' was. I didn't want to draw any fire on me."

The mayor leaned back and put his feet up on the windowsill. For several minutes, he sat staring out at the city. Finally, he turned to face Mrs. Byrd. "We're headed into another goddamned war with those krauts," he whispered. "I feel it in my bones. I wonder if F.D.R. has as much crap in his job as I get in mine."

"He gits even more," she said, standing to leave. "And he has to sleep with Eleanor at night. She's even uglier than me!"

They both laughed and adjourned.

In Chicago, Francine arrived at the Dearborn Station and transferred to the LaSalle Street Station. The cab took a circuitous route through the loop and she got a glimpse of the Christmas decorations on State Street. Large white celluloid candles hung from each lamppost, streamers of gold colored garlands waved in the wind, and every store window was lighted in keeping with the theme. On each corner stood a Salvation Army Santa next to a cardboard chimney, ringing a bell to attract offerings for the poor.

Francine had lived in Chicago until she was a teenager. She never liked to recall anything up to that point. She purposely dismissed any thoughts of this part of her life, and down through the years she developed a mental block about it.

Now, she was in Chicago again. It was a joyous season with Christmas approaching. Her stay need not last more than the time between trains, yet she was drawn to see some familiar landmark.

The old neighborhood would be too severe for her to handle. Her school was probably still the same, but she had no desire to come face to face with any of her old teachers. She could imagine the conversation with anyone who could remember her misfortune. Then, she remembered a pleasant scene. She and several classmates had cut class one spring day and had gone to the Lincoln Park Zoo. It was a great day for all of them. They laughed and ran, feeling free as the air. One of the boys did an imitation of the baboon and they all followed suit, rocking with laughter.

"Drive me through Lincoln Park," she said.

"Yeah," the cabbie answered, looking at her in the rearview mirror. "Any place special?"

"Just take the road through the park," she ordered.

"That's out of my usual. Wanna pay up front?"

"Don't worry, I got the dough," she stated as she threw a five-dollar bill onto the seat next to him.

"Anything you say," he answered as he worked their way into a northbound traffic lane.

Seeing the park was not what she expected. Her memories came from spring. Now, it was winter.

Everything looked barren. The leaves had dropped from the trees, and the scene was devoid of color. Even the buildings appeared cold and foreboding. She didn't need much of this to be irked.

"Okay," she said. "Wheel it around and go back to the Loop, I've got a train to catch."

The cab turned back to the south. She saw nothing more of Chicago. She was deep in thought. As the train lurched across switches leaving the yards, she looked over her shoulder at the skyline in the haze. Even then, she saw nothing. Chicago had faded back into the past.

The Merriwethers were excited about the coming of Christmas. Lacey was too young to realize much of what was happening, but Val was beginning to like the idea.

Melba had hung paper bells on the cords of the window shades. They moved slowly about in the draft from the frosted glass. Val made noises and pointed to them, always wanting to touch.

David's family never celebrated much on Christmas, but they sometimes decorated a small tree several weeks before the holiday. Melba's family, by contrast, waited until Christmas Eve when the tree and all its decorations mysteriously appeared during the night, along with filled stockings and gifts.

After much deliberation, the Merriwethers decided to decorate two weeks before Christmas.

They bought a small tree and a string of colored lights. When one burned out, the tree went dark. Finding the bad bulb took a great deal of time.

"David, help me," Melba called. "I've tightened every bulb and they just won't come on!"

"I'll walk down to the drug store and get some bulbs," he responded.

"See if you've got enough for some tinsel," she called to him as he left the apartment.

David stomped down the stairs and out of the house. He had turned at the corner and was out of sight when a cab pulled up in front and stopped.

Francine paid the driver and stood at the curb looking up at the old building. If it had changed at all, it was for the worse. It seemed larger and darker than before. The railing was gone from the porch and the wind blew in through the ill-fitting door. Cooking odors and the smell of wet diapers met her nostrils as she climbed the stairs.

Francine hesitated on the landing and listened. Melba was walking about in the apartment. Little Lacey was asleep, but Val was sitting on her potty-chair jabbering away and shaking a string of large beads. The sounds brought a chill to Francine. Maybe she should not have come this far. Maybe she should turn back. She could turn and go. No one would ever know that she had been there. Val gurgled and threw the beads rattling to the hallway. Melba went in pursuit.

"Why do you do that?" Melba said aloud as she stooped to retrieve the beads.

"Why do I do what?" Francine asked, looking through the railing at her.

Melba's face told of her shock. "Who's there?" she asked.

"Got a bottle of beer?" Francine said smiling at Melba's obvious perplexed position.

"Francine? Francine, Is that you?" Melba asked.

"Right as rain," Francine answered as she bolted up the last few steps.

Both women collided at the top and threw their arms about each other.

"Francine, where did you come from?"

"The Golden State, Pumpkin. Where's my kid?"

"Val. Val, baby, your mama is here!" Melba cried as she pulled Francine into the apartment.

The noise frightened her, and Val began to cry.

"Oh, we scared you. Here let me introduce you to your mommy," Melba soothed as she lifted the bare-bottomed child from the potty chair.

"Val . . . . Oh, Val darlin'," Francine said, holding the child to her chest and starting to sob.

The noise woke Lacey and she started to cry, too.

"Oh, Francine," Melba said. "Look here at my baby. This is lil' Lacey, named after Mama."

Francine nodded, but did not look. She was holding Val, tears racing down both cheeks.

For a long while both women stood holding their babies while rocking back and forth. Val and Lacey finally were settled down and Melba showed Francine how to wipe a dirty bottom and apply a diaper.

It took the combined efforts of Melba, David and Aunt Pearl to keep Francine in Riverport. She was not accustomed to motherhood, and she wanted to bolt and run. Day by day they worked with her, and day by day she became more attached to Val. Things finally began to settle down late in December. The apartment was much too small for the five occupants. David was weary of the floor for a bed, and Melba realized they should sleep together at night.

Then came a break. Uncle Shorty decided to retire at the end of the year. He had inherited a small farm in Arkansas and it was his plan to live there. This became good fortune for the Merriwethers when it was announced that they could rent the bungalow in Riverport for a modest amount. It was further decided that January 15th would be moving day.

The day after this news, Melba and Francine were caring for their children and reviewing events.

"I'm so excited," Melba said. "To think that there will be room for all of us. A place of our own. Aunt Pearl and Uncle Shorty certainly are good Christian folks. God bless them."

"I remember when they threw you out on the street," Francine reminded. "Who's changed the most, us or them?"

"A blend of understandin'," Melba answered. "Tolerance and God's love. It conquers all."

"I don't expect that we'll see the day when Uncle Shorty gets so tolerant that he takes to drinkin'."

"Francine!" Melba admonished. "That is an absurd thought!"

"Good thing there aren't many like him or Jacob Wasserman would have to switch to wine and champagne for communion and ship launchings."

"Never come the day. Never come the day," Melba said shaking her head. She took a clean diaper and folded it.

"I've never asked," Francine started. "Did the checks continue to come from Canada?"

"Yes, and David and I have saved every cent in an account for you."

"What? You were to supposed to use it to live on! You mean you've been supporting Val on your own slim budget?"

"We got by . . . didn't think we should forge your name. Just signed ours and put 'em in the bank."

"I can't believe they are still sendin' 'em, and I can't believe you and David didn't use the money. How much work did the girls get at the distillery this year?"

"Most of us got three and a half months this fall. Startin' next spring we can draw the new unemployment checks."

"I get a dependent's check from Roddie's military, and Val is a dependent of his too. Oh, Melba, I'm so screwed up," Francine complained as she sat down at the table and poured herself a cup of coffee.

"Well, you're back with your child, and I just know things will get better from now on!"

"I can't move with you into Pearl 's house. I just can't sponge off your good fortune like that. But I can't handle Val alone. What'll I do?" Francine cried.

"I got it," Melba answered. "Val can move with us, you keep the flat. When we git called back to work, you can git forty winks over here, but be with Val at our place when she's up and about."

"Would you work it out with me?"

"Always have," Melba said, squeezing her hand.

The first Christmas party was in the afternoon of the twenty-fourth at Jesse's house. Her husband, Clark, had decorated the outside of the house with boughs of evergreen. Inside, each window shade supported a red paper bell, and the small tree in the living room was decorated with glass ornaments, popcorn threaded onto a length of string made a streamer around the branches and waving circles. Jesse had hung mistletoe from the light fixture in the center of the room. More pine boughs decorated the archway between the living and dining rooms, and the table held plates of homemade cookies and fruitcake. In the center, a large bowl of Tom and Jerry's sat surrounded by glass cups. On the buffet, Jesse had lined bottles of all the products manufactured by the Jacob Wasserman Distilling Company. It looked like a sales promotion for company products, and stood out in mute testimony to Jesse's ability to steal from her employer.

"Well look who's back in town!" Jesse exclaimed when she saw Francine walk in. "Merry Christmas, stranger," she cried as she threw her arms around Francine and squeezed.

"Hi, Jesse," Francine grinned. "Gotta drink for an old coworker?"

The women began a line of chatter, oblivious to their surroundings as Clark took their coats and laid them on the bed.

Clark turned on the radio and got some Christmas music from a station in St. Louis. Several other couples from the plant came in and the crowd began to grow. One couple brought a relative visiting from Detroit. He was a solidly built blond about twenty five years old, who had just returned from a trip abroad. Francine became attracted to him and got engrossed in his tales of Europe. He had visited France and Germany and made his return trip to the United States aboard the air ship Hindenburg. His description of the voyage made Francine want to go to Europe by dirigible.

Melba was changing Lacey's diaper in the bedroom when Francine joined her.

"Hey, Pumpkin, would you do me a favor?" Francine asked.

"Let me guess. You want me to watch the kids while you go off with this blond fellow for a few glasses of beer," Melba predicted.

"Please, honey, I'm not havin' the best time here, you know."

"I understand. Just don't miss the party at Aunt Pearl's place tonight, and be sober. In fact, don't even smell like alcohol. Eat a pound of Red-Hots if you have to, but be sober at Aunt Pearl's! What's this guy's name, anyway?"

"Kurt somethin'. It's a foreign name. I didn't get it all when I was introduced. He's here to do business with the Centipede Company. Something his people want to contract for some kind of tractors."

"And does this Kurt somebody have a means of transportation?" Melba inquired.

"A Duesenberg. An honest-to-God Duesenberg," Francine laughed, as she slapped Melba on the butt and left the room.

"I bet he's got a Duesenberg," Melba mumbled through clenched teeth that held the safety pins for the diaper. "I'll just bet he has, just like

I'd bet this baby won't wet her pants for the rest of the evening. A Duesenberg indeed."

Val had gotten involved in the glittering ornaments under the tree, and Jesse had extracted her several times when one of the guests suggested the child be somehow distracted from the temptations.

"Clark," Jesse said. "I've got an old rocker from my childhood up in the attic. Would you please go up and get it? Dust it off up there, before you bring it down here. I think it's back by the chimney," she said to her husband's back as he went off toward the attic stairs.

Dave was in the kitchen showing a couple how to make a 'Dagwood' sandwich, Jesse poured drinks as she darted around the house. Several of the guests seated on the couch began to hum Christmas music with the radio, and about the time Clark reappeared with the small rocker, they broke out in loud singing. The sudden noise alarmed Lacey and she began to cry.

"We know we are not good, but do you have to complain so loud?" one of the women joked.

This provoked a burst of laughter and more singing. Val was seated in the little rocker and was shown how to move back and forth in it. She caught on quickly, and rocked in the chair most of the afternoon.

David studied Melba's appearance as compared with the other women. He wished he had given her the new dress he had gotten her for Christmas. The one she wore was drab and a bit slobber-stained around the right shoulder. Her stockings were cotton, not silk like the other women wore. She had done her hair with the familiar curling iron, and it seemed to protrude out from the sides of her head and not hang down in cascading curls, as he preferred. All in all, she was a picture of poverty and to him a Queen of Glory. He only wished he could afford better fare for her, but she seemed happy in this group of familiar faces.

Somehow, both babies fell asleep on Jesse's bed. When it came time to go to Aunt Pearl's house, Melba and Dave got busy gathering up the paraphernalia. Clark offered to drive them. Jesse had begun to show signs of the drinks, and she elected to stay with the remaining guests. Clark had loaded the car, and the Merriwethers and Val were just getting in when Jesse bolted from the house waving a wet diaper over her head.

"Oh, no you don't," she laughed. "I know the old wives tale about leaving a wet diaper so the hostess is next to be pregnant."

Melba blushed. "I didn't do it on purpose," she said.

"Purpose or not, this mouse ain't havin' no kids!" Jesse said.

Clark sat behind the wheel, thinking how much he wished they did have children.

The second Christmas party was at Pearl and Shorty's home. It was a contrast to the first.

For one thing, it was more traditional, and certainly more religious. There was herbal tea and hot chocolate for drinks. Pearl had baked traditional German cookies and made a beautiful, rich Stollen iced with whipped cream and covered with nuts. It was almost too pretty to cut.

Melba unwrapped the babies and checked their pants for dampness before getting them settled on the couch. A knock at the door preceded Francine's entrance into the house. She waved to someone outside and a car motor purred from the scene. Dave looked out the window. He had never seen a Duesenberg before.

"Hi Pearlie," Francine shouted as she darted to Pearl and threw her arms around the enormous woman.

Melba held her breath. Was Francine drunk?

" . . . And Merry Christmas to you too," Francine said, turning on Shorty and giving him a hug. This caught the small man figuratively and physically off balance. He nearly fell to the floor. Francine caught him under the armpits, righted him and brushed off his shoulders. Shorty regained his composure, tugged at the bottom of his vest and smiled an embarrassed grin.

"It's a time to rejoice," Shorty said, looking at Pearl for endorsement.

"Amen to that," Pearl said as she placed a stack of dishes on the table.

The house was warm and beautiful. The living room had a fireplace and mantle. Pearl had hung stockings for all of them on the mantelpiece. A picture of Jesus dominated the opposite wall where Pearl had hung embroidered Bible quotes and church bulletins. Tiny bells hung everywhere. Most of them were sleigh bells, and they jingled every time Pearl bumped them in her movement about the house. There was an advantage to being so rotund. In this case, it made music.

Melba shot a warning glance at Francine and she settled down. They surrounded the table, standing with bowed heads while Shorty said the prayers. He gave the usual grace and added words about Christmas, peace and victory of good over evil. Then, he asked for the blessings of the Lord on the house, soon to be occupied by Melba and David.

Francine bit her lip to keep from crying.

Prayers over, Aunt Pearl served the food and the guests were seated.

Outside, it had started to snow. A Cadillac sedan pulled up in front of the house. Four men wearing large hats sat inside. One of them got out, put his arms around an enormous basket of fruit and walked to the door.

Pearl was standing when they heard the knock. She went to the door and opened it.

"Lord have mercy," she cried. "It's my lamb, Heinie!"

"Merry Christmas," he said, handing her the basket.

"Come right in here, young man," she demanded. "This makes my Christmas a happy one."

Heinie was pulled across the threshold and into the room. He saw the seated guests and started to bolt. Pearl had him in her grip, and guided him into the room.

"Look, Shorty, it's my boy Heinie come home on Christmas Eve!" she cried.

Shorty and Dave stood and shook hands with him. Melba nodded and the babies both gurgled infant noises.

"Can't stay, Pearl," Heinie said. "We've got business in St. Louis. We're on our way now."

"Honest?" Pearl asked.

"Honest," Heinie answered.

"Let me fix you and your friends some Christmas goodies," she insisted as she went to the kitchen and returned with a roll of waxed paper and a paper bag.

"That's not necessary," he complained.

"It will be something for you to snack on while you drive," Pearl said.

The bag was filled. She topped it with a church paper and followed him to the door.

"Thanks. Happy Christmas," Heinie whispered as he stepped into the night. Pearl stood in the open doorway waving as the car pulled away and disappeared into the night.

"God bless you, my sweet boy," she murmured. "God bless you and keep you."

CHAPTER ELEVEN

TREACHERY, PASSPORTS AND REVENGE

Besieged by the crusade to socialism and the causes of society's oppressed minorities, the country survived the first shock of the Great Depression and tottered into a recession. If that was not enough, nature delivered a drought and the Dust Bowl forced farmers to swarm to the West, while labor forces pitted physical violence against management and demanded recognition.

Overseas, Franco pushed Spain into a civil war while Mussolini attacked backward tribes in Africa, and Hitler destroyed his opposition and goose-stepped across his neighbors.

This growing problem of world lawlessness caused America to slowly turn from domestic issues to international matters. President Roosevelt warned that these foreign issues threatened America.

In Riverport, the locals directed their frustration toward the German families within the community. It mattered not that these people had lived here for three generations. The fact that they clung to strange customs and language identified them as foreigners. Most of the town looked down on the "krauts." Those with German ancestry took a low profile and isolated themselves from public activities. It went so far that the annual Oktoberfest was cancelled and not resumed until late in the 1950s.

A.J. Adams won the Republican Primary in March, and notwithstanding the popularity of F.D.R., won the general election in November. This would not have been unusual, but this time the Jacob Wasserman Company had contributed heavily to his opponent. The mayor might not have known about the distillery's involvement if the opponent's campaign manager hadn't gotten drunk at Madam Byrd's.

A.J. Adams was working in his office late in the evening when the telephone rang.

"City Hall," he rasped into the mouthpiece. Actually, he would not have answered it at all except that he was expecting a call from home.

"Mr. Mayor?"

"Yeah, this is the mayor," he barked.

"This is Sadie."

"Sadie Byrd?" the mayor asked.

"We got a bad connection?"

"Yeah, I can hardly hear you. Where are you?"

"In my cathouse, hon. You got company?" Mrs. Byrd asked.

"No one here but me and the bats," the mayor answered.

"Good," she said. "We got a drunk down here that says he's a big shot in the last election, but nobody remembers seein' him before. He's upstairs, braggin' about how much money he handled in the city election campaign."

"Is this the first time a john lied to one of your whores?"

"No, but it's the first time anybody ever tried to cash a Wasserman check for more than one thousand dollars!"

"Wasserman check?"

"Now we got a good connection." she cooed.

"Who's the payee on the check?" Adams shouted.

"Your erstwhile opponent. That's another reason why we won't accept it," she said.

"Tell your girl to keep him occupied until I get there, if she has to go around the world to do it!" Adams roared.

"What're you gonna do with him?" Mrs. Byrd asked.

"I'm gonna give him the third degree."

"Now, you behave. I got a reputation to live up to. I don't want nothin' unpleasant around here. Maybe you'd better bring your brother-

in-law along. I'd feel safer if I had a good cop down here tonight." she
suggested.

"Don't you bother none about the details," the mayor grunted as
he strained to put his coat on and hold the telephone simultaneously.
"You just do as I say!"

Mrs. Byrd slowly put the telephone back on the hook. She really
wished she had not called at all.

The light in the room was very dark. The air smelled of cheap toilet
water and human sweat. In the center of the room stood an iron
Simmons bed with wire coil springs. It pitched and rolled as if it were
creating the breakers on the high seas. There was the continual grunting
and puffing of the labor of love as the john and the prostitute thrashed
about. Neither of the naked revelers saw the wave of cold water hurling
through the air. The beam of a desk lamp directed on the scene
accompanied the sudden cold shock.

The man stood on the bed, dripping with water, shock and disgust.
The woman rolled off the bed and disappeared under it. It was too dark
behind the lamp to see who was holding it. When the naked man dove off
the bed toward the light, it moved out of his reach and several people in
the dark hustled the man out of the room and down the back stairs.

It was a cold night by the river when Dr. Barstow left his office and
walked across the company street to his white Cord. He nodded to the
guard standing outside the gatehouse, and opened the door of his auto.
Inside the car, bound hand and foot was the man from the cathouse.
He was naked, and alive, but very cold. When Dr. Barstow and the
guard removed his gag, the doctor recognized it as containing a company
check from Canada. No one at the distillery ever knew how the man
was put in the car, or for that matter how he got onto company property
in the first place.

It was not surprising that A.J. Adams and Dr. Barstow never were
seen dining at the club together after that.

Work at the distillery picked up, and Melba and Francine got the
last five months of the year full time. When the New Year arrived, they

were eligible for unemployment benefits under a new governmental insurance program.

The babies were a constant responsibility. At times, Melba thought Francine was improving as a mother. This seldom lasted because Francine periodically wandered off and avoided her obligations.

Kurt Luftmann, the blond fellow Francine met at the Christmas party, came to town with increased frequency. Each time he appeared, Francine abandoned her domestic role and stayed away from home. Finally, Melba decided to talk to Francine about the impact of her conduct on Val. It was early one day before going to work.

"Francine," Melba began. "I know there are a lot of differences in the way you and I do things, but there is one place where we are alike."

"You are goin' to preach!" Francine said, looking at her friend's face. "I can tell by the tone of your voice that you are goin' to *preach!*"

"Not preach," Melba corrected. "It's just for the good of Val. She misses you so when you are not here."

"I'm usually around when she's awake," Francine said.

"How many times a week?" Melba asked. "You've been gone three days this week already."

"I've been thinkin' about goin' to Europe," Francine announced as she lit a cigarette and blew the smoke toward the ceiling. "Kurt has lots of relatives over there, and he wants them to meet me."

"Europe!" Melba exclaimed, "What am I to do about Val if you go to Europe?"

"Maybe I'll take her along."

"You and who else? You can't care for her here at home. Is this Kurt hiring a nanny to take along?"

"He might, his uncle is paying our freight. Maybe he will pay for the nursemaid, too. Kurt's relations are very well off. They have a lot to do with the Zeppelin stuff over there."

"Zeppelin? You mean they fly around in those balloons?"

"Not balloons. They are like ocean liners in the sky. They have all the comfort of a big ship, except they go by air."

"Are you out of your mind?" Melba asked. "You don't mean to say that this guy has proposed that you go across the ocean on one of those flying cigars?"

"We've talked about it. Skip it for now. I'll let you know if we make any plans."

"An airship!" Melba cried. "You'd really ride in one of those gas bags? You're either crazy, or a complete daredevil, and maybe a little of both. Wait 'til I tell David about *this!*"

The increased international tension and particularly the criticism of the Germans caused Kurt to put his Duesenberg in storage and drive a Buick. He picked Francine up without coming into the house and they went to a roadside honky-tonk for food and beer. He was more quiet than usual, and she filled the silence with chatter. She talked mostly about her daughter.

He sat listening to her, his steel blue eyes focused on her face.

"What do you know of your ancestry?" he asked. "Are any of your forefathers from Europe?"

"Ireland," she answered, going on with her story about Val.

"Are any of them Jewish?" he inquired.

"Jewish? What kind of a question is that? My family has been Catholic as far back as we can remember. Why ask that question now – does it make a difference?"

"If we go to see my family, I must first know something of your family. It is a trait of the old country to examine blood lines of the people we know."

"They will want to see my pedigree?"

"I'll check your pedigree. You can show them your pretty face."

Francine had experienced the brashness of Roddie, and the nervousness of Bud with a few short affairs thrown in, but she had never before experienced the dominance she got in her relationship with Kurt.

In the first place, he was the strongest and best-developed man she had ever known. He worked out daily and constantly improved his muscular anatomy. He was so wrapped up in this aspect of his physical appearance, that he often went out of the way to display his physique. He never missed an opportunity to strip to the waist or roll up his sleeves to expose some of his muscle. He had a handsome face, and soft blond hair, which seemed so fragile that it was inconsistent with the rest of him.

If his body was not intimidating, his attitude was. He never had raised his voice around her, yet every word he spoke fell upon her ears like a sharp command. She could not understand what kind of a spell he was casting over her, but she was not moving away from him. In fact, even with his brutish force in lovemaking she believed she was beginning to fall for him. Actually, she was starting to like his way of doing things.

Val was now eighteen months old, and Lacey was one year old. Both girls were walking and getting into everything in the house. Lacey was smaller than Val, but she tried to mimic everything the older baby did. Val was not as quick to share her toys or food, but never failed to come to Lacey's aid if needed. They were always inseparable and even slept at the same time. It was not surprising that when one of them had a problem, the other had the same situation. This included a severe case of chicken pox.

Melba noticed the bumps forming on Val's chest and she then examined Lacey to find the same thing. Dr. Wein recommended a family doctor just starting to practice in Riverport. He was a younger man and made house calls. After coming to the cottage and seeing the patients, he left some calamine lotion and explained to Melba the agony of itching when these bumps dried and scabbed over. The new doctor was very thorough. He was giving Melba instructions about the care of her charges when David walked in.

This is my husband, David Merriwether," she said.

"David, this is our new family physician, Dr. Edwin Maloy."

David shook hands with the doctor.

"Good to meet you doc," David said. "Why do we need a doctor?"

"The children have chicken pox, David. Dr. Maloy is telling me how to treat the disease."

"Chicken pox?" David repeated. "How did they get chicken pox?"

"It's a childhood disease, but if you've never had it I'd recommend you stay away from them until their fever breaks," Dr. Maloy said.

David reluctantly moved his shaving things and some of his work clothes to the cellar on the doctor's advice. It was the first time he and Melba had been separated overnight since they got married.

Melba tried everything to keep the kids from scratching. She even tied mittens on their hands, but Val was used to sucking her thumb, and this caused her to cry constantly; and to call out for "Seen," which was what she called Francine.

The health department came out and nailed a large red quarantine sign on the front of the house. It was a tough experience for all of them, but in a little over a week, David was allowed to move upstairs and back to Melba's waiting arms.

The next day at work, David had a hard time staying awake. He blamed his loss of sleep on the kids, but the truth was, he overindulged in Melba's favors once they got back together. David had jokingly called the night a real "baby maker." He did not know how right he was.

The Wasserman Company had been unable to determine how their property could be invaded and desecrated without a solitary clue. The security people had worked on many possibilities, but all of them proved worthless. The specter of such a trespass haunted Dr. Barstow. The matter had caused the Canadians to doubt his capability, and he was feeling the heat from his superiors.

Oscar Keel, U.S. representative and friend to the distilling industry, made a special trip to Riverport. His secretary arranged for him to meet with Dr. Barstow the next day. If Dr. Barstow had not watched the arrival of the congressman, he would not have known that Benjamin Howard Bentley, Treasury agent and watchdog, met him at the depot.

The meeting was held at the club. A private dining room was set up at one end of the building with instructions that there were to be no interruptions, particularly by any city officials. Keel was a politician, and he was not going to put himself in an awkward position. He appeased the Canadians by hearing Barstow out, and he stayed off the toes of the politically popular A.J. Adams by visiting him at City Hall. Through his efforts, and with the aid of some new federal laws, Keel promised protection to the distillery without affronting the local officials. It was fortunate for the congressman that foreign tensions had precipitated legislation protecting materials of national significance. Alcohol somehow came under the wing of this act. It followed that the distillery being a producer of alcohol was entitled to be so included. To add a touch of authority, two agents of the Federal Bureau of Investigation came to the plant and lectured the guards on security.

The company installed three strands of barbed wire atop the already imposing fence, and got the city council to post "no parking" signs along Apple Street. The officials of the railroad promised to leave no cars standing near the plant, except for late afternoon hours when livestock would be loaded at the stockyards. Now the distillery looked like a penitentiary, and Dr. Barstow was appeased.

A.J. Adams was content that he had baffled the Canadians, and isolated them in one smooth move. The "goose that lays the golden eggs" was now out in the open where everybody could see her. With all the commotion, the only loss was the liquor store run by the mayor's relatives. Not to be outdone, Adams got them jobs collecting personal property taxes in the industrial blocks along the river. Of course, the distillery was in this category.

With the demands for grain to feed the world's hungry ever on the increase, the price of farm products began a slow rise to continue for two decades. This increase in cost prompted the distillers of alcohol to look about for a substitute material for their product. The popularity of things Russian began to appear. These stalwart people seemed to he allied with our national causes, and promised to be a barrier to the expansion of Germany. Little was known of these allies, except that they danced sitting down and drank a ghastly drink called vodka. It did not take much research to learn that vodka could be distilled from potatoes.

A portion of the advertising was allotted to touting this "new" drink. After all, it did not possess the telltale odor on the consumer's breath like other hard liquor, and therefore it was a natural for those who wanted to keep their thirst a secret.

Carloads of potatoes appeared in the rail yards. The distillery began producing vodka in bottles bearing labels looking like Russian playing cards. A new line was invented for the drinking public.

The two goons who had killed Arlo reappeared in the back streets of Riverport.

They stayed away from the red-light district and the skin shows, and watched the activities of A.J. Adams. The justice of the peace having offices across the street from City Hall had a heart attack, and his office was unoccupied. His misfortune had been announced in the local newspaper, so it was commonly known that the office was vacant. It did not require a Jimmy Valentine to pick the lock and enter.

The location was perfect for their purposes. From this second-floor position, they could look straight across the street into the mayor's office. If their intent was to assassinate the mayor, they had plenty of opportunities, because "His Honor" frequently worked alone late at night, making a good target for a rifle shot from their perch. However, that would be too obvious, and they wanted to do their work in such a way that some other person would be suspected.

The first floor of the building housed a popular and very active night club and gambling casino. The pair had not learned that the Strickler gang operated this club, which they avoided because it was so crowded. Instead, they cut down the alley behind the building to a smaller tavern on the next street. Here, they bought beer, cigarettes and sandwiches. Except for their forays for supplies, they seldom left their lair.

It was obvious that they waited for a particular occasion. Finally, on Monday night, they prepared to do their dirty work. They forced open the window, which had been painted shut for a decade. Setting up a small tripod, they affixed a long-barreled rifle to it.

The older man had just parked their getaway car right by the back stairs. He was heading up when Heinie and some of the "family" pulled into the alley and parked behind the casino. It was dark and Heinie could not have seen the goon, but in the still air, he heard the wheezing hacking cough of this asthmatic henchman.

Heinie stopped short between his car and the building. His associates went for their guns, but he motioned for silence. Pete Mandel came alongside Heinie and whispered, "what's goin' on?"

"Shut up and listen," Heinie growled.

"Just a stray cat," Pete said.

"Maybe, maybe not."

From the top of the stairs came the cough and wheeze before the door closed behind the man.

"Hear that?" Heinie asked. "Where'd we hear that before?"

"Just some guy coughin'," Pete said.

"There's somethin' about that cough," Heinie mulled as he turned and went in the back door of his nightclub.

Inside, a card game was in progress under a green shade. One of the players stood to let Heinie have his chair. The big Dutchman sat down and picked up his cards. He was scowling as he examined his hand and knocked once on the table. The dealer nodded an acknowledgement, and dealt to the players.

Down the street, Mrs. Byrd pulled up with a group of girls for Dr. Wein's office. The girls got out chattering and disappeared up the stairs to the doctor's place. Mrs. Byrd looked at the city hall, and walked to the entrance. A.J. Adams was clearly visible through the open window in the lighted mayor's office. The goons crouched down behind the gun.

After several minutes, Mrs. Byrd came into view inside the mayor's office. She dropped down into an upholstered chair and engaged in conversation with the mayor. The plot was evident. Now was the time planned for the execution of the mayor. Mrs. Byrd was fingered to be the patsy. After the shot, the gun could be placed inside her car, and she would be blamed for murder. A simple plan for eliminating two former enemies of the liquor business!

Heinie sat looking at his cards. Somehow, he felt as if Arlo was sitting in on the hand. Arlo? Why did he feel his presence so strongly at this time? Then he thought of the sound of the man with the wheezing cough.

"Gott in Himmel!" he shouted. "It's that bastard that shot Arlo!"

Every man in the room sprang to his feet. Some of them raced into the street in front of City Hall, and the rest followed Heinie into the alley.

"Don't let those bastards out alive!" Heinie commanded. "Pete, git me that machine gun in the trunk. Wait for me, I want to be the first. I want to slice 'em up with lead!"

Pete quickly fetched the Thompson. Returning, he found Heinie on the second-floor porch behind the building. He gave him the gun.

The commotion of the men rushing about in the street below

distracted the goons inside. The marksman embraced the rifle, mustered the concentration he needed and was just squeezing the trigger when Heinie broke down the door to the J.P.'s office and sprayed the place with bullets. The goons turned toward Heinie and opened fire with handguns. Heinie gave the Thompson another squeeze and another burst splattered the room.

This sudden bedlam and ricochet of bullets put A.J. Adams and Mrs. Byrd to the floor. They faced each other in the well, under the mayor's desk.

"My rosy red ass!" the mayor cursed.

"What's goin' on?" she asked, crossing herself.

"Don't ask me – sounds like a war out there in the street! Stay down while I call 'central'. Where the hell is that chief when I need him?"

Heinie continued firing bursts into the J.P.'s office and the goons answered each burst with a barrage of return fire. The crowd in the street fired pistols in the air like a bunch of revelers at a celebration.

It was evident to the goons that they were in a losing position. They could not go out the front window and drop to the street because of the men down there, and it certainly was not possible to get past Heinie and his raging machine gun at the door.

They found an alternate route, through the ceiling and into the attic.

The infuriated Dutchman came charging after them. Pete and the boys followed like a pack of hounds.

The roof of the building was sharply pitched and built of slate.

The goons crawled along the edge, seeking a line of retreat. They came to a dormer and window. The goon with the cough was hacking and wheezing. They forced the window and it opened. In the darkness they saw the face of Faust, for Heinie stood in the dormer, machine gun in hand!

The first man jumped from the roof and died in the alley. The coughing man tried to crawl away, wheezing desperately in panic.

Heinie handed the machine gun to Pete, and pulled a large pistol from his coat. With sudden calm and determination, he took aim and fired. The goon hunched, gasped, and dropped over the edge to the pavement alongside his accomplice.

Heinie stood on the roof and spat down on them.

Before the police arrived from their station across the street, it was over. The men in the street and on the roof were gone as suddenly as they had appeared. Silence prevailed, and the quiet air was laden with the acrid scent of burnt powder. The alley smelled of garbage. The police discovered the dead goons and started their investigation.

A.J. Adams soon got the picture of what happened. Mrs. Byrd went back to the red-light district where it was safer. His score settled, Heinie went to the cemetery to talk to Arlo's gravestone. Pete and the boys had chores, so they returned to the farm.

The next morning, one would have expected an extra edition of the local newspaper. Instead the headline told of national news.

On page six was an article about two men from Chicago who had tried to burglarize a downtown business and were killed in the attempt.

David had planted a garden behind the shed where Aunt Pearl and Uncle Shorty had always had their vegetable patch. It was the first time he and Melba had ever tried growing plants. They took great interest in the project and got a lot of help from the neighbors. Melba and David had never realized before that rabbits like to eat the same plants that they grew in the garden. Melba was concerned for the welfare of the cottontails and would not let David kill them. A letter from Pearl and Shorty advised them to surround the garden with some chicken wire from the shed. This proved to be only partially successful, but it helped.

Melba wore a sundress and bonnet when she worked on the patch. Some of the younger girls in the town were starting to wear shorts, but the practice was held in low regard for anyone over the age of twelve. David found an old straw hat with a wide brim hanging on a nail in the cellar. It was punctured in several places, and sweat stained around the headband. The first time he wore it, Melba had to laugh. She said he looked like a real country bumpkin.

"Do not," David protested.

"Hayseed," she taunted.

"Tote that bale, swing that hoe," he commanded.

"Yassuh, massuh," she answered, bowing.

When she straightened up, she pushed him over backwards between rows of onions.

"Here now!" he protested. "I'll make you eat one of these."

"Got to catch me first," she shouted as she took off running across the yard around the shed.

David sprang to his feet and took off in pursuit. She threw a bucket toward him and he stumbled over it as Melba was racing full tilt alongside the house when she crashed into the chest of a man walking toward the back yard.

"Oh," she cried in surprise. "I didn't know there was anyone here. Excuse me. Are you hurt?"

"Only because you don't know who I am," the man replied.

Melba stepped back to get a better look at him. He had raised a mustache and was several inches taller, but he looked like . . .

"Boyd?" she exclaimed. "Boyd, is that you? Oh, Boyd, it is you! Oh, David, come meet my brother Boyd!"

Boyd stood laughing at her when David appeared, still holding an onion in his hand.

"Who?" David asked.

"My very own brother, Boyd," Melba replied. "I want you to meet my brother!"

"Oh, hi," David stammered, letting the onion drop to the ground and wiping his hands on his pants. "I'm David, Melba's husband."

"How about that," Boyd said, shaking David's hand. "My sister married and living in the city. Glad to meet you. Mom told me where you were living. I came up on the traction."

"I thought you were living out West somewhere," Melba explained. "Why, I haven't seen you for years. Are you married?"

"No, I've been kickin' around the country and decided to come home for a while."

"Is anyone with you?" she asked, holding the screen door Open for him to enter the house.

"No, the kid that left Logan with me got killed when he fell under a freight train in Kansas City. He never made it to California. I met with some other guys and traveled all over California. It's a lot different than around here."

Melba lifted an apron from a chair so he could sit down.

"How's work out there?" David asked.

"About like anywheres else. Them's what got it keep it, and them's what don't, stay broke."

"Are you goin' to look for work around here?" David asked. "I could maybe get you in the apprentice program."

"I expect to hang around for a while, but do me a favor. Keep it under your hat that I'm even here. I wouldn't want any of my crowd to catch up with me."

David and Melba stared at each other. It hit them simultaneously. He was on the lam!

CHAPTER TWELVE

THE ZEPPELIN, A DROP-OUT, AND A BIRTH

Except for fancy autos, Francine was not one to dwell on material things. Now, there was another exception – she had gotten a passport. She hurried to her apartment and took it from her purse. She read it and held it out at arm's length, then she held it under her chin and gazed at her image in the mirror. She practiced handing it to an imaginary official and rehearsed pulling it from her purse with aplomb. Then, she held it to her chest and danced around the room. She felt as if this document would be her magic carpet to explore the world.

She was unable to revel in this excitement alone. She telephoned Jesse from the corner drug store to see if she was home.

"You sound excited," Jesse said. "Don't tell me you really have found Jacob Wasserman and married him!"

"Better than that," she replied between deep breaths. "I got something to show you."

"Let me guess," Jesse continued. "It *has* to concern a man to get you so excited. You've adopted a eunuch and are on your way to Egypt."

"Almost. I got a passport!" Francine announced.

"Clark knows a guy in New York who has a license to drive an auto!" Jesse said.

"*Really,* Jesse. I've got a genuine United States passport!"

"Why do you have a passport?" Jesse asked.

"To go to Germany!" Francine shouted into the telephone. "I'm goin' to Germany!"

"The way things are over there?"

"Kurt is taking me to meet his relatives in Friederickshafen. We will be back before winter."

"You'd better be back. Your boat could hit an iceberg!"

"Not *boat*, we are goin' by *airship!*" Francine squealed.

"Have you been drinking?"

"I'm stone sober. We are going to New York by train, and then by bus to Lakehurst and off into the clouds!"

"I think we better talk about this. Why don't you come over for supper tonight? Have you told Melba your plans? What about your baby?"

"I'm going to tell Melba when I get the right opportunity. She will keep Val for me while I'm gone. I'm sure she will."

"Don't blame her if she kicks you in the ass!" Jesse warned.

"Wouldn't you go if you had the chance?" Francine asked.

"Those things are full of gas, aren't they?"

"Sure. But I'm not afraid. I'm looking forward to it." Francine giggled. "Bet you never slept with a man above the clouds."

"I think your brain is a cloud." Jesse said. "See you tonight for supper."

In the following days, Francine was very busy. She spent more time than usual with Val, and stayed home more than she ever had before. She had lied to David and Melba, saying only that she was going to New York and would return in a week.

Finally, the day came for her departure. Half the shift from the distillery came down to the train station to see her off. It was not every day that one of theirs took such a trip. Melba stayed at home with the children. She believed Francine's story, and she did not want Val to create a fuss when she saw "Seen" going away for a week.

"Take a bottle of Jacob Wasserman along," Jesse told Francine, "and get that Hitler guy drunk."

"How about it if I just bring him back home with me?" Francine giggled.

"Do that, and we will all shove him into the river," one of the barrel jockeys hollered.

"Remember, we'll go back to work at the end of August," Jesse reminded.

"Don't mention it," Francine frowned. "I want to enjoy this moment forever."

"Bye, bye, beautiful," Jesse said, slapping her on the rump as she stepped up onto the stool to board the train for New York.

"Bye," called Helen, and Marge, friends from the bottling line. "Send us a postcard."

The train jolted to a start, and Francine hung onto the handrail, waving as the coach moved across Main Street and disappeared around the bend of the track.

Kurt met her at Grand Central Station. As planned, they took a bus to Lakehurst and then a cab to the airport. It was early afternoon when Francine stepped from the cab and got her first glimpse of the Hindenberg.

"Jeez," she cried. I didn't know it was *that* big. How big *is* that thing?" she asked.

"In your measurements it is about eight hundred feet long," he said, smiling with pride. "Isn't it magnificent?"

"How fast does it go?"

"About eighty miles per hour. The advantage is that we will have a very smooth ride and go directly to Europe. We will take a circuitous route over there as we are not permitted to fly over England or France."

"You act like this was your airship," she said.

"My uncle is one of the top persons in the Zeppelin Company," Kurt said. "He is aboard the Hindenberg now. He is our host. Not many people are allowed to fly in this ship – just fifty passengers on this trip. Come, we must go to the hangar for advanced instructions before we board."

Francine was so fascinated by the enormously grand appearance of the cigar-shaped giant hanging in the sky, that she stumbled looking over her shoulder as she followed Kurt.

"I've never seen anything so big," she said. "What keeps it from going up without us?"

"It is tethered to the conning tower," Kurt said, as he guided her into an office in the hangar.

She was so excited that when an official asked to inspect her passport, she handed it over without a thought. Thus, her rehearsal was wasted. He returned it and she put it into her purse.

Dr. Eckener, a principal official of the Zeppelin Company and usually captain of this airship, gave the passengers preliminary instructions. Francine nearly changed her mind about going when they told the passengers that smoking was prohibited anywhere on the ship.

"If and when your country sells us helium," the captain said, "it will be permitted to smoke, because helium, unlike hydrogen, is non-explosive."

After the talk, each of them was assigned a number and told to board. Even numbered passengers would go to the starboard side and odd numbered passengers would go to port. Francine was glad that she and Kurt both had odd numbers. She did not want to be separated from him in this strange experience.

When she first saw the airship, she thought the gondola was for the passengers. She was amazed to find there were two stairways lowered down from the ship to the surface. Kurt smiled with pride as he guided her up two long flights of stairs into the belly of the ship.

Inside were almost all the luxuries of an ocean liner. There was an upper and lower deck. The upper deck was primarily for passengers and contained a lounge, dining salon, reading room, and promenade.

The staterooms were in the center of the ship, on the lower deck. Here, they were located against the hull and had windows slanted outward at a sharp angle. The rooms were small but well designed. Below the windows was a storage place and along the wall perpendicular to the hull was an upper and lower bunk. One could stand at the window and look down on the scene below.

Kurt led Francine to a window on the promenade to watch the liftoff.

The German crew took up their stations to trim the ship while some seventy American Naval personnel operated the tower and anchor line. Two blasts from a horn signaled their departure. There was a flurry of activity on the ground, and along the catwalks within the ship.

Nacelles attached to the hull supported the diesel engines that made the propellers churn the air.

Francine felt the muscles of her stomach twitch at the excitement as the great airship became buoyant and moved away from the mooring tower. Like a silent whale, the ship rose into the sky, circled the field, and left Lakehurst behind.

The captain enjoyed "grandstanding" and he made it a point to fly over New York before heading out to sea. The view of the world below was beyond description. It was like riding on a magic carpet to float above the city, looking down on the tallest buildings and then to move across the harbor and finally the ocean. Francine stood affixed to the deck, looking down through the window glass. It seemed unreal to be so suspended in the sky.

"How long does it take?" she asked Kurt.

"Ordinarily, it takes two days to Frankfurt. But we have a good tail wind. This trip may be a record-breaker," he said. "Let's have a drink and enjoy the view before it gets dark. Come, let's go to the lounge."

The lounges contained tables and chairs, and at the far end a baby grand piano where a man sat playing popular songs. Francine and Kurt watched the waves on the ocean below, as they reflected the setting sun, and listened to the music.

"Want to get some rest?" Kurt asked.

"I'm so excited, I'm not sure I can," she answered.

"Let's go to your stateroom and see what we can do about your enthusiasm," he suggested with a handsome grin.

It wasn't a very subtle hint. But the excitement of the day had gotten her adrenaline up and she thought it might be a good way to relax.

"Lead the way. I'm ready," she said.

Once inside the stateroom, he began kissing and embracing her, and again she thought he was getting a little too rough to be romantic. She tried to slow the tempo, but he was too big and strong for her to control that. Before she knew it, he had her out of her dress and underclothes. With one arm wrapped around her waist, he started biting at her nipples. She became frightened and tried to pull away. He tightened his hold and fell forward onto the bunk on top of her writhing body.

"Kurt, stop it!" she demanded.

He continued nipping at her skin wherever he could put his mouth to her. She tried kicking and hitting, but her strongest blows seemed to go unnoticed. In desperation, she turned to her hands and knees on the lower bunk and tried to crawl away from him.

He got a viselike grip on her hips and she could feel his penis thrusting at her from the rear. She let out a stifled cry as he entered her.

Her upper body was off the bunk and across the window where she could look below at the tranquil sea. She decided resistance was more painful than surrender, and she lay staring down at the water, jolting forward each time he thrust. His violence seemed a contrast to the tranquility of the scene below. She was beginning to think this was not going to be the fun trip she had expected.

A.J. Adams took a large gold watch from his vest pocket and stared at the timepiece. It was nearly noon. Could it be that Congressman Keel was going to stand him up?

Seated at a table, Adams selected a cigar from his pocket and lit it.

Would Keel have the audacity to turn his back on the mayor of Riverport? He discounted the idea. Keel was too politically wise to make such a faux pas. Something must have come up to delay the congressman.

It was nearly half past twelve when Oscar Keel came rushing into the club.

"Please accept my apology," he began. "I was on the other side of the river and the damned bridge was up for a boat. Traffic was lined up for a mile."

"Good," Adams exclaimed. "Now you see why we need legislation to get us another bridge."

"You've made your point," Keel said as he sat down at the table. "Is this why you wanted to see me?"

"You know better than that," Adams snorted.

"Then *why?*"

"Oscar, I want you to drop out of politics," Adams said, blowing smoke across the table.

Keel looked at Adams and frowned.

"You heard me right," the mayor continued. "I called you to this meeting to tell you that."

"Are you going out of your mind?" the congressman asked. "Do you think for one minute, after all these years in the House that I'd just drop out because *you* wanted me to?"

"No, I wouldn't expect you'd do it just because I wanted you to do it. But you see, Oscar, I've lost confidence in the management of the whiskey factory. It seems they got some kind of strange idea that Riverport needed someone else to be mayor of our fair city and they got caught red-handed walkin' both sides of the street in the last election. Now, as a fellow politician, you know how bad that can be."

The congressman shifted uneasily in his chair.

"Now," Adams continued. "Ordinarily a mistake like that wouldn't affect you in any way. You don't work for the Wasserman Company and so you are not involved in what goes on between me and the Canadians. Right?"

Keel did not answer. He knew Adams was building up to something big.

"For Christ's sake, Adams. Are you drunk?" Keel asked.

"No, not with alcohol, and not with power, but I've got you by the balls and I'll squeeze only if you don't do as I say."

"I'm not going to listen to your unfounded bullshit," Keel growled, ready to leave.

"Better sit back down, Oscar. My next statement may come as quite a shock."

The congressman returned to his chair and listened for the bomb to drop.

"That's better," Adams said, smiling at Keel's uneasy reaction.

"Damn it, mayor, let's get on with it. I haven't got all day, you know."

"I'm kinda insulted that you never told me about your experience as a government gauger back before Prohibition," Adams started.

Keel jolted upright in his chair.

"What the hell are you rambling on about?" Keel asked.

"Oh, I've got it all documented. I've even located some of your old cronies out on the East Coast. Seems you liked another name much better than the one you use now," Adams taunted. "Those folks called you 'theef' like a sound the bluejay makes. You know, a bluejay puts his eggs in another bird's nest so he doesn't have to raise his own. Seems like those folks knew about you a long time before you became a Midwesterner."

Adams took a long draw on his cigar and exhaled. "A couple of years ago, some farm trucks blew up down by the river, and the whiskey people got antsy as hell." Keel stared in stony silence. "I found out why the trucks got fried, but I couldn't understand why the distillers got so upset. I started checking into local history, and that's when I found out that you came here as a grain buyer about the beginning of Prohibition."

Keel was growing slightly redder by this point. "You became prominent, particularly with the farmers. After a few years, you just about had the grain business sewed up in these parts. You bought up many of the grain elevators and brokers in this part of the state. You got so popular with the country folks that you were a 'shoo-in' when you ran for Congress, and you've been re-elected ever since."

"That is an *entirely* unfounded observation," Keel protested.

The mayor smiled. "Now, I'm not one to criticize an opportunist. I fancy I'm one myself. But it just kept *gnawing* at my mind about those trucks and about the half-Nelsons put on the farmers around here."

"Now just a goddamned minute," Keel said, putting his hand out toward Adams. "I'm not going to sit here and listen to your warped impression of the history of the world."

"Not the history of the world, Oscar – the life and times of Oscar Keel, boy wonder. Now – after we get our distillery, I'm grateful for the taxes, but I'm still curious about some things. I start ferreting around and the Canadians decide they want to get someone else elected mayor of Riverport. I suppose I goofed when I asked questions of the bank in Ontario – they probably tipped off your friends. So, they decide I'm getting too close and I better be removed. They secretly sponsored my opponent, thinking I'd be easy."

The mayor had a glint in his eye as he continued. "Well, I wasn't. But I *was* still curious. Turns out our government tax man, Bentley, knew about your days in the whiskey business out East. He also heard you were hooked up with distillers who moved to Canada to avoid

Prohibition. They went to Canada, and you came to Riverport." Keel tried to speak, but at this point he didn't have a prayer of breaking into the mayor's roll.

"Back then, I was flattered to think our little town would be so lucky. We get a high-roller like Oscar Keel, and then after F.D.R. makes alcohol legal again, we get us a distillery. But now, I think about the strong-arm stuff laid on the farmers, and I find out that they've borne a heavy yoke all along. In fact, I find out that our farmers in particular have had a *hammerlock* on them at the grain elevators. This, coupled with your control of grain prices and enormous campaign expenses makes me wonder if you *are* the saint everybody thinks you are."

"Now stop right there," Keel demanded. "I'll sue you for defamation. I'll break your back politically if you start spreading this bullshit!"

"Don't threaten me, Oscar. I'm not the one out on the limb. While I'm searching for the source of this money that springs eternal whenever you make a move, I discover that a grain company in Canada paid for those elevators! Well, nothing so strange about that. Every school kid knows Canada is big in grain production. Then, I find that *this* grain company's owned by a foxy old guy named Jacob Wasserman. Kaboom! The whole picture snaps into focus. Advance man Oscar Keel is sent by Wasserman to soften up the market *and* make legislation favorable to the booze business. All of it right here under my nose in Riverport! Damn, what a power play! Oscar, I love it. The only thing I regret is that I didn't see it all fifteen years ago. As it is, if some petty gangsters hadn't gotten riled up about their jukeboxes and blasted a couple of farm trucks, I'd have never even started looking."

"What is it you want?" Keel asked tensely.

"Well, I want you to get in touch with your friends up north and tell them that I won the election . . . and the ball game. Tell them I'm going to be reasonable. We are going to go right on making the best damn 'alkie' in the world, and my people are going to enjoy the employment that endeavor brings to our fair city. We're going to enjoy all the taxes we are legally entitled to enjoy."

"What's your point?" Keel asked.

"There are two thorns in my side that make me upset. One, is that Dr. Barstow. He better git. The other is my suspicion of a U.S.

representative who would pull such a pile of crap on my people. Like I told you when you came in, Oscar, I want you to drop out of politics."

The two men sat watching each other, Keel staring so intently that his eyes began to water. Adams puffed on his cigar and smiled.

"I just can't believe that you would do this," Keel mumbled as he rose and left the club.

It took some time, but the mayor had his way. Dr. Barstow was relieved of his command and recalled to Canada. Oscar Keel announced his retirement from politics and a return to the private sector. The Jacob Wasserman Distilling Company sent Bud McKenna to Riverport as general manager of the Riverport Plant, and Oscar Keel became general manager of the entire Wasserman Company.

The new bridge across the river was named the Adams Bridge. The mayor was on the schoolyard of a grade school playing softball with the kids when an aide told him that news.

"The whiskey business isn't all bad," Adams said as he caught a line drive and threw it home.

"No sir," the aide agreed. "Are you about ready for me to drive you back to City Hall?"

Besides being taller and having a mustache, Boyd was different in lots of other ways. Melba noticed that he had acquired several tattoos on his arms, and a couple of scars on his neck. His wily mannerisms worried her most. He had the habit of looking at people from the corner of his eye. Melba did not like that. In fact, she began to worry about her brother being a bad influence on David. Whenever she heard Boyd telling tales of his exploits, she wondered if his stories would cause David to want the same.

Finally, Boyd went too far. He asked David to help him carry a case of beer from the store and David agreed. It was after 10:30 p.m. when they came home, and she demanded to know why. They had gone to a nightclub with a striptease for entertainment. Boyd did not expect David to spill the beans under pressure, but it did not take Melba ten minutes to learn where they had been, and that David had gotten a little drunk and touched one of the girls in the show.

It was the first time David ever heard Melba shout. She was not so much angry with David as she was shocked that he would be so easily misled.

When she finished with David, she cornered Boyd in the kitchen and shouted even louder at him.

"*WHATEVER possessed you to take MY HUSBAND to such a low-down FILTHY place, and to encourage him to get PERSONAL with those AWFUL WOMEN?*"

"Oh, grow up sis," Boyd protested. "It probably was the most fun the guy has had since he's known you."

The camel's back was broken. Melba flew into a rage, dogging Boyd's steps around the kitchen, finally slapping a sandwich from his hand and telling him to get out. David simply sat in the living room. He had never seen Melba act like this before.

In less than an hour, Boyd was packed and out onto the street. David wondered where he would go, but did not ask for fear of rekindling Melba's ire. After they went to bed, David tried to put his arm around Melba, but she pulled away. Their first spat was turning out to be a big one. He made a mental note to stay away from the bawdy end of town.

Up to this time, Melba and David never had a telephone. In fact, none of their friends had ever had one.

But David was working every day now, and felt the need to keep in touch with his pregnant wife, who was due in November. After a serious discussion, it was decided they could afford a two-party line for $3.50 a month. They thought having a telephone would make them feel in touch with the outside world, but though it often rang for the other party, but had never rung two short rings for them.

David went to the corner drug store and used the pay phone. He told the operator the number he wanted, and she rang – two short rings.

"Hello," Melba answered cautiously.

"Hi, is this the Merriwether residence?" he asked.

"David, is that you?"

"Hi, Pumpkin," he shouted into the mouthpiece. "How about this for the lap of luxury! Now, we can keep in touch wherever we are."

"You come home this instant," she demanded.

"Be there in a flash," he said. After he hung up the telephone, he stood smiling at it. He felt the pride of accomplishment.

Arkansas was home to Pearl and Shorty. They had been raised there in their early days. Now, they lived there in retirement. Some of their neighbors were old acquaintances, and the rest were just good ol' folks. They never met a stranger. Shorty was already deep in church work, and Pearl, after failing to organize a chapter of the W.C.T.U., got involved in charity for the poor.

When they got Melba's letter about her pending birth, Aunt Pearl packed a traveling bag and kept it ready.

Across the ocean in Friedrickshafen, Francine was beginning to miss the American way of life. The Germans were highly regimented. There was an official title for everyone, and a uniform to go with it. The most noticeable were the Hitler Jugend because there were so many of them. Kurt's relatives seldom talked politics in her presence, but their attitude could be felt in the air. The German people had been nearly starved to death by their organized opposition after World War I, and they were out to get even. Francine could tell she was sitting on a time bomb, and she decided she better get out.

"When will we go back to America?" she asked Kurt.

"I've taken out papers to stay here," he announced.

"Stay here? What about me? Did you think I'd stay here with you?" she demanded.

"I can get my relatives to arrange the papers," he replied.

"I'm not staying. I didn't intend to *stay* over here. I'm homesick for my friends."

"This would be a much better cause for you than to return to America," he answered.

"What do you mean, 'better cause'? This isn't my cause *or* yours. We are American and have no interest in their problems."

Kurt hit her in the mouth.

She stood staring at him. A trickle of blood appeared on her lip and ran down her chin.

Francine left Friederickshafen that night and went to Berlin where she cabled Bud to help her come home.

Before the end of the week, she was aboard an ocean liner leaving Bremen. The boat could not go fast enough for her.

Dr. Maloy had predicted that Melba would deliver in mid-November. As expected, the distillery began bottling in August. Melba was called back and worked until October 10th when the company nurse, Hazel Mathews, pulled her time card and sent her home. Jesse drove her home, stopping at the union hall to get a withdrawal card.

"I won't get a turkey this year," Melba protested. "The rule is that you have to be working November 15th to get one!"

"Don't worry, kid. I'll get you one if I have to steal it off the truck." Jesse promised.

"You'd better stop stealing things from the plant," Melba warned. "If they ever catch you, your name is mud."

"I'm only borrowing things," Jesse said. "If I wanted these things for keeps, I'd buy them."

"Joke if you will, I just don't want to hear that you were hauled off by the plant guards. Think what a shame all that would be."

"Green kid. That's what you are," Jesse teased, as she pulled up to the curb in front of Melba's cottage. "By the way, Bud McKenna is back. He's going to be the top dog at the plant. It seems the reason we haven't been seeing Dr. Barstow around is because he is not in Riverport anymore. Rumor is, the Doc got fired."

"Bud back in Riverport?" Melba pondered aloud. "That should be news to Francine. They were very close, you know."

"*How* close is the question," Jesse cracked as Melba got out of the car.

"Close enough that I bet you can't get her fired," Melba taunted.

"Close enough that she doesn't have to work as hard as the rest of us," Jesse said.

"Thanks for the ride home. Keep me in touch," Melba said as she got out of the car and closed the door.

Francine got safely back to America and returned to work at the distillery. Bud was indeed the top dog. He resumed his clandestine romance with Francine and rented a nice apartment for her and Val.

Melba had doubted Francine could take care of Val alone. But somehow, Francine was better able to cope with the role of mother now. Melba speculated that it was Bud's presence and his devotion to Val that caused the change. Whatever the cause, Val and her 'Seen' began to live together and to learn about each other.

Dr. Maloy was gifted. On November 15th at 7:30 p.m. Melba went into labor, and David rushed her to the hospital. Jesse sat with Lacey as she waited – Francine could not be found. Thirty minutes later, a nine-pound baby boy was born. The proud parents named him Earl, after Melba's biological father.

David was more experienced now and was able to handle the details with the hospital and Melba's return home. He held the door of the taxi as mother and child departed for home. Jesse and little Lacey were waiting when they got there. David had phoned Logan to tell Melba's family of the birth, and he had sent a telegram to Aunt Pearl and Uncle Shorty.

Church work was too demanding for Shorty to leave, but Pearl caught a bus and was on her way. Twelve hours later, she arrived in Riverport where David met her at the bus station.

"Hi, Aunt Pearl." He greeted. "Was the trip tiresome?"

"No, but those seats aren't built for my frame. I've got bruises from ridin' that bus."

David put her suitcase in the taxi and then helped her.

"The baby looks just like lil' Lacey, except this one's a boy."

"I can't wait to meet the lil' rascal," Pearl said, wrapping her shawl around her for warmth.

"You won't have to wait for long." David promised as he noted some packages Pearl brought with her. "We'll go straight to the house." He had started to say "straight home," except he remembered it was really Aunt Pearl's place, and more hers than his.

From the minute Pearl entered the premises, everything took on a new dimension. They watched in disbelief as things were scrubbed, scoured and organized.

Most of her efforts centered on the baby. She sterilized anything that might come near the child, including the walls, floors and furniture.

Little Lacey remembered Aunt Pearl and followed her around the house like a stray pup. Melba was able to concentrate on the new arrival, who adjusted as well as Lacey had done at the same age. But there was a difference. Earl cried more, messed more and spit up more than his sister had done. It was a good thing that Pearl had come to help. David was working every day and could not be home much.

One day, about mid-afternoon, the baby was sleeping. Melba was drowsing and Pearl was peeling apples for the evening meal, when Francine, Val and Bud came to see the new baby.

Francine hastily introduced Bud to Pearl and tiptoed off to see Earl.

Val was delighted to see Aunt Pearl, and climbed onto the large woman's lap. Pearl shoved the paring knife and materials out of reach and embraced the child.

"Eat," Val grunted, trying to reach the apples.

"Of course." Pearl agreed, giving the child a slice of the fruit.

Bud sat in a chair across the table.

"What line of work are you in?" Pearl asked.

"Manufacturing," Bud answered carefully. Francine had warned him about Pearl's feelings concerning alcohol and "demon rum."

"Do you make anything for the war in Europe?" Pearl asked.

"Yes, I guess some of our products do go to Europe. In fact, we will soon make an ingredient that is used in the production of gunpowder." (Wasserman had just signed a contract to make alcohol for the government.)

"How can people contribute to the suffering of others without a tinge of conscience?" Pearl asked.

"It is a matter of perspective. I like to think we are aiding the rescue of thousands of enslaved Finns and Polish people. It is a case of meeting force with force."

"God forgive you." Pearl moaned looking upwards and folding her hands as if to pray. "Have you never heard about turning the other cheek? If God be for us, who can be against us?"

"That's a nice thought, but the forces of evil would soon swallow all of us if we did nothing to resist. I am in favor of armed resistance. A 'fight fire with fire' sort of thing."

"If God wanted us to resist, He would tell us to do so. It is *His* word we should follow. We should love one another and not fight our enemies. It is murder to kill another human being, and doing so because of patriotic demands does not make it any less murder."

Val was reaching for another piece of apple. She stood on Pearl's lap, bumping her chin on the table.

"If we did nothing, that baby would grow up under a dictator, if indeed she got a chance to grow up at all. That 'hands off' attitude would he national suicide. Thank goodness we have a president who can see the dangers of what's happening in the world."

Mention of the President caused Pearl's blood pressure to skyrocket. Ordinarily, she was noncommittal about politics, but living with Shorty all those years had rubbed off on her. He did not like F.D.R. and neither did she.

"War is not the answer. We should find peaceful answers to our national problems. Besides, that child already lives under a dictator. He's no better than Hitler or any of the others. Roosevelt is our dictator!" she screeched.

The noise in the kitchen brought Melba and Francine from the bedroom.

The lines between the isolationists and the interventionists were clearly drawn across the nation and had come to focus here in Melba's home. And another issue was soon to arise.

"Sin," Pearl screamed, jutting her chin out from her fat neck. "The wages of sin is death!"

"Trying to appease the Germans is death, too," Bud said. "And I'm damned happy to have as much of our production as possible to be dedicated to alcohol for the war effort."

"*Alcohol!* Do you have something to do with alcohol?" Pearl demanded.

"We *all* have something to do with alcohol!" Bud shouted.

"Lord, forgive us," she gasped, looking again at the ceiling. "The serpent reappears to us in many forms. We must not yield to its temptations. It will cause the damnation of us all." Pearl bowed her head and cried.

Francine walked to her and put an arm around the older woman's shoulder.

"Don't fret, Pearl. We are not all damned to the hell like you think." Francine consoled. "You must learn to be tolerant of others. I'm sure that is one of the rules of your religion. Haven't I heard you say, 'Live and let live'?"

Pearl sat silently sobbing. Francine picked Val up from the big woman's lap and moved toward the door behind Bud.

"See you around," Francine called over her shoulder as they departed.

CHAPTER THIRTEEN

THE FUZZY FORD, THE WORLD SERIES, AND THE WAR

If ever there had been a time to look back to, it would have been when the children were small and cute.

Little Lacey was walking and talking and getting into anything that was not nailed down. Earl was beginning to sleep nights, and had come out of the colic. Work at the distillery had increased, and Melba was on a job requiring less stamina than before. All in all, she got about seven months' work each year, and the rest of the time she stayed home with the kids and collected unemployment benefits.

Their home was looking good. She and David were able to buy some furniture and now had a complete bedroom suite. They had repaired and painted a table for the kitchen and put some furniture in the living room. Their proudest possession was a Philco radio in a dark wooden cabinet. This was their source of news and entertainment. It was this electric wonder that carried the details of the Louis Braddock fight. David and his friends listened on June 22, 1937. That night Joe Louis became the World's Champ, a title he was to hold for many years to come.

Next, they bought a used General Electric refrigerator with a round drum top and a little foot pedal which opened the door when your hands were full. Lacey also discovered the little pedal, which meant the refrigerator was often found open.

Aunt Pearl and Uncle Shorty paid a local company to convert the large coal-burning furnace to an automatic stoker unit. For the first time in their experience, it was not necessary to fire the furnace every time they needed heat. Now, they filled the hopper once a day, removed the cinders and set the thermostat to the desired temperature. Automatic heat! Home comfort at its best!

One of the carpenters working with David had a car for sale. David looked at it and tried it out on the road. It was several years old, but in good condition. One of the major selling points was the fact that it was a two-door and thus safer for transporting small children. The owner let David take it home for Melba to see.

He drove it up in front of the house so that she could view the entire auto as she approached it.

"David" she said, "Where did you get this automobile?"

"A guy at work wants to sell it," David answered. "It belonged to his father-in-law, who died recently. It needs a coat of paint, but it is in good shape otherwise."

They walked around the car looking at the fading black paint and rusting wire wheels. Melba noticed the thermometer in the radiator cap was cracked.

"I'll get a new one at the junk yard." He promised. "Look, Pumpkin, it's a Ford. We have every reason to be sentimental over a Ford, and here's one we can own!"

"Oh, David I don't know," she mused. "I know it would be a convenience, but the expense is something we have to worry over. I might not get as much work as we expect, and then we'd be in a real fix."

"There'll be plenty of work – they say at the union hall that the new bridge will be built this year. Do you have any idea how many months' work it will take to build forms for all that cement?"

"I think we should talk about a house of our own before we think about an automobile," Melba replied.

"With this car we could go to see your folks once in a while. You know how your mother is always asking about the kids. With a car, you could take them there so she could see them." he said.

David had made a sale. The thought of driving to Logan in her own auto clinched the deal. They paid seventy-five dollars for the car, and the seller threw in two extra tires and a Ford wrench.

They cleared out an old shed behind the house to serve as a garage, although it was evident that the vehicle was no stranger to the elements.

The alley behind the shed was not paved, and plenty of dust flew when cars passed the property. David waited for a warm, dry evening when he thought it would be too late for traffic in the alley. Then he sprayed the alley with water, set up electric lights in the shed and prepared to paint the car. Melba had agreed on a dark green and had promised to help as soon as the children were asleep. David used old papers to cover the areas he did not want to paint. A friend had loaned him a compressor and spray gun. He was ready to glorify the old car with a new coat of enamel.

"David," Melba called from outside the shed. "How do you expect me to get in there? You've got the door sealed shut."

"Here, honey, crawl under this old tarp," he replied.

"Why all the old newspapers?" she asked as she appeared inside the shed.

"To keep down the dust. It takes this paint about six hours to dry. I don't want dust to land on the car in that time."

"Have you ever done anything like this before?" she asked.

"Naw, but it's easy. You just start the compressor and spray away," he explained.

They both felt the spirit of adventure as they made a last minute check on details and started the compressor.

David made a sweeping arc across the back of the auto. The green paint reflected the light from the surface of the auto. It looked great to the two novice painters.

"Look at THAT!" David exclaimed. "Is that a great color or what?" he asked.

"It looks keen to me," Melba answered.

"'I can't wait to see the whole car that color," he said as he made more sweeps at the surface. The paint hissed from the nozzle and flowed across the metal of the car, seeming to transform the tired old relic into a glistening new machine.

"Let me try a spot or two," Melba pleaded.

"Here, but be careful of runs. If you get too close or apply too much paint, it will run and cause an awful mess."

"This is fun," she squealed as she moved the spray gun back and forth across the surface of the car. "I think I really do a much better job than you. My work has a prettier gleam to it."

"It's just the way the lights are located," he answered.

They were both staring at the mist coming from the paint gun and were not aware that several large moths had flown into the shed, beating their wings on the bulb and reflectors of the lights. Next, the millers flew about the shed and ultimately onto the auto.

"Oh, David," Melba squealed as the first of the bugs got a coating of green paint and tracked it across the newspaper.

"David, those bugs! Stop those bugs from flying around! Oh, David, they're ruining the paint!"

He grabbed a cloth and whipped it about in the air to scatter the insects. This only caused the moths to fly about in crazy patterns and to increase in numbers. Soon, the air was thick with them, flying about in a frenzy. The car began to collect them on the wet surface. David and Melba stood back and watched in despair as the auto took on a fuzzy look as the moths became stuck on the sticky surface.

"Oh, boy," he moaned. "We've got the only furry Ford in town. Maybe it'll start a trend."

At the distillery, improvements were being made. The union had pressed for better safety in the parking lot, and the Wasserman Company had installed new streetlights, making the lot as bright at night as it was in the daytime. New sidewalks helped the pedestrian traffic. No longer was it necessary to walk along the railroad tracks to get to the main gate at the distillery.

Inside the plant, new bottling machines were installed on three lines. The new machines were less noisy and a whole lot faster than the old ones. Some of the women did not like this because it required them to work faster to keep up with the machine. The conveyor system was reworked, and steel mesh was installed at critical points where cases might fall onto the workers.

Many new women were hired and Melba soon had significant seniority. She used it to bid on a job at a reclaiming table. Now, her job was to salvage tax stamps from broken bottles. The best part was that she now was off the conveyor line and could sit while she worked. Francine, on the other hand, had been assigned some new work in the executive offices. Her friends seldom saw her and she did not take coffee breaks in the cafeteria, but instead went to the dining room with the executives. Melba sometimes got a glimpse of her in the parking lot where she had a reserved space and arrived later than the others.

On the south side of town in a small cottage, Mary Hooligan, sister to the late bridgetender, lived on her modest budget. She took in laundry and sewing as a livelihood. The street in front of her house was unpaved and without curbs. It was more an oiled pathway than it was a street. A chuckhole developed in the surface in front of Mary's house and every time a car went by, it thumped in and out of this hole. This caused the house to shake and made Mary worry. Fearing the vibrations would damage her house, Mary notified her alderman, but he stopped at the tavern and her concern never made it to City Hall.

In church on Sunday, she saw A.J. Adams. (Unbeknownst to the public, he attended services in three separate churches every week.) Mary told the mayor of her problem. Although it was the Sabbath, the city crew repaired the problem before the day was over. This was not an unusual effort by the city. A.J. Adams seldom let the sun set on any problems that affected his constituents.

To further improve the city, the mayor got radios for the police cars and a new ladder truck for the firehouse. No special assessments were needed to provide for these new luxuries. The distillery, through real estate and personal property taxes, kept the city coffers full.

In the fall, during the World Series, the mayor, with help from the newspaper, installed a screen on the front of City Hall. It was painted green in the outline of a baseball field. The street was barricaded to vehicle traffic and when it was gametime, the block was filled with anxious sports fans. Amplifiers broadcast the radio report of the game, and workers behind the screen simulated the path of the baseball on the field. The crowd made a strange appearance standing in the street looking up at the front of City Hall. Of course, A.J. Adams always had words to say during the seventh-inning stretch. It should not be supposed that the mayor would miss an opportunity to speak to his electorate.

Production at the distillery was booming. The need for drinking alcohol had increased. Both the domestic and foreign markets soared. It was not possible to make the better grades of bourbon fast enough because of the aging process needed to cure it in charcoal barrels. This is why the production of vodka and gin increased.

In addition to the usual lines, the distillery had a contract with the government to make alcohol for the war. Workers began clearing the first floor of one of the rack houses.

"What's goin' on here?" Melba asked Helen and Marge as they walked past the scene.

"It's a bomb shelter for F.D.R.," Marge lied, giggling.

"Maybe it is going to be a lounge for the employees," Helen suggested.

"Maybe it will be the new U.S.O. for the soldiers from camp," Melba speculated.

"It's goin' to be a new production line," a voice behind them said. They turned to come face-to-face with Francine.

"Francine!" Melba squealed. "I haven't seen you in a month of Sundays."

"Hi Pumpkin," Francine greeted, putting her arm around Melba's shoulder. "Big things are happening around here. This is goin' to be a line for packing medical kits for the army."

"What kind of medical kits?"

"Small ones that every soldier can carry on his belt," Francine answered. "I was at the meeting when we made the deal with the government. Now, the entire plant is protected for the war effort."

"War effort?" Melba asked. "We're not at war with anyone, are we?"

"We're just that far from it," Francine said, holding her finger and thumb so close they almost touched.

"It don't look good, does it?" Helen asked.

"It sure don't," Marge agreed.

"How's Val?" Melba asked.

"Growing like a weed. Sorry we haven't been over. Bud got the place all fixed up for us. Then, he got a woman to sit with Val when I'm workin."

"Which ain't much of the time," Melba said, smiling.

"Which might be more than you know," Francine said. "We have to go up to the home office on this government deal. Would you keep Val while we're gone?"

"Of course, Lacey will be happy to see her again."

"I'll let you know. It looks like we'll be gone over her birthday. I don't knew whether to celebrate before or after we get back."

"Wait until after you git back. It will give the kids something to look forward to." Melba suggested.

"Oh, by the way, would you he interested in movin' up?" Francine asked Melba.

"Movin' up where?" Melba asked.

"The company will need a new supervisor on the medical kit line. One word and you've got the job."

"Oh, Francine, I'd have to talk to David before I did a thing like that. I'd have to leave the union, and you know how David believes in union!"

"It's a big step up, if you want it," Francine said, waving as she turned into the administration building.

"You wouldn't have to ask *me* twice," Marge said as the women walked toward the bottling house.

Lincoln Public School was an imposing two-story red brick building. A dirt playground containing some swings and a sliding board surrounded it.

Inside, it smelled of floor polish and disinfectants. Each room had an outside wall with high-silled windows and two walls with slate blackboards. The fourth wall was a billboard for posters and papers created by the children.

Wide, dark halls and yawning stairways connected the rooms. Along both sides of the hallway were rows of hooks supporting hats, coats and other wearing apparel.

The office housing a secretary and the principal was located just inside the main entrance.

THE DISTILLERY | 199

One entrance was the girls' and the other the boys'. These doorways were so marked overhead in carved stone.

On school days, the building bristled with action. Classes were assembled and dismissed by the ringing of bells. With the movement, and the buzzing of voices, it was like a giant beehive. Lower-grade students were moved about in single file so that stragglers could not wander off unnoticed. Students in the upper grades seemed to move about like tiny organisms under a microscope.

When they were in the schoolyard, Val and Lacey played together. The five months difference in their ages caused Val to start school in February and Lacey in September. Although in different classes, they always looked for each other.

Val was inclined to be the leader, but Lacey was the more popular. These differences caused no problem between them.

They confronted adversity as a team. Val, being older, usually took the fore, but Lacey was not one to retreat. Once, a third-grade boy chased Val across the school yard with a garter snake. He made the mistake of coming within range of Lacey, who tore the writhing reptile from his grasp and flailed him with it. Both girls cried afterwards, but the boy never bothered them again.

The girls did not avoid group play – they participated in hopscotch, jacks, skip rope and tag – but they preferred to spend recess talking to one another. It was always a special treat to stay at each other's house overnight.

Val was taller than average, having dark hair, blue eyes and dimples like her mother. Lacey was shorter and had brown hair and freckles. These differences led people to believe they were much different in age. It also made their strong association seem more unbelievable.

It was a cold Sunday in December. The weather was clear, the sun shining. Things were pretty much routine in Riverport. David had a neighbor friend who operated a ham radio. They often tinkered with the set together. They enjoyed talking to other hams in distant places. To extend the range of the transmitter, it was necessary to improve the antenna, and they worked on this all day.

Dusk had descended when the two men went into the cellar and sat down at the transmitter. Wendell, the neighbor, turned on the receiver to allow the tubes to warm. The first voice they heard was an official of the federal government.

"This is the F.C.C. The United States has gone to war. All hams will cease operation until further notice."

The two men sat in start shock looking at each other.

"Gone to war?" David said.

"That quick?" Wendell asked. "With who?"

"I'd better get home," David murmured, putting on his jacket and leaving.

"*War!*" Wendell said, turning off the switches on the radio set. "War with who?"

Melba was waiting when David got to the porch.

"Did you hear?" She asked.

"We heard someone say the United States had gone to war!"

"It's true," she said. "The Japs have bombed Pearl Harbor."

"Where's that?"

"It's in Hawaii. They say our whole fleet is sunk. Oh, David, it's just terrible!"

David raced to the Philco and turned it on. President Roosevelt was speaking to the American people: "With confidence in our armed forces, with the unbounding determination of our people, we will win the inevitable triumph, so help us God!"

The President named it a "day of infamy," and indeed, it was. It changed the lives of everyone.

On the local campus, the college "brains" began to fashion solutions for the future of mankind. The trend gained momentum, and several large universities got involved.

It was resolved to meet in a consortium in Chicago. Delegates came from many communities.

When the local people returned to Riverport, they were convinced that the manager form of government was the city's only hope for the future.

If A.J. Adams ever made a political mistake, it was when he underestimated the effects of this craziness.

Now at war, the townspeople banned together as they had never done before. Crowds formed for war bond sales and aluminum drives. It was imperative that the country conserve things ranging from rubber to sugar. Gasoline rationing became a necessity, and sacrifice was the price.

David had mixed emotions about being deferred from the draft because of his dependents. He wanted to do something.

Melba told him he already was involved in the war effort, making barracks for a new army camp.

Security increased at the distillery to the extent that one would have supposed it was the next target of the Japanese. The guards questioned everyone entering the plant and nearly dismantled vehicles before they were admitted onto company property. Lights were directed on the undercarriage of freight cars coming into the plant. The employees contained a quiet hysteria about the war. Everything was suspect, even the workers against each other.

"I don't like it," Melba said to Jesse as they entered the cafeteria. "Everything has changed for the worst. People just don't trust each other anymore. We are not only fighting those Japs, but each other."

"Everybody is pretty jumpy," Jesse agreed.

"I can't imagine that there are any spies in Riverport," Melba speculated, as she looked up to see Francine running across the room toward her. Francine's face told her there was an emergency. "What in the world?" Melba started.

"Melba, Melba," Francine cried, throwing herself across her seated friend. "I got a telegram. Oh, God, look!"

Melba took the crinkled paper from her hand. Jesse leaned toward Melba to see the message. It said Sgt. Roddie Dixon had died as a result of enemy action at Pearl Harbor, December 7th, 1941.

All three of the women clung to each other and wept.

CHAPTER FOURTEEN

THE DEATH, A KISS,
AND THE PROBLEMS

After Val started to school, Francine took more interest in the child. She shopped for the girl's clothing and school supplies. It was not unusual for Bud to go along.

Riverport boasted three department stores, and Francine was familiar with all of them. She bought dresses, ribbons and accessories. The war had caused shortages, so things like shoes were rationed. The shoes available were drab and lacking in style. While she did the best she could, she often stopped for cocktails. Bud noticed she sometimes showed the effects of the drinking by slurring words, and talking too loudly.

At least money was not a problem. Roddie had left ten thousand dollars in insurance, and Francine had deposited these funds for Val's future. Her salary at the company was very generous and Bud paid for nearly everything she and Val needed.

Val was staying at Melba's for the weekend, and Bud and Francine were on a shopping, and drinking, trip.

"I can't get used to being seen in public with you," Francine said. "I still get jumpy when we meet anyone from the plant."

"You'll get over it in time," he answered. "Everyone knows I'm getting my divorce this week."

"Have you heard from your attorneys in Canada?" she asked.

"Yes, everything is agreed on."

"I just can't imagine you being free," she mumbled as she stopped to examine a table of socks.

"It seems like an eternity, getting all the details worked out," he said. "I've had some problems with the thing from the start. It is a relief to be out of the marriage, but I do care enough about her to worry over her welfare up there."

"It's her home," Francine reminded. "She has her parents and no children to care for."

"Thank God for that," he agreed. "She has good chances to remarry."

"How about me?" Francine asked, studying his face for a reaction. "Do I have a good chance of getting married again?"

"The best. The very best," he answered, taking her by the arm and moving into the next department.

When there was work, Melba and David left home before seven in the morning. Aunt Pearl took charge of the house and children. She enjoyed having something to do.

Val and Lil' Lacey were inseparable. Val liked it when Francine dropped her off at Pearl's so she could walk to school with Lacey. Half a dozen children walked together in a group. They had been cautioned about the crossing at Lincoln Road.

Each classroom contained rows of seats, high windows, slate blackboards and a pump organ. Each teacher was expected to play the organ and lead the class in singing. This awkward procedure was probably the reason Lacey never liked music. She became an expert at pantomime, moving her lips in synchronization with the voices of the other students.

The school bell rang for the start, for assembly, for recess, and for dismissal.

"I like the bell that rings for us to go home," Val said to Lacey as they walked across the schoolyard at the end of the day.

"It is the best bell of all," Lacey agreed.

"Did you see Herbert get spanked?" Val asked, eyes gleaming.

"Yeah, but it made me sad," Lacey answered. "I felt sorry for him."

"He had it comin'. He broke the globe."

"He didn't break it, he just knocked it over and put a dent in India," Lacy protested.

"He's clumsy. He walks like a creep," Val complained.

"My mother says he can't help it, and we shouldn't make fun of him," Lacey warned.

"Anyway, he broke the globe and now we can't find India," Val continued.

"I saw Nancy shove him," Lacey mumbled.

A boy named Billy ran up shoving Val from behind.

"Stop shovin' people," Lacey warned.

"She ain't your sister," Billy replied.

"She's my friend!" Lacy shouted back.

"Here comes Herbert," Val announced.

"Ya, ya, Herbert got spanked by the principal," they chanted.

"Did not!" Herbert protested.

"Did so."

The group sauntered along the street toward Lincoln Road and home.

Melba sat at the kitchen table folding clothes and softly sobbing.

David came into the house. "Hi, Pumpkin," he said, noticing her tears.

"Oh, David," she moaned. "I almost wish we hadn't installed a telephone."

"Why are you crying?"

She turned and through her arms around him. "Oh David, it's Dad . . . he died!" She began to wail.

"Your dad . . . died?"

"The call came half an hour ago."

David sat down. "My God! What happened?"

"He didn't feel well . . . Mom *tried* to get him to stay home, but he went to work anyway."

Melba tried to compose herself before continuing. "He passed out at the pottery . . . and they brought him home in his old truck. Mom put him to bed and sat with him . . . and this morning, he started moaning and thrashing about . . ."

David wished helplessly that he could change what was coming next. "When she tried to comfort him, he tensed and died in her arms."

There was near silence as Melba cried quietly for a few moments more before getting up from the table. "Mrs. Benson is staying with her and running the house. I've got to get down there as soon as I can."

"Have you told Aunt Pearl?"

"I didn't want to wake her. She'll want to go when I do."

"Me too," he said sadly.

Melba poured him a cup of coffee and sat down next to him.

Harold Stark's funeral was a solemn, simple event. He was dressed in his only suit and tie, and placed in a wooden casket which sat on sawhorses in the middle of the living room. Cloth was draped around the base. Flowers picked by neighbors and put into vases surrounded the bier. The room was dark and sad.

Friends and relatives came carrying food and condolences. The sideboard was heavily laden, but few had any appetite. Melba and David stood on either side of Lacey, who wore a simple black dress; her hair tied in a bun at the back of her head. A tall man, hat in hand, followed by a white-haired lady, entered the room and gazed at Lacey.

She looked at him, extended her hand and started to cry.

"Oh, Melba, it's your father's brother from down south. Oh, Jefferson and Ella, how good of you to come."

The man embraced Lacey and stood whispering to her for several minutes. Tears flowed down her cheeks and the white-haired lady offered a handkerchief.

In the afternoon, the minister conducted a funeral service at the casket. The local American Legion Post performed graveside services. They fired their rifles, folded the flag from atop the coffin and presented it to Lacey. This gesture caused Melba to come apart and she wept violently. Harold Starks was laid to rest.

After the funeral, the mourners followed Lacey to the family home. Mrs. Benson and other neighbors had set food out and made coffee.

There was little conversation. Melba introduced her mother to the guests from Riverport. Jesse and Clark followed by a surprising number of distillery workers. Helen and Marge offered condolences for the group.

Aunt Pearl, handkerchief in hand, sat on the couch sobbing. Uncle Shorty, Bible in hand, stood along side of her.

Melba and her mother whispered support to one another and forced smiles upon the passing procession of mourners.

"Is Boyd not here?" one woman asked.

"We don't know how to get in touch with him," Lacey sobbed.

"How sad," the woman moaned, stepping aside.

The tension began to lessen and the conversation took a less solemn air as the house filled with people.

David stood with his arm around Melba, who maintained her composure until Francine stepped forward and embraced her. Melba lost control again and wept.

"It's tough, Pumpkin. Go ahead and let it out," Francine whispered.

"Oh, Francine, there was so much I wanted to say to him, and now it's too late." Melba sobbed.

"I think he knew what was in your heart," Francine consoled. "Not everything needs to be put into words, you know. He probably had wished he'd told you what was in his heart as much as you did. I'm sure you understood each other. It just wasn't the kind of relationship that was big on talk. He loved you. You know that."

Melba shook with grief, sobbing into Francine's shoulder. David offered his handkerchief as Uncle Shorty read aloud excerpts from the "Good Book."

Francine walked Melba away from the guests and into the kitchen where they stood facing the sink. Through the window they could see the back yard. Melba's eyes fell on her father's truck. Like an old friend, it stood waiting for a driver who would never again take the wheel.

"It looks so sad," Melba remarked. "He was so dependent on that old relic. In a strange way, it represented his defeats and victories. When he got it, he'd lost his only chance to own a car. It was a gift and a sacrifice that seemed to depict his whole life. He always had to make do with whatever was dealt to him. Now, he is gone and the old truck has done its job."

"David, will you drain the radiator before we go? No tellin' if he had enough alcohol to keep it from freezin.'"

David nodded, handing her a cup of coffee.

Trudging through the war made time seem to stop. There was no lack of patriotism. Everyone was involved in the war effort, and every family had a relative in the service. Small cloth flags hung in the windows, displaying a blue star for those who served. Each family prayed that a gold star, for those who died, would not replace the blue.

During such solemn days, with time suspended, Val and Lacey not only survived, but also grew toward maturity.

Aunt Pearl decided to take the girls with her on a return trip to Arkansas. The prospect of a change during summer vacation excited the pair. They had never been away from home, and in fact, had never been anywhere, except Riverport.

Just getting to Arkansas was project enough. Uncle Shorty had collected boxes of items to be taken "home," so the trip would have to be made by auto.

"Do you think that ol' car will make it down there?" David asked Melba.

"Oh, ye of little faith," Melba said. "That ol' car has made the trip so much that I reckon it could go by itself."

"What about these city kids gettin' along down there?" David inquired. "It's a lot different there than here."

"Why, you ol' worry wart," Melba chided. "Can you think those girls can be in any safer hands than with Aunt Pearl and Uncle Shorty?"

David stood looking into his coffee cup. "You've got a good point," he said.

The trip lacked comfort and speed, but the sight of new horizons proved exciting enough to keep Val and Lacey upbeat and active. Once, they whistled at a group of soldiers standing along the road. This brought a sermon from Uncle Shorty. The girls crouched down in the back seat and giggled.

Their destination was a strange sight. The entrance road was unpaved and dusty. The hills were hidden in thick patches of pin oak and hardwood. The house, a crude dwelling with unpainted wooden walls and tin roof, seemed to be smaller than more familiar dwellings.

Surrounded by open yard and unfenced property, the place suggested a freedom never before experienced by the girls.

In the process of unloading the car, three local boys appeared from the woods and volunteered to help.

This was excitement enough, and Val and Lacey knew immediately that they were going to enjoy being here.

Aunt Pearl set about to make the house inhabitable and to introduce the girls to the primitive conveniences of the place.

"I'm afraid to go out to that lil' shed to go to the toilet at night," Lacey confided to Val.

"You'd be even more afraid if you knew those boys can see you from the woods," Val commented.

"No!" Lacey exclaimed. "How do you know that?"

"I've seen them. I waved to the biggest kid. He waved back, and they all ran off out of sight."

"Let's tell Aunt Pearl," Lacey whispered.

"What? And spoil all the fun? Think again, kiddo, I'm likin' the whole scene."

"I don't know. Seems like Aunt Pearl ought to know," Lacey commented, shaking her head.

It was a different world without electricity. There was wood to chop and carry to the house. There was water to be pumped from the well and carried to the kitchen. In the yard, there was a kettle to heat, and laundry to be washed by hand. Daytime was not for sleeping, and nighttime was for going to bed.

Come Sunday, it was down the road to church with Bibles, hymnals and picnic baskets of food. Aunt Pearl approved appearances and Val was made to remove her lip rouge. To say the event was strict was an understatement. To say the day was boring was an absolute certainty, until the familiar faces of those boys appeared at the picnic table. Mr. and Mrs. Chumney were as devout as Lacey's kin, stern people bearing up under the hardships of life. Uncle Shorty told how the boys had helped him unload. Nervous smiles graced the faces of the youngsters as they each stepped forward to be introduced to Val and Lacey.

Woody, the oldest, was raw-boned and homely. His dark hair was long and unkempt. His speech faltered and he often paused to collect his thoughts. Aunt Pearl later commented that he was "not too tightly wrapped."

Hamma was so named because, as a child, he always pulled a claw hammer behind him as he toddled about the cabin. The nickname stuck long after the family forgot his given name. Unlike his older brother, he had fine features and made some effort to groom himself, mostly by brushing his teeth with baking soda and his hair with a homemade comb. To compliment this, his grin was massive and seemed to enlist his entire face.

Clete, the youngest, was short and stocky. Blond-headed, he bore no resemblance to his family. Surly, he went about crashing into people and things. Melba likened him to a wooden croquet ball, ricocheting around the gathering. This boy seldom spoke in sentences, but was given to make loud guttural noises, particularly when excited.

Thus went Sunday at the church. Afterwards at home Lacey and Val reflected about the day.

"That Woody gives me the creeps," Lacey confided. "He just sits and stares at us."

"He's harmless," Val answered. "It's Hamma that I like."

"*Like!*" Lacey exclaimed. "What is there to like?"

"He's the best thing I've seen in these woods."

"You better think about hushin' up before Uncle Shorty hears that kinda talk."

Val smiled into her pillow as the night took over.

Aunt Pearl usually hung her clothes on the fence to dry. With the girls' additional laundry and the practical non-existence of a fence, there was a problem.

"No other woman has a clothes line," Shorty complained.

"Cleanliness is akin to Godliness," Pearl quoted. "I need a clothes line!"

"Oh, all right, but tain't my fault if'n yo'all cuts your necks walkin' across the yard."

Shorty stretched a wire clothesline from a large oak tree at the back of the lot to the corner of the house.

Laundry day became a drawing card for the Chumney boys. Their faces could be seen peering from the woods as the wash was hung. Pearl used a metal scrub board in a tub in the kitchen, as Val and Lacey carried baskets of wet clothes into the yard. Val was at the far end of the yard whispering to Hamma, who stood hidden behind the trunk of the giant oak tree. She was hanging wash when Hamma reached out and snatched Pearl's brassiere off the line. Val grabbed at it and missed, and then went in pursuit as he skipped off through the timber. Lacey saw this and followed.

Hamma ran deep into the woods and turned on Val. She collided with his outstretched arms, and before she could recoil, he pressed his lips to hers then ran off out of sight!

Val blinked her eyes. He was gone.

"Val," Lacey called as she came up to her. "What in the world got inta him?"

"Yeah," Val answered, smiling as she looked in the direction of his retreat. "You' see that? He kissed me! Kissed by a boy!"

"Did he hurt you?" Lacey asked.

"No way. He kissed me! My very first kiss! WOW!" Val cried, picking up the brassiere and walking back to the yard.

Lacey was confused. How could Val be so thrilled over an attack on her person? Life was getting complicated.

They agreed not to mention the matter to Pearl and Shorty.

Val and Lacey had different reasons for enjoying summer in Arkansas. Val was eager to see Hamma, and Lacey was compiling a recipe book of Aunt Pearl's best dishes.

When school was out for the summer, both girls were packed and ready. This routine repeated itself all through the high school years.

Initially, the girls negotiated with Pearl and Shorty for a better Sunday schedule.

"We jest can't sit in church all day Sunday!" Val exclaimed.

"It's the Sabbath and we are the devout," Shorty replied.

"Lacey and I are not children. We will run off and go back home," Val threatened.

"And I'll let the hounds loose an' track ya down!" Shorty shouted.

Lacey could see the issue developing into open hostility.

"Uncle Shorty, wouldn't it be better if we learned about Jesus while attending Sunday School?" she asked. "We could walk home after Sunday School and have supper ready when you and Aunt Pearl returned from church Sunday evening."

It took fortitude, but Shorty finally capitulated and agreed conditionally to endorse the plan.

Val could see the possibilities. If Hamma could escape his family, they would have most of the day together!

Melba would be free to explore Aunt Pearl's notebooks, and copy the pages she sought. It was a good plan, indeed.

Permission to date was more difficult. Shorty took a firm stand against the idea, saying the girls were too young.

"Not while livin' in my house!" he proclaimed.

"You said yourself that the folks down here were better stock than those up home," Val reminded. "Why do you object to my associating with these God-fearing young people?"

"Oh, Lord," Pearl said, turning to Shorty, "We was younger than these two when we got married," she recalled. "Would you say we was too young?"

Shorty was trapped. Permission was granted for dating in plain sight or when chaperoned.

Val hugged everyone in the room and then ran outside to check the clothesline.

The shortage of manpower in the Treasury Department and the ever-increasing thirst of the public gave rise to an expanded activity in bootlegging. This was particularly true in the southern states, which offered endless wooded hill country, often without access road or trail.

All the materials were available except bottles. The alcohol produced was of uncontrolled quality, but the savings of $10.50 in tax per gallon made it appealing to the consumer. This was a loss to the tax collector as well as ever-increasing competition to the legal manufacturer. The problem was severe in the two decades following World War II.

Thieves broke into a warehouse in Harrison and stole a truckload of tires. These were precious items at the time. A manhunt of immense proportions was instituted. The high sheriff of a southern county found a clue and telephoned the city.

"What have you got?" asked the official in Little Rock.

"We got a boy who's spotted a stack of tires off'n a rural road," the sheriff responded.

"Are they new tires?" Little Rock asked.

"Sure are," came the reply.

"Our agents are on the way."

"Don't hurry. They ain't goin' nowhere," the Sheriff commented.

"Who discovered them?" Little Rock inquired.

"Jist a boy."

"Do you know his name?"

"Ain't important."

"The hell it isn't. He could know how they got there!"

"He don't."

"Did you ask him?"

"No need," the High Sheriff responded.

"Why are you being so evasive?" Little Rock queried.

"Ah cain't tell you his name, 'cause it ain't important."

"Do you know who he is?"

"Shore do, but if yo'all want the tires, don't press fo' the name of the boy who found them."

"Relieve my mind, why are you protecting his identity?"

"Jist an ol' boy walkin' along th' road, and he seen them from the road, stacked up in the weeds."

"Why don't you tell us who he is, Sheriff?"

"Cause he's a bottle watcher."

"A what?"

"He walks the roads lookin' for empty bottles to sell to the moonshiners. If I give you his name, it could lead to the man who needs the bottles."

"We understand." came the response. "Your boy's identity is unimportant to us. Thank you, Sheriff."

Small, legal distilleries had a problem disposing of the mash after a distilling run was made. These small plants did not run every day. Local farmers feeding livestock were ever alert because the "slop" was meted out on a first-come, first-served basis. When steam rose from the stacks at the distillery, the trucks would line up waiting for the byproduct. These trucks blocked entrance to the plant, and all too often it was necessary to referee disputes among the drivers.

One farmer saw a solution. A passing agent admired his well-stocked cattle pens and drove to the house.

Inside in the kitchen sat a young lady before a battery of Motorola radios.

"Hello," greeted the agent.

"Hello," the woman responded without turning away from the radios.

"What's all this?" asked the agent.

"Everyday life in the cattle business." she responded.

"Pretty fancy equipment for a cattle farm."

"Pretty fancy cattle farm," she answered. "Okay, Johnson, git over to Number 3 plant. They got a run about finished."

With this she took off her headphones and turned to face the agent.

"This is my family's spread," she began. "We got tired of the hassle at the plant gates. So we put radios in our trucks. When one of the local distilleries runs mash, they call us and we get the 'hot slop' first choice. It pays off for us and the whiskey people. They love us, and we love them," she said pulling back the curtain to see the crowded cattle pens. "Our trucks are busy day and night, and so am I," she said turning back to the radios.

"Quite an operation," the agent mused as he left the farm.

The Jacob Wasserman Plant at Riverport was one of the largest. When they started another building at the site, it hardly was noticed, but it started a new facet of business.

214 | JOHN ARCHER

The company was well aware of the potential for feed from the mash left by the distilling process. Their chemists and engineers had drawn a plan.

The machinery installed in the new building had nothing to do with the distilling of grain. It was a processing facility to dry and pack animal supplement for agriculture. Inside the new building, the mash was dried for poultry feed or cattle feed. Enthusiasm ran high on the day this new operation was inaugurated.

The employees were mustered for the occasion. A company spokesman on a platform talked into a megaphone, as the workers filed through the new addition.

Melba found Francine with the office personnel, and joined her in the procession.

"Why all the big hoopla?" Melba asked.

"The company is improving its image," Francine answered. "It's really a farce."

"Why so?"

"Everybody has known for years that cooled mash is good feed for animals. Instead of practically giving the stuff away, they'll bag it, give it a fancy name and charge high prices for slop that used to be worthless," Francine explained.

"How does this improve the company image?" Melba pondered.

"They wear the white hats," Francine smiled. "They pay the farmer for his grain. They suck out the alky. Then they dry it, bag it, and sell it back to the farmer because it's supposed to be better for his stock.

Melba wondered if Francine was echoing Bud's attitude or if she was irritated for some personal reason. The new product seemed to be a good idea to Melba.

Working in a distillery had its advantages, if you were an alcoholic. The product was readily available at no cost to the consumer.

The Wasserman Plant had its share of such people. Opened bottles were stashed any place they could be hidden. Many of the employees brought a thermos to work. Some actually contained hot coffee or soup. At the end of the shift, most of these thermoses contained eighty proof bourbon going out the gate.

A favorite trophy was the miniature bottle made for the airlines. The women of the bottling line hid these in their purses, bras, and panty girdles. For those more daring, decanters and larger bottles were smuggled from the plant.

The guards at the gates often pulled surprise searches at the end of a shift. The second shift was critical because it was dark when these employees left work. If such a search was in progress, those in the front line shouted that a search was under way.

There was no turning back to the building to hide stolen bottles, so a hail of them would fly through the night, over the fence and into the river. The crash of glass sounded like tinkling bells on the rocks along the bank, but everyone was "clean" when they got to the gate.

This product loss was small by comparison when a drunken tank man turned the wrong valves and shot eight thousand gallons of four-year-old tax-paid bourbon into the river. Fish went belly-up for miles downstream.

Coal began to be hauled from distant states because of new laws about sulfur content and environmental impact.

It was not uncommon for the distilling process to be completely curtailed for lack of well water. Sometimes river water was used!

The machinery at the Riverport Plant was fast becoming obsolete and costly to maintain.

The union had pumped up the pay scale. Workers now made four times their earnings when the plant was founded. If this was not enough, the drinking public was developing a preference for beer and wine!

The company had decisions to make. Then Jonathan Hackette, the new C.E.O. stepped into the chaos. He announced that he and his staff would hold a press conference in Riverport in two weeks!

CHAPTER FIFTEEN

THE ELIMINATION, THE FRUSTRATION, AND THE BIZARRE NIGHT

The national election of 1956 was formed along party lines. Dwight Eisenhower was re-elected to a second term.

At the local level, the mayor form of government was pitted against those proposing the manager form of government.

Surprisingly, a multitude of supporters appeared for the college theory. A crafty old professor imported from a foreign country just after the end of World War II inspired most of these people. His chief credential was his accent, and his appointment to the faculty of the college. It was fortunate for him that the war had destroyed European records from his country of origin. The college and the community accepted his letters on their face and without verification.

It mattered not to the electorate that their beloved mayor held the city in balance. Things had always gone so smoothly in City Hall that it was not contemplated that they would do otherwise.

When the election was over, the mayor had lost!

The morning newspaper headline proclaimed, "IKE WINS!" On one of the back pages, the local news told of the victory of the manager form of city government. The business section of the paper told of the pending visit by officials of the Wasserman Corporation. Subtitles announced the newly appointed officials, Chairman, Richard (Bud) McKenna, C.E.O. Jonathan Hackette, and further along, Secretary of the Board Francine Dixon!

Reporters raced to City Hall to interview A.J. Adams.

He was standing in his office looking out of the window when the clerk entered.

"Mr. Mayor," the clerk said.

"Yes," Adams answered without turning.

"The press is here to see you. Some local, some from Chicago."

"Come to gloat, I suppose," Adams answered. "Show the bastards in."

The clerk opened the door to the group of newsmen. They crowded into the office, notebooks in hand, pencils ready.

"Mr. Mayor," one of them asked. "It is rumored that you will clean up the city before you leave office. Is this true?"

"Clean up what?" Adams asked. "Clean up the so-called intelligentsia upon the college campus?"

"You sound bitter. Has the lost election caused you to be bitter?"

"Now, get one thing straight. I'm not bitter, I'm just plain mad! I've given my all for this town and I think the city runs pretty smooth. I admit we got a red-light district and we got more taverns than most towns, but I point with pride to the fact that we have control over crime in this town."

"What about the attempt on your life a while back?"

"Baloney, that was just warring factions from the big city who thought our boys would be easy. It was a couple of random shots by a couple of petty burglars."

"What will you do when you are out of public life?"

"Who said I was out of public life? I intend to be in the limelight more than ever. You'll see more of A.J. Adams from now on than ever before. Remember, I don't have to live by the rules now."

"Does that mean you will oppose the new form of government from outside City Hall?" a reporter asked.

"You bet your rosy red ass!" Adams said as he bit off the tip of a new cigar and left the room.

It was the last month of the year. Winter bore down on the earth. Snow fell day and night. The wind howled through the city streets, blinding all those who challenged the weather.

Mrs. Byrd wiped the moisture off the window to look outside. "This weather is the pits," she murmured. "I should move down south and get away from all this." There were no johns in the street. Business was poor. "This is one fuckin' strange night," she said, rocking back in her chair.

It was *indeed* a strange night. Down on the banks of the river, activity defied the elements. There was much happening at the Jacob Wasserman Distillery.

The officers of the company had changed, but the room had not. It contained the same long wooden table surrounded by high-backed leather chairs. The beamed ceiling and tall entrance doors were just as they were in 1934 when Francine and Jesse presented the installation awards.

The only improvement seemed to be the younger faces at the table. Francine, the only woman, sat next to the C.E.O.

Every member had reviewed the problems of the Riverport Plant. After Francine made the roll call, Jonathon Hackette stood at the head of the table and read from a report.

"This location has been like an old relative," he began. "We must decide whether to sustain it, or send it to the 'home.'"

He turned pages, read, stopped, and continued. "To sustain this location will demand large investments on our part. The question is will the return merit such an investment? This location still offers the raw materials and labor force to support continued production. We expect our market will bear up under the present sluggish activity. What, then, shall we do? Each of you has a prospectus. The secretary will take a roll call vote."

Francine called the names of the board, and the officers. There were a few dissenters, but by the large, the group voted to modernize the Riverport Plant and continue its operation.

Francine recorded the vote, and gave a sigh of relief. Riverport was saved!

Though she was exhausted, she phoned Melba with the news. "Hi, Pumpkin," she greeted. "Did you know this was our lucky day?"

"Give me reason to rejoice," Melba answered, looking at the clock.

"Yours truly just left the board room where the issue was whether or not to close the Riverport Distillery!"

"Oh Francine, was that a possibility?" Melba asked.

"It was almost a certainty. These guys are not like the bunch that started this 'joy-juice' factory."

"You say this was our lucky day. Did they decide to keep us open?"

"Not only that, but to modernize the place as well!"

"Hallelujah!" Melba cried.

The city manager had taken over City Hall, and the payroll ballooned. There was a new director or administrator for every function of city operation. New departments appeared overnight and strange new faces came from all over to help improve the City of Riverport. With these new expenses old taxes were raised and new ones sought. There was a wheel tax, an entertainment tax, a beer tax plus a sales tax. Many consumers crossed the river where the taxes did not apply.

A school in New York recommended the new city manager. His experience was attained while attending classes on political science. His name was Franklin Fagg. He strongly preferred to be called Frank, but behind his back, he was called by other names.

After taking the helm, he looked for a project to create status for himself. He needed to make a reputation. Knowing sex to be bad, he decided to rid the town of its red-light district. He invited a national magazine to do a story on the cleansing of Riverport.

The magazine sent a crew to interview and photograph the town and its people. They did human-interest stories on a variety of people, but they were *always* steered away from A.J. Adams.

He sat in his private office, puffing on a cigar, and smiling.

A whole week had been spent doing the story about the former "red-light" district. Photos were taken of the closed buildings and the barren streets where prostitution once prevailed.

Cab drivers and bartenders were interviewed, and they told of the absence of vice as the result of the new manager's efforts.

It was a great story. The magazine could see a feature here.

Before leaving town, the magazine crew and the city manager met for dinner at the country club. Praises were sung, and the effort was hailed as victorious.

While this celebration was taking place, the sheriff and fifteen state troopers raided ten houses and rounded up some eighteen working prostitutes.

This news put a halt to the celebration at the country club. The magazine people packed up and left town. So much for a feature story.

A.J. Adams and Mrs. Byrd watched the police vans bringing the arrested prostitutes to the station. As soon as bond was posted, they left the building.

"That's a helluva news story there," Adams said, pointing to City Hall.

"Specially since I had to round up a bunch of girls for the occasion. Some of them ain't been off the bus more than an hour," the fat lady commented.

"*That's* the story that won't get out," Adams said, looking her squarely in the eye. He lit his cigar and blew smoke skyward.

She knew he was pleased because he was smiling. He seldom smiled. At least not like he was smiling now.

Making men happy seemed to be Mrs. Byrd's purpose in life. It was her turn to smile as she lumbered down the steps to her car. "That'll teach 'em to fuck with an expert," she said to herself as the car pulled out from the curb to take her back to her "house."

The Riverport School Board was building a new, modern high school in the affluent area of town, on the bluff. It was a magnificent plan. The building was a sprawling two story stone and brick structure containing all the latest innovations.

The first feature to catch the eye was the large parking lot behind the building. The old school had made no allowance for parking because students did not have autos when it was constructed. Times had changed.

The new school gymnasium was larger than the old one, and bleachers framed the basketball court. Sports had become popular with the public. Team spirit and ticket sales were to be considered.

There was a special section for the athletic department. Showers and lockers for the athletes and a private office for the coach were included in the plans!

The school board had accounted for everything, except a name.

A special meeting was called for this purpose. In their search for a name, past presidents, military leaders, scientists, and pioneer names were considered.

A caucus considered all possibilities. One of the board members suggested, "In as much as we have agreed to share our new chemistry lab with the local college, and they have agreed in exchange, to fund that part of the school, why not pick a name associated with the college?"

"Let's not confuse the public," another member interrupted.

"We need to name our school after someone associated with the college.

"How about the college president?"

"Yes, it will appease all concerned."

At that precise moment, an urgent telephone call changed it all. The president of the board listened and paled. He hung the receiver in its cradle and turned to those in the room.

"One more hour," he said, "and we would have made asses of ourselves!"

"How so?" a member asked.

"That was the police department. The man for whom we were to name our new school has been arrested this evening in Chicago."

"Arrested? For what?"

"He was engaged in an unlawful sex act – with one of his male students!"

The hour was late. The urgency to select a name for the school was intense!

"How about a stalwart public servant?" a member asked.

"Who do you have in mind?" the chairman asked.

"A.J. Adams!"

Silence prevailed while this possibility was contemplated.

"Yes, A.J. Adams," the board agreed.

This is how the school board came to name the new high school after the former mayor.

Because of the late hour, the news was not released until the next day.

After Francine's telephone call about the board meeting, Melba was too excited to sleep. She tried to lie still so as not to disturb David, but she began to twist and turn.

David opened one eye and peered at her from his pillow.

"What's goin' on?" He asked.

"Oh, David, I'm sorry I bothered you, but I'm uptight about things."

"Like what?" He asked.

"That was Francine calling to say the company is going to modernize the distillery. I'm worried about how that will affect employment."

"It should make things better for you."

"I'm afraid it will lead to layoffs," she frowned.

"It wouldn't affect you. You've got twenty years of seniority. Besides, Francine will protect your job for you."

"It's not *my* job I'm worried about," she moaned.

"Who else?" he asked, raising his head from the pillow to sit up in bed.

"I didn't want to tell you, but Francine and I got some shocking news today."

This got his full attention. He turned to stare down at her. "News about what?"

"It's a long story, but you know how the grapevine works at the plant. Carl Cassel in personnel runs the downtown hiring hall."

"Go on," David insisted.

"Well, he heard these two young ladies talking."

"Come on!" David protested. "Get down to the nitty-gritty."

"These girls had a long discussion about their mothers not approving if they took a job at Wasserman's."

"Teetotalers?" He asked.

"Far from it."

"What then?"

"Well, they both qualified, and Carl called Francine because he wanted her approval before he hired them."

"Is that part of her job?" David asked, sitting up and wrapping his arms around his knees.

"No . . . but this case is different."

"Melba. Quit beating around the bush and come out with it," he groaned.

"Well, Francine called me, and we talked it over . . . and decided to tell Carl to go ahead."

"Fine, fine; now Wasserman has two new employees. Can we get some sleep?"

"David," she cried, putting her head on his chest. "They were Lacey and Val!"

"Ouch!" he exclaimed, sitting straight up. "And you're telling Carl to hire them?"

"Subject to your approval," she said.

"Looks to me like you and Francine have already made the final decision. I'll go along with whatever you say. What the heck, they are both old enough, and the pay is the best in town. What's to ponder?"

He gave Melba a squeeze, kissed her and flopped down on his pillow, facing away.

Now *he* was the one who could not sleep!

Mrs. Byrd tried to scrape the frost from the window. It was too thick to yield to her fingernails. She took the spoon from her coffee cup and pushed it back and forth across the glass. This made a small opening in the white frost.

"I feel it in my bones," she said. "This is one bizarre friggin' night." Pulling a shawl across her shoulders, she shivered and rocked back in her chair.

It was quite warm and comfortable in the Presidential Suite of the Lafayette Hotel. Francine wore a dressing gown and little else as she sat on a quilted stool in front of the vanity. Her long, black hair glistened as she brushed it away from her face.

Bud McKenna wore a smoking jacket and sat upright in bed reading *The Wall Street Journal*. He rustled the pages as he absorbed the headings about business.

"I think Mr. Hackette likes my looks," she said, still brushing.

"He'd like any broad's looks. He's not to be trusted around women."

"He was very courteous to me," she said, turning to face Bud.

"And why *not*? He knows you are *my* woman. He wouldn't dare get cute with you. He was just petting the cow to get to the bull."

"Well, thank you very much! That's no credit to my good looks. Maybe he was sincere when he told me what an exquisite beauty I am," she pouted. "And what's this stuff about me being *your* woman?"

"You *are* my woman," he answered without looking away from the newspaper.

"I remind you, we are not married!"

"And I remind *you* that you wouldn't have a pot to piss in if it weren't for me. Christ's sake, I even got you appointed as secretary of the company!"

"Things that are important to you are *not* that important to me. I am a red-blooded passionate woman. Your whiskey factory is just another stinkin' old waterfront eyesore," she hissed, walking to the bed and reaching for him under the covers.

"Besides, now that you mention 'whiskey,' I've got some very secret information I will share with you, if you admit you are *my* woman," he said, holding her hand away from his balls.

"What could you know that I wouldn't know. I was at the meeting tonight, and at your side every moment."

"This is something about the future," he whispered, pulling her body close to his.

"You must never breathe a word of what I'm going to tell you. The market for hard liquor will not survive another decade. The future is in beer and wine. We can't invade the brewery business because it is too tightly controlled by the "beer kings." This leaves only the wine market. The wineries are small by comparison, and basically unorganized. They would be less competitive if we invaded their market. I am authorized to spend millions of dollars buying up California grape vineyards so that we can, in coming years, produce new labels in domestic wine!"

"What about all that business tonight to modernize the Riverport Plant?" she asked.

"A necessary business venture. We get tax breaks on that transaction, and by so doing, we don't telegraph our punch on the California caper."

"Why does it have to be such a secret?"

"California land is already high-priced. What do you think those bastards would do if they knew we wanted to buy in?"

"How long will it take to buy up the land?" she asked.

"Years. The wineries have to be built after we have enough land for grape production – we won't be able to buy from local agriculture like we did from the farmers here in the Midwest. We have to be able to grow our *own* crop."

"*Years!*" she said. "Are you going to be out there for years?"

"No, *we* are going to be out there for years," he said putting his lips to her and holding her for a long kiss.

"We?" she murmured. "Live in California? Oh, there is so much to be considered."

"Only thing to be considered is: Are you *my* woman or *not?*" he asked as he rolled her on her back and started licking her nipples. He knew this was one move she could not resist.

She moaned, ran her fingers through his hair, and pulled his face down on her chest.

About the only things A.J. Adams kept when he left were his roll-top desk, sleeve garters, and his green eyeshade. He sat at his desk in his private office, looking across the street at City Hall.

Benjamin Howard Bentley sat at the desk next to A.J. Adams.

"Your replacements are adding onto the building," Bentley murmured, looking over Adam's shoulder at the scene across the street.

"They'll do anything to spend the taxpayer's money," Adams said without looking away.

"I almost wish I was going to stay in town, just to see how things turn out," Bentley moaned. "My department is determined to see me in retirement. This recall for my services to Chicago is just a ploy to give me the gold watch and my walking papers."

"At least you get that!" Adams commented. "As an elected official I git diddly squat for my services to the city."

"I have only one regret for my twenty years in your fair city. I never *could* prove a really good case against your old pal, Mrs. Byrd. We even checked on the three farms she has in the southern part of the state, but a different nephew owns each of them, and each one can prove he bought the land. The towel caper proved a small unreported income and we agreed to take 'time pay' in restitution."

"I thought the new city fathers had cleaned up the vice in this city," Adams said in mock surprise.

"Oh, yes, I asked her how she could come up with the money for payments if the city had her shut down. She winked and said she was giving green stamps."

The very, thought of this made both men chuckle.

"As long as I'm leaving town, I guess I can tell you now," Bentley started. "When I arrived here, years ago before World War II, this burg was crawlin' with federal cops.

"Here?" Adams exclaimed. "What *kind* of federal cops?"

"Almost *all* kinds. J. Edgar Hoover had his FBI agents thicker than hops up in the north end of town. Army Intelligence crisscrossed the county, competing with Navy sleuths. It was a regular Chinese fire drill."

"Horse hockey," Adams shouted. "Why haven't I heard of this before? What were they doin' here?"

"International intrigue," Bentley answered. "There was a segment of this town that was first and second generation German immigrants. The Centipede Tractor Company had a secret contract with the Germans to manufacture conning towers on a tractor base, to dock dirigibles and pull them into their hangars. It was one hell of an idea. Our government feared your local company, in order to promote lighter-than-air craft, might somehow deliver helium to the Nazis. Didn't you know that the top names of the dirigible company visited your city long before that catastrophe in New Jersey?"

"Are you pullin' my leg?" Adams asked.

Bentley enjoyed the response he was getting from Adams. "Then, you *really* didn't know what was going on, right under your nose?" he asked.

"Horsefeathers!" Adams exclaimed. "How can you verify this bullshit?"

"Ask the Navy. They still have one of the towers in service in Akron, 'Made in Riverport' molded in iron on its sides."

Adams reddened. He stared at Bentley and turned back to the window, pushing back in his swivel chair, clenching his teeth.

"Sorry," Bentley smiled. "I always thought that you knew something about this."

Adams reached out and shook Bentley's hand. "Godspeed," he whispered and turned back to the window.

Adams was despondent. "How could these things have happened?" He leaned forward and put his head on his desktop.

In the morning, the sun came out and the fresh new snow made Riverport appear cleansed and pure. It was as if God had renewed and forgiven the city by the river.

Delegates from Wasserman Company left the Lafayette Hotel and went to City Hall to reaffirm their faith in the city.

A.J. Adams lay with his head on his desk. He did not see the Canadians enter City Hall. When the courier came to tell him about the new high school, he did not respond to the knock on the door. It had been a very *bizarre night.*

Printed in the United States
1503800001B/429

9 781413 421460

Born in an industrial environment, the author earned his education working in heavy manufacturing, railroading and distilling. In the United States Army during World War II as a combat scout in the European Theater, he survived three separate campaigns. Wounded in the Battle of the Bulge, he was awarded the Purple Heart. Returning to civilian life, he married, and raised a son and daughter.

Managing casualty claims, he earned a Law Degree at Drake University and was appointed by the State of Illinois as a Special Agent. Retired, he presents this fictional account of young women confronting life in an alcohol factory.

In America's earliest days, distilling grain was an accepted occupation. "Moonshine" was consumed from mansions to cabins. Pioneers heading west carried jugs for social, medical and bartering purposes.

Uncontrolled bootlegging during Prohibition sometimes caused death or blindness to the consumer. The repeal of Prohibition attracted corporate entities to again make and market alcoholic beverages.

During the Depression, women found employment at the distilleries. Against a backdrop of corporate espionage, powerful gangsters, politicians, and prostitution, this is how Melba and Francine met and bonded for three generations.

Meet them and learn how alcohol affected all that became involved with The Distillery.

ISBN: 1-4134-2146-6

9 781413 421460   (20658)

90000>